COLD HANDS

AND OTHER STORIES

COLD HANDS

AND OTHER STORIES

JEFF DUNTEMANN

Copperwood Press • Colorado Springs, Colorado
2010

COLD HANDS
AND OTHER STORIES

"Cold Hands" first appeared in *Isaac Asimov's Science Fiction Magazine*, June, 1980.
"Marlowe" first appeared in *Alien Encounters*, Jan Howard Finder, Editor, 1982
"Drumlin Boiler" first appeared in *Isaac Asimov's Science Fiction Magazine*, April, 2002.
"Inevitability Sphere" first appeared in *Isaac Asimov's Science Fiction Magazine*, September/October, 1978.
"Our Lady of the Endless Sky" first appeared in *Nova 4*, Harry Harrison, Ed., 1974.
"Whale Meat" first appeared in *Starwind Magazine*, August, 1977.
"Born Again, with Water" appears here for the first time.
"Drumlin Wheel" appears here for the first time.
"Roddie" appears here for the first time.

The Cunning Blood (excerpted here) was published by ISFiC Press, 2005 and is available through Amazon.com or by special order from any bookstore. ISBN: 0-9759156-2-2. Hardcover, 360 pp. $28.00.

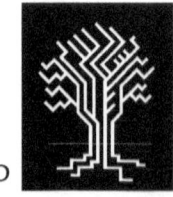

COPPERWOOD MEDIA, LLC
COLORADO SPRINGS, COLORADO

For Delores Ostruska,
who gave me her daughter—
and made me her son.

CONTENTS

INTRODUCTION

I'm not well-known as a science fiction writer because I haven't written all that much science fiction. I think it's interesting that I sold my first SF story and my first technical article in the same month, way back in late 1973. The story took an *immense* amount of work and time, critique and polishing and rethinking and rewriting. The article took me one long afternoon, and I sold what was essentially my first draft. That turned out to be a strong trend: As the years ticked past, my nonfiction output exploded, while my fiction output remained about what it's always been, a new story every year or two. 35 years later, the tally stands at 14 technical books solo and portions of ten or twelve in collaboration with other authors (all of them on computing) plus about 250 nonfiction articles and essays, balanced against 21 completed SF and fantasy stories (of which 12 saw print in paying markets) and one published SF novel.

A close friend who enjoyed my stories a great deal told me once, "You've got to get serious about science fiction!" Alas, dear lady, I *am*—and that's the problem. I take the challenge of SF very seriously. I don't even begin a story unless I get an idea worth spinning a yarn around. I do the research and (when necessary) the math, and then I take as much time to write the story as the story demands. Some stories demand more than others; I've had the occasional short in play for well over a year. And sometimes I get blocked. "Born Again, With Water" sat unfinished in a drawer for nineteen years, until I pulled it out in 2007, mulled it over during a number of long walks, and then completed it. "Drumlin Wheel" happened in fits and starts over a seven-year period. I rewrote "Whale Meat" completely three separate times since first finishing it in 1974.

I admit it: That's not the way to build a reputation. Still, it is in no way evidence of any lack of devotion to the field. It may have been a blessing, in fact, since I haven't been tempted to crank out tonnage merely to make ends meet. What I've written has been well-received, and I still get the occasional fan letter for stories that first appeared in 1982.

I also get notes from time to time asking, "Please, where can I buy a copy of 'Cold Hands'"? For a long time the best I could suggest was to haunt used bookstores and SF convention huckster tables for yellowing magazines and dogeared anthologies. In the last few years, short-run publishing technology and ubiquitous Web access has opened another path: Gather 'em all between covers and put them where people can buy them.

Hence this book and its predecessor, *Souls in Silicon*. Between the two books, all my SF and fantasy that I've been happy with is now back in print, and with any luck will be forever. I'm still writing SF (just as I'm still writing technical nonfiction) and with any luck, by 2032 I'll have enough new short stories to fill a third volume. (If you think I'm kidding, you don't know me well enough!)

In the meantime, next year I will publish *Firejammer*, the short novel I wrote for *Isaac Asimov's Science Fiction Adventure Magazine* and finished just as the magazine was shut down. I'm scoping out a shared-world anthology with a few other writers, taking place in the universe of "Drumlin Boiler" and "Drumlin Wheel." I've actually made a little headway on the sequel to *The Cunning Blood*. (Getting an agent or, heaven knows, a publisher, could really get the fire lit.)

Whatever. Stories happen. I'm here when they do. Thanks for reading me all these long years, and stay tuned.

Jeff Duntemann
Colorado Springs, Colorado
May, 2010

COLD HANDS

1980

COLD HANDS

I

Ed Graczyk sat before his easel in the cool Maine evening, painting the sunset. He had had arms once. In those days he had been a Combine employee, Combine-born. In Titan orbit he had piloted a tiny steering tug, single-handedly orienting monstrous sausage casings for filling from the Titan ramscoop, and then orienting them for the long pull to Earthspace.

Things go wrong. A leaking oxygen tank near the stern of his skeletal craft had thrown it off trim, edgewise into a soft container of endless tonnes of dirty methane. The resulting inferno had cost him a lot of skin, and both arms below the elbow.

The skin they had replaced. The arms were gone forever.

Ed painted a lot. It was good therapy. His prosthetic arms were very good: ingenious metal things which responded to swellings in the muscles in his shoulders. The more he used them the better they would respond. Still, the hands were little better than claws. They were without touch or any but the grossest motion. Ed adapted, and painted, and did software work in his little geodesic dome for a firm in Augusta. He was as content as a man who had been brought back from the dead should have been, but in the deep Maine nights he wished he could see untwinkling stars again.

Evening light would be gone soon. Dusk was robbing his canvas of its color. When Ed heard the unfamiliar whine of a turbine car on his gravel approach, he guessed that the Bipartisan Economic Combine was coming to visit him, and he was right.

"Mr. Graczyk."

"That's me."

The big car emptied itself of two men. Both wore slate gray, the Combine's color. One was a solidly-built fellow with a receding hairline and a healthy tan. He smiled as he approached. The other was shorter, and very thin, and wore a hood tossed over his head. What skin Ed could see was pale, untouched by the sun. Both men walked with the slow, cautious gait of the centrifuge-born and -raised, overcompensating for coriolis forces which were not there. Ed put his brush down.

"I'm Herb Sussaine. Combine PR," said the smiling man. "This is Thomas Rector, Combine R&D out of Adam Smith Nexus. We're glad to see you've established yourself."

Ed grunted. "It's not what I'd like to be doing."

Efficiency had made the Combine's fortunes, and efficiency drove it. Ed's inborn talent for spacecraft course correction had put his efficiency rating in the top one fiftieth of one percent. Without arms, he could no longer make his talents work for the Combine, and like all unprofitable employees was sent to Earth with best wishes and a lump-sum settlement.

Sussaine's smile widened. "We know. It's been a long time, Ed—how many years now? Six? Hardly seems like it. After you left us R&D realized a lot of good men are lost to disability every year. It's a shame to waste a good brain for lack of a good body. We want you back—and R&D will give you arms again."

Sussaine handed Ed a glossy plastic sheet. The instant Ed saw the complicated image for what it was-a blowup of a mechanical arm identical in all outward ways to a human arm—he knew he could never be satisfied with his Earth—given prostheses again.

"I'm impressed."

"I should hope so. This device can do anything an organic arm can do, and more. Forty-nine hydraulic levers in each hand, and sixteen more in each arm. All interlinked through a microprocessor equivalent to some of your better spacetug guidance systems, on a chip three millimeters by two. The chip is interfaced to your nervous system directly. The hands will respond as your old hands used to. About sixty thousand piezothermic diodes embedded in the plastic skin provide touch feedback to your nerves through the processor. On top of that, there will be a direct microwave link from the hands to the ship's computer. Our physiatrists have programmed several thousand basic hand-arm actions into the ship's compiler. The computer will smooth out the kinks from coordinated hand movements when it recognizes a common function being initiated. Even better—" Sussaine pointed to the palm of the hand in the diagram. "—each hand has an 'eye' in its palm, which images in color and three dimensions, to further assist the computer in guiding your actions. Think of the advantages of working in tight spots and with very small objects! It will be like having an extra set of eyes."

Ed scanned the drawing, tracing incredibly fine wires, outlines of tiny hydraulic pumps, the minuscule power supply, the hair-fine diode sensors scattered across the palm and concentrated on each fingertip. He had been nodding as Sussaine explained the vanous features, and when the lecture was finished he stared into the deepening night. The other man, who had said nothing until then, tossed back his hood.

"Do you want these devices, Mr. Graczyk?" His voice was deep and very soft.

Ed looked at Rector. The man's head was shaven clean in a popular Combine style, ghostly white behind piercing eyes. "Of course I want them. I wanted them when I saw the drawing. I don't need a sales pitch. But you can tell me what you people stand to gain by this. The Combine doesn't make a habit of philanthropy."

"We certainly do not," Rector said. "See it this way: When you pushed blimps for Titan Hydrocarbons, you saved us thousands of tonnes of fuel every year, and hundreds of man-hours of labor. What you did alone is done by a crew of three now. This project has been expensive, but if it enables you to work for us for only six years, your remarkable efficiency rating will absorb all costs. After that it will work wholly to our profit. The computers at Physiology Central give you forty more productive years at .7 G average. The savings that represents is something to consider."

Ed rose, smiling. "That sounds more like the Combine I know. Do I get my old job back?"

Rector shook his head. "We're going to try something new. You'll be flying the tanker *King Lear* in cislunar orbit, distributing liquid hydrogen, oxygen, and water to several stations and plants we have found awkward to supply by conventional methods. You'll be picking up water from the smaller stations, which use fuel cells, and giving it to the larger fusion-powered plants which generate no water on their own. Your mass will thus be continually changing, and this kind of problem has never been easy to deal with. We trust that your approximations will be better than anyone else's. Aside from your work itinerary, the contract is standard."

Ed looked at the proffered contract. "Hmmm. My signature is poor these days, and I haven't got a thumbprint."

"Toeprint will do. When can you leave, Ed?"

Ed looked away toward his little dome. "Can you wait ten minutes? I never got out of the habit of living out of a footlocker. But first...tell me something. Why bring a PR man along? No offense, Herb, but I know your job: You deal with these crazy Earth people. I'm a Combine man. Always have been."

Rector looked up at the first stars. Several of the great orbiting stations and plants were drifting across the sky, brilliant white points. "A precaution. Furloughed Combine employees have picked up some objectionable attitudes down here in the past. Earth can be like that, and we couldn't be sure about you. Herb could tell me if you had grown a little too...Earthlike."

Ed chuckled. Night was complete now, a nearly palpable darkness. "Maine is the nearest thing to space that Earth can offer. I never really left."

Ed turned and followed the gravel path back to his dome.

II.

Barefooted and chewing a wad of gum, Ed Graczyk drifted from handhold to handhold in *King Lear*'s crawlspace on his semi-daily inspection tour. Docking with Golwing Nozzles Plant 7 was three hours away. Fifty kiloliters of liquid hydrogen to be dropped there, and then it was a leisurely climb to the first of three R&D stations in wide lunar orbit. Ed had the entire schedule committed to memory.

Terminal 19. Last one. Soft plastic flesh gripped the handhold while Ed considered the small hole set into a plate beneath six guarded controls. A jack. For a most unusual sort of plug.

He curled all his fingers but his second-to-last (something he could never have accomplished with their organic forerunners) and plugged the finger firmly into the hole. He closed his eyes and weighed the feelings coming in on the finger. The six monitor voltages which surfaced in Terminal 19 had become a harmony of textures, six separate sensations which Ed could only compare to running each finger of one hand over a material of distinct and different texture. The feeling of harmony was important. If any of the six voltages had changed value, a weird tactile cacophony would alert him to a misadjustment in the system. By adjusting the six controls above the jack, the sensations could be brought back into harmony, and proper operation obtained again.

The adjustments were independent of sight and hearing. Even if blinded and in a vacuum, Ed could service his ship and bring it back to port.

The six textures marched in step. Ed removed his finger from the jack and dusted his hands symbolically. R&D had done a good job. Just below each shoulder a polished steel band encircled each arm. Above each ten-centimeter strip was flesh and blood. Below each was steel and synthetic, but in the minimal light of the crawl space Ed could see no difference.

Ahh, but when they moved—the hands did not jerk, twitch, or tremble as organic hands did. They flowed. With the ship's computer assisting, every movement of every tiny finger-segment was coordinated to the movement of the whole. And when Ed would reach for a screwdriver, the computer would recognize the action and guide the hand to graceful, perfect completion of the act.

A finger touch against a handhold sent him drifting toward the center of the ship, past a wall of gray panels, beams, and dim light-spots. To the other side of him, behind a thin steel mesh, the ship's centrifuge turned silently. He swung feet-first through the frictionless magnetic repulsion bearing at the center of the centrifuge and began the twelve-meter clamber ever more strongly downward.

"*King Lear* from R&D Six."

Ed settled himself into the control couch. "Come in, Rector. Good copy here. Just got back."

The efficiency engineer seldom wasted energy and bandwidth on video. The screen remained dark. "Our physiatrists just handed me the printout on the latest data set on your arms. They tell me coordination and reaction time have reached the expected plateau. I had hoped they might have kept on improving, but…well, they did better than we predicted. It looks as though nothing we can do will improve the hookup. Do you like them?"

Ed grinned. "Love 'em. Every sausage-bumper should blow his arms off for a set of these."

"What I should have asked: Will you be able to create that sort of rapport you once had with your spacecraft through the prostheses? That rapport is crucial to regaining your efficiency rating."

Ed flexed plastic fingers on the couch arm. "It's not a matter of 'through' anymore. One way to define machinery is that it's 'out there', and I'm in here." He thumbed at his head to a blind vidicon. "The hands aren't 'out there' anymore. I can think with my fingertips again."

Rector's soft voice sounded pleased. "That's a good deal better than we had hoped. With all your data in, we've gotten most of the glitches out of a mechanical leg and an entire lower torso-leg combination for double amputees. We'll probably never lose a good man to a disabling accident again. What's your ETA at Golwing?"

"Mmm...hundred thirty-eight minutes, unless I decide to fine tune again."

"I got a request from Plant Manager Pilsen up there. He's heard about the project and wants to see your hands. Golwing's a fair-risk plant and has its share of disabling accidents. Interest in this sort of thing is high over there. You have the usual half-hour contingency time you never need. Pilsen wonders if you'll stop in for a 'small demonstration.' I told him I would ask, but I warn you, half the plant will be there to gawk."

"Tell him I'll do a video show for the whole plant. Nobody gets left out that way and I get an excuse to stay in here."

"Good. I'll relay. Rector out."

Golwing Seven hung above a waxing Earth, bright steel in the sunlight. Ed watched it grow on his screens. The plant was a thousand-meter cylinder girdled by two centrifuges rotating in opposite directions. Docked at both ends of the cylinder were a scattering of freighters and supply ships. *King Lear* was approaching from the "north" or receiving end. A small pockmark in the wide expanse of shadowed metal was winking at him with its docking strobes. Ed would insert *King Lear*'s nose in the center of the docking collar, and automatic pumps would withdraw the proper amount of the proper fuel from *Lear*'s huge tanks.

It was not a difficult maneuver. A computer could do a fair approximation, but Ed's courses invariably saved time and fuel.

The docking collar slowly grew to a bright-rimmed hole with a blinking eye in the center. Ed peered at the screen and rubbed his eyes with one hand. Something looked wrong with that collar. There was a dim trace of gray in one side of that central hole.

The scene grew dizzily as *Lear* bore down. The course programmer fired another set of braking blasts. When the exhaust gases cleared away, Ed saw what was wrong with the collar: a suited human figure was curled inside.

Ed hit three buttons and touched his throat mike. The braking jets fired again. "Golwing, there is somebody in my damned docking collar! What are you going to do about it?" He was less afraid than furiously angry. The laws of physics did not forgive such idiotic behavior.

The comm tech was incredulous. "Confirm your message, *Lear*: 'Someone is in my docking collar.' Is that correct?"

Ed was sweating. "Don't question my sanity! There is a body curled up around the docking strobe of my collar. A million tonnes of tanker is going to plug into that hole in one minute! What the hell are you going to do about it"

"We can't do anything in a minute. Stop your approach with the full emergency forward brake program. We'll send out a detail."

Ed saw the scene in his mind: *Lear*'s nose jets a small sun, throwing a six-gee reaction forward toward the collar. *Lear* would stop in ten seconds. And the detail would find a greasy ash in the collar.

Ed reached to one side of his console and fired a signal flare directly in the course of *Lear*'s travel. The flare struck the plant's plates a meter to one side of the collar. It flared brilliant red for a moment and was gone.

The last of the braking jets fired. *Lear* coasted slowly toward the collar. The figure shifted in the collar but remained. Ed fired two more flares. At such close range, their concussion must have been heard throughout the plant.

Then the figure moved. In the last seconds to docking Ed watched it clamber up to the edge of the collar. Then the bulk of the ship hid the collar from view. The scene remained in Ed's mind: a human being climbing frantically over the collar's ring of extended docking fingers...

Chunnnnnnnnnnnnnnnng!

Lear heaved back and forth for several seconds as the ring absorbed the last of the tanker's momentum. Then, red lights flashed on the Unplanned Occurrences board. The computer sized up the situation:

FOREIGN OBJECT WEDGED BETWEEN DOCKING FINGER NINE AND DOCKING COLLAR. DOCKING INCOMPLETE.

"Christ," Ed muttered as he scrambled madly up the ladder toward the airlock.

Less than a minute later, in a special emergency suit that left his plastic hands ungloved, Ed blew the emergency hatch near Lear's nose and bore down on the docking ring. Filling his helmet were screams, throat-racking screams.

The screams of a young woman.

Ed hit the plates feet-first where the woman was trapped, a husky spring-puller in his hands. The woman's left leg was crushed between the jointed docking finger and the mating groove on Lear's nose. Air was silently issuing from her rup-tured suit, mingled with tiny spherical droplets of red that soon froze cold pink.

Ed braced his feet against *Lear*'s nose and jammed the spring-puller into the breakaway spring mount. He pried violently to one side. The finger hesitated, then with snapping release gave way and swung outward.

Ed threw the spring-puller away into the void and began unfolding a transparent casualty bag. He stuffed the scream-ing, thrashing woman into it as though she were a load of laundry, and pulled the pin on the attached cylinder of air. The bag expanded to a fat pillow that rapidly frosted over on the inside.

Pulling his burden by a corner, Ed tramped across the plates on magnetic soles to a cast-wide hatch from which the detail had begun issuing. Ed waved them aside with what looked like a hand exposed to the vacuum of space. Ed pushed the bag ahead of him into the lock and climbed in after it.

When pressure rose in the lock and the anteroom beyond, he heard her screaming: "I want to die! Let me die, damn you!"

Helmet tucked under his arm, he watched medics anesthetize the girl and struggle to reassemble the crushed knee joint and shredded muscles surrounding it. He knew before they began the incision with blue-hot laser pencils that they would have to amputate. Ed had been down that path before.

The plant manager approached him, a hunted-looking little man with shaven head and sunken eyes. "Mr. Graczyk, that was incredible. You had her in the bag before we could get a crisis team suited up and out the door. It must have been your hands…"

"Shut up," Ed snapped, turning on the man. He had begun to tremble so hard he almost let his helmet slip away from him. "How many more potential suicides are working for you? How long will it be before somebody decides to detonate a few ounces of pyroform under his mattress and sets half a centrifuge on fire?"

Pilsen looked down. "She was on probation."

"And now she's off. It almost cost us my tanker…and a lot of machinery on this end of your plant. If it had, she wouldn't have been the only one out of a job."

Ed looked back toward the girl. The ruined leg was gone, the stump covered with a plastic cocoon. The medics were wheeling her away. "There's still lots of ways to die, love," he said under his breath. "Lots."

III.

Out beyond Saturn, Ed's arms were burning again, his entire body wrapped in fiery hell. He thrashed in the void, but the flames would not go out. It was worse than fire; it ate at him to the center of his bones. It stung every blood cell moving through his veins. Fire, he was on fire and falling slowly into the Sun…

Ed Graczyk awoke. But the fire was still there.

He stared at his hands. From the nerves inside the stumps of his arms he could feel the fire coming, creeping in consuming waves from his plastic fingertips to the center of his brain. He twisted the hands around, and stared into the little black spots set into the centers of his palms: his hands' eyes. He almost thought he could see tiny flames flickering inside those dark circles.

Then the fire went out. From the comm console beside his cot, Rector spoke to him.

"Ed, you're awake. What's the matter? We thought we'd never rouse you."

Ed stared at his hands, then looked to the comm console. "You did that? I thought they were going to eat me alive!"

The efficiency engineer spoke calmly. "We rang buzzers, flashed the cabin lights, had the computer sing songs you hate. Nothing worked. You stayed asleep."

Anger roared up in him, like the flames he had felt licking his guts. "So? What if I decide I want another hour's sleep? I don't think I've ever missed an inspection tour in my entire career."

"It's not in the contract."

"It's never been in any contract I've worked under."

Rector said nothing for a long time. "Ed, your contract specifies eight hours sleep per duty period. The itinerary spells out retiring and rising times. It's all there. You signed it."

It was said coldly. Ed forced himself to be as cold. "A contract is an agreement specifying conditions to be met by the contracting parties. I agree to guide this ship to specified points at specified times and do specified tasks along the way. That's my job. You supply my pay. That's your job. I have never derelicted my job. You have not derelicted yours. We, both of us, have kept that contract."

"The itinerary is part of the contract."

"Getting up at 06:00:00 is *not* a part of my job!"

"No, Ed, not quite that simple. Your job is to maximize output for given input. That is the job of every person who works for the Bipartisan Economic Combine. Human function is an equation with a very large number of variables. Some of those variables we leave up to you—course correction, obviously. If we could do that better than you we would not pay you to do it. Other things—diet, sleep schedules, rest schedules, work schedules—have been plotted very precisely according to your biorhythms. We have men who specialize in such things. We have entire departments devoted to nothing but optimizing sleep schedules. We assume they can do their job better than you can. Or we would not have hired them."

"I'm tired," Ed said. "The Golwing incident shot my nerves."

"There are drugs for that in the medconsole."

It was true. Ed nodded, feeling sheepish. He had never thought of it. Before his next sleep period he took a double tranquilizer, and awoke five minutes late with flames engulfing his dreams. He wretched from the pain until he remembered to point the palms of his hands toward his sweating face.

"What the hell do you think I am!" he roared at Rector.

"You're a Combine man. You work for a living. You maintain a high level of competency in keeping with your salary. You forgot to set your alarm."

That, too, was true, but Ed's anger got the better of him. "Fold it five ways, Rector. I'll take a burn-specific before I turn in."

Without warning it struck, for only a moment: a resonance of absolute agony ringing up and down his entire nervous system, as though he were a bell struck by a red-hot hammer, echoing until he wished for death. By the time he could scream it was gone.

His arms tingled coldly, well up into his shoulders. Ed looked, unbelievingly, at the palms of his hands. There was warning in Rector's words:

"We will accept your resignation at any time."

Ed had to bite his lip to keep back what he was thinking. If the hands could watch, they could probably listen as well.

You'll have my resignation, but not the way you think!

IV.

Lots of ways to die—the thought came to Ed often as the days passed. It came on the heels of the crazy dream that made him feel alternately exhilarated and ashamed. Rector was wrong in assuming that Ed Graczyk was the same man who had once nudged methane blimps around the solar system. Still, Ed told himself that he was a man, and deserved better.

Indecision made his mouth dry while he browsed through *King Lear*'s engineering manuals. He had done that often before, simply for curiosity's sake, to be better acquainted with his ship. Now he was looking for something, nothing in particular, but he knew that it would announce itself when he found it.

One evening, the crazy dream crystallized on the page of an engineering manual, and left Ed with an agonizing decision. To betray the Combine by his own hands... He swore, and then laughed. His hands would have nothing to do with it.

Several times each day Ed left the centrifuge for various parts of the ship. To re-enter, he had to pass through the center of the two-meter diameter frictionless magnetic repulsion bearing which held the rotating centrifuge away from the stationary ship's core. It was an automatic action: reach hands into the meter-wide opening, grasp handholds there, and swing body with a clockwise twist into the rotating tunnel within. Ed began adding a new, strange action to the procedure.

Each time he swung his body into the tunnel, he pulled his mouth up against the line where the rotating bearing met the stationary core. With his tongue he pressed a wad of chewing gum into the six-millimeter gap where intense superconducting magnetic fields held the two surfaces apart.

Some weeks later, Ed woke from a deep sleep with crawling nausea wrenching his stomach. Another slow, slithering lurch threw his body against its sleep tethers. A low, nearly subaudible moan came down to him from the center of the centrifuge, and his nose picked up the acrid smell of burning insulation. Moments later the malfunction alarm began sounding, and Ed was climbing out of his cot, trembling all over. No going back now.

He did not have to feign grogginess. Rector's thin, peering face met his at the comm console. It was not like Rector to be using video. Ed felt himself being scrutinized.

"Ed, the centrifuge bearing is beginning to seize up. We don't know what, but something leaked into the gap. Shut down the centrifuge and get on it."

Ed waved a wordless salute. He leaned over, ripped the cover from a guarded switch, and threw it home. As though some velvety hand had grasped the rim of the centrifuge, it slowed to a smooth halt. Ed heard the emergency flywheel coming up to speed with the angular momentum from the centrifuge. His weight lifted away from him, and he gripped a handhold while trying to shake himself awake. Eddy currents induced in the moist chicle had heated, dried, and eventually hardened it until the heat of friction made it burn. Ed had made odds with himself that the coolant control circuitry feeding the super-conducting magnets within the bearing would not be able to respond to such an impossible situation, and he was right. It was hard to suppress a smile as he read to Rector a list of micro-circuits that had overheated and burned out.

"Fix those microcircuits *first*," Rector was saying. "If too much of your coolant bleeds off as gas, you won't have enough to go around. The computer won't work without it."

Ed tried to look worried, but the only thing worrying him was how to make the rest of his liquid helium coolant boil and bleed off into space. He headed for the tool locker.

Every part of Ed Graczyk was shaking except his hands. This was a new Ed, one he himself had never suspected could exist. To damage his own ship...he shivered, but continued tucking tools into a belt kit. Only his hands didn't know what he was doing. Smoothly, expertly, they executed their motions. Almost by themselves. Ed swallowed hard. The hands did not share his pangs of conscience. Ed finished filling the kit, and clambered barefoot up a crawlspace to Ship's Circuitry.

Circuitry itself was a crawlspace of sorts: a narrow channel between wide walls of hexagonal panels, each dimpled with reactionless bolt wells and printed with a large code number. Ed drifted between the walls, pushing with his fingertips against occasional handholds. Part of his mind was unhurriedly looking for panel VV47. The rest was steeling itself to what it intended to do. The arms were controlled by the ship's computer. The computer had to go. Once it was gone, the computer on Ed's shoulders could take care of the last step in his plan.

The computer was helpless without its main memory, stored in superconducting magnetic bubbles frozen into hair-thin sheets of tellurium. Ed's trick with the gum had caused a good part of Lear's liquid helium to be lost. It hadn't been enough, as Ed had more than half expected. There was another way.

A last finger's touch slowed and stopped him in front of panel VV47. All coolant controls, including main memory's, were behind that one panel. He only had to reach for a tool with one hand, steady himself with the other, while he did…what he had practiced so often in his head.

Quickly, smoothly, he plucked the little reactionless bolt driver from his kit and shoved it into one of the hexagonal wells in the corner of the panel. Through his hands he felt the socket inside the driver's nose fit over the head of the bolt in the well while the outside of the nose gripped the sides of the well. One hand easily squeezed the two halves of the handle together, and the bolt came loose.

The computer tie-in, as always, was working very well. Ed felt he need only begin the operation, and the hands would take it from there, almost automatically. They plugged the driver into the second well, squeezed, and repeated the operation for the other wells without Ed having to think about it. Ed was sweating heavily. He could feel drops growing on his forehead, fat drops with no place to fall.

With a grace that was almost poetry, Ed's hands pulled the panel away and stuck it to a velcro patch nearby. Four eyes peered into the crowded space behind the panel. Stack upon stack of tiny microcircuit boards filled the half-meter-wide hole. A sour taste of tension came into Ed's mouth. Nothing but circuit boards. No fat bus lines, no husky switching diodes, none of the components that his memory told him were also behind VV47. The manuals had betrayed him in his own betrayal. And the centrifuge bearing was still full of chewing gum.

Lots of ways to die, he thought, *and I bet they know some I don't.* He closed his eyes, forced panic away, and hoped his hesitation would not be noticed by Rector and the hands. When he opened them he found himself looking at the panel immediately above the one he had opened. It read: VU47.

Something in his subconscious started screaming: *A U can look like a V.* It was there, only one panel away. Perhaps a quick check; preventive maintenance? Hardly; that was what computers were for. It would smell like a month-old egg. That left only the hard way. And he had better start soon.

The reactionless bolt driver was hanging in the air where he had parked it. Ed reached into the hole without hurrying and pulled a stack of boards free of its connector. As it came loose, he let his elbow nudge the driver gently upward.

Ed glared at the drifting driver as it approached his face. He wondered if his hands could hear as well as see. He leaned toward the driver, checking to make sure his palms were down. *Now I have to keep them that way.*

When his lips brushed the driver's handle, Ed inhaled sharply. He caught the tool in his teeth and worked it around so that he could work the thin split handle between his jaws. Ed bit down, felt it turn easily. The bolts would give him more of a fight.

Two intricate tasks to do at once. Madness! Ed wanted to laugh, but the driver filled his mouth. He peered down past the driver to the stack of circuit boards in his hands. The hands knew what to do. Ed privately thanked the Combine's phys-iatrists. He started the hands on the action of unclipping the boards from the stack connector. The hands recognized the action and took over. While the stack came free like a deck of cards, Ed leaned forward and plugged the bolt driver into the first bolt-well on panel VU 47.

He bit down hard. The effort made his molars ache, but the bolt came free with a snap. Two more squeezes removed it. He hoped the hands would not notice the lurch as he swung his head to one side and plugged the driver into the second well. That bolt gave up easily.

His hands were smoothly riffling through the freed boards. Ed watched with one eye and half his mind. He was already maneuvering the driver to the fifth bolt well when the proper board appeared. Ed cautiously directed his hands to the belt kit, where they removed the replacement microcircuits and an insertion tool. Simultaneously he jabbed for the fifth well, missed, and then plunged it home. He bit down. Nothing. Another hard bite met only solid resistance and a spreading ache in his jaws. Ed glanced down and helped the hands place the insertion tool over the first bad circuit. All the time he was working the tool further back along his jaw for more lever-age. Ed tensed himself and clenched his jaws in a tremendous spasm that was all he felt he could exert. The bolt released, the driver slipped, and Ed bit down hard on his tongue.

Tears welled up in his eyes, and even the hands paused. Ed tasted blood, and swallowed hard. Bad time to scream, and with the driver in his mouth he might choke. His hands effort-lessly removed the bad chip. They positioned the new chip and snapped it into place. Ed felt desperation growing with the pain in his mouth. He jabbed the driver into the last well.

And knocked it out of his mouth.

First, panic. Then came the flood of cool analysis that had made him what he had been, once. *No space mechanic ever lets his tools get away from him.* Rector knew that. Convection cur-rents could make a tool start drifting away. Ed casually reached out his left hand, snatched the driver, and parked it near his shoulder with just enough drift to carry it toward his face. Ed sucked the tool into his mouth and positioned it with a burning tongue. He had the second bad chip out and was positioning the new one. Quickly! Ed forced himself to be calm and inserted the driver into the last hole. The bolt resisted. He noticed a thread of blood and saliva creeping horizontally out of one corner of his mouth. Ed bit savagely, and felt the ragged crunch of a bicuspid chipping against the hard plastic of the driver's handle. The bolt gave way.

Ed simultaneously restacked and clipped the boards and pried the newly freed panel up and out of the way with the metal shank of the bolt driver. The hands knew what they were doing. Through tearing eyes Ed looked at the newly exposed circuitry.

It was all vaguely familiar. Several aluminum bars carried heavy currents to and from the cooling and pumping units handling the liquid helium which cooled the computer's main memory. It had to be the *right* one, and the decision would have to be made in seconds. The proper bar carried a harmless six hundred amps at five volts, but there were bars carrying two and three hundred volts. Which, which...

An inquiring buzz arose in the nerves of his arm-stumps. Rector had sensed something going on. The hands snapped the board stack back into place. The buzz turned into a rasping burr on the edge of discomfort. Ed's anger boiled over.

Now!

Ed clamped his eyes shut and plunged his head forward toward what he hoped with all his heart was the right bus bar. The steel shank clicked against the bar and the tip brushed the frame.

A small explosion echoed in Circuitry. Sparks burned Ed's face and closed eyelids. The driver was welded to both bus bar and frame, sizzling and arcing. The lights around him dimmed Many went out altogether. Alarms began to wail in the distance.

"Go to hell!" Ed screamed at the alarms, and threw a screwdriver away into the gloom. He heard it caroming from one panel to another.

As though in answer, the hands began to devour him. Lightning coursed down his spine and ate its way back up to the base of his brain. Ed screamed. Molten lava was streaming out of his hands into his shoulders, flowing down to settle in his lungs and diaphragm. Tiny jaws were tearing at every muscle in his body. He curled himself into a fetal position, thrashed blindly between the walls, felt his heels dent the thin metal panels. A fiery yellow cloud congealed at the center of his brain and began eating its way outward, devouring his consciousness as it went. *Kill me, then, and waste your damned expensive hands!* he thought through electronic agony.

The pain gradually died away. Every muscle in his body ached at its passing. Ed shook his head and slapped his cheeks to clear his mind. Was the computer finally dead? It had to be! But the hands maintained a coarse rasp that pulsed every so often into pain. He knew what they were telling him: *Go back to the centrifuge.*

Rector's face was at the comm console, angry.

"Sabotage of Combine property is a capital offense, Ed. You'll probably have to prove insanity to save your life now."

Ed's tongue lay thick in his mouth. He swallowed blood. Speech was painful. "Shove off. I've never been saner in my life. If you decide to kill me, I'll just crank open a hatch…

Ed saw the foolishness of that. Rector was impassive. "I don't think so."

Ed shrugged. "So I didn't kill the computer?"

The small shrewish face never showed hatred; Ed thought it had grown more intense. "Main memory lost cooling, and blanked when the plates went ohmic for lack of helium. We will beam back what was lost after you've replaced a few more parts."

"Then why do the hands still work?" Ed flexed his fingers. The strange expertise provided by the computer was gone, but they followed orders, from both Ed and his employers.

Rector smiled. "They have an independent radio link to R&D through the Cislunar Repeater Network. We put more into those hands than we mentioned. Now get to work."

The hands pulsed one hot pang for emphasis. Ed's eyes watered, and he turned away from the comm console.

For two days Ed worked without daring to scratch his nose. He knew the Combine had a five-man crew watching every move he made, each with his own individual pain button. Ed had felt it more than once. Sometimes it made him smile. They were frightened of him, based on what he had done. It was a shame he could do nothing more.

He had been a careless saboteur. With a little more planning it might have worked, and he could have been on his way to the Iron Republic of Mars. For bringing in the *King Lear* he could buy citizenship and a thousand hectares of newly terraformed land—not that he wanted or needed the land. The Iron Republic had nearly as few spacemen as it had ships. Even if Ed had only his nose to guide a ship with, they would let him stay in space.

Now, after repairing his ship, he would report to Curie Station, be arrested, tried, and probably executed. He continued to work only because work was as much a habit as living.

"You know, Rector, I think you're as crazy as I am," Ed said once before beginning a short sleep period. "You spent a fortune making me three-quarters of a superman, and then drove me insane with the fine print of a contract. Is a contract worth the life of a good worker?"

Rector answered without video. "You're not insane, Ed. You're an Earthman. Earthmen don't respect contracts. And contracts are the only things that make the Combine work."

Before dropping into sleep, Ed thought: *Yes, he is absolutely right.*

Sweating heavily, Ed removed the last bolt from the top plate of the superconducting memory unit. A hiss of helium gas sang around the loosening gasket. Ed pried with a screwdriver. A last gasp of gas, and the lid swung upward.

The unit was a Dewar flask filled with microscopically etched tellurium, chilled to zero resistance by liquid helium. The temperature controls had been ruined, and the unit could not keep itself colder than one hundred degrees Kelvin. Still, a blast of arctic cold met his face as Ed sized up the huge squat pressure tank. The tellurium sheets were arranged like the spokes of a sparkling wheel around the hollow at the center of the tank. That was the liquid helium reservoir, empty now. Thirty centimeters down were the ruined controls.

Ed pulled some tools from his kit and parked them in the steaming air over the reservoir. Pliers in hand, he leaned over the empty space and peered downward. He backed off very quickly.

Wobbling up to meet him was a meter-wide bubble of liquid helium.

Ed gasped in surprise. It was the last of several thousand liters of helium that the device was meant to contain. Most had boiled into gas and had been bled off into space. The bubble rose on convection currents, cloaked in a veil of condensing water vapor and atmospheric gases. It started to bubble and froth as heat from the air reached it. As much as Ed had depended on liquid helium for computer functions, he had never before seen it. The cold air biting his cheeks seemed almost hot. Cold could destroy as well as flame. Better.

Ed screamed a choking scream of defiance, and plunged his arms to the elbows into the sphere of deadly cold.

Instantly the fires began, roaring out of his arms to wrench and twist his body in unbearable agony. He screamed again, biting his wounded tongue, but focused every jot of concentration in his body on keeping his arms within the steaming bubble. His legs kicked involuntarily. His whole body throbbed to the tune of pain the hands were playing on his body. He closed his eyes and tried to shut out the pain, and kept thinking: *Die, freeze, die!* The yellow cloud of oblivion began to condense in his head again. He could not allow that to happen. *Die, damn you!*

The feeling crept in from his fingertips: a crawling numbness that devoured the pain that was devouring him. It spread up the tiny golden wires and steel shafts inside the hands. The fingers twitched and twisted for a moment as sudden superconductivity sent false pulses racing through freezing motors. He saw the hands bend in a grotesque clawlike position, and freeze.

The pain was gone. Only cold numbness remained. Ed was breathing fast as he pulled his hands from the boiling helium and stared at them. The pink plastic was frozen a brittle white. Quickly, quickly!

The bubble, much smaller now, had drifted off to one side. Ed raised his right arm over his head, and brought it down as hard as he could on the edge of the thick-walled memory unit. The arm cracked off and continued downward, smashing the delicate tellurium plates. Bright fragments tumbled about in the air. He raised his left arm and brought it down even harder. It shattered into several pieces, which caromed off the memory tank and hit his face. They burned him with their coldness.

Ed stared at the jagged plastic stumps steaming on the ends of his arms.

He was free.

V.

Ed laughed. They were offering him amnesty in return for the *King Lear.* He had held a video two-way with Rector and Sussaine, the Earth-specialist PR man, for more than twenty minutes. Behind them Ed could see the computing machinery and gray-uniformed tacticians of a Conflict Center. Ed realized grimly that the Combine was a lot for one unarmed man in an unarmed tanker to take on.

But after thinking for a moment, he stopped worrying.

"Come on, Herb," he told Sussaine, who was doing all the talking. "The moment I step clear of my ship I'll get a twenty-one gun salute right through the head. And while we're talking promises I'll make you one: As soon as whatever you have tailing me gets within boarding range I'll blow myself up. Seventy percent of my mass is liquid hydrogen, kerosene #3, LOX, and assorted hypergolics. I'll make a nice fireball, and do my damndest to take any followers with me."

Sussaine tried to look smug. "We have three S-class Gray-stingers on an intersecting course. Their laser cannon are lethal at two hundred kilometers."

Ed shook his head. "Graystingers chasing old *Lear*? I don't think so. Let's do a little Combine arithmetic. I've been boosting at a constant quarter-G for almost four hours. I have enough fuel to do that almost forever; hell, I'm *all* fuel. Bringing a Graystinger up to Battle-Green takes two hours, and for three ships costs maybe ten percent of what I'm worth. To catch me with that head start would take two solid fuel strap-on boosters per 'stinger, at a cost of another ten-percent per booster. Paying a 'stinger crew battle grade for a week is another ten percent of *Lear*'s net value. Fuel, wear, and refitting the 'stingers after a long chase would probably be another fifteen or twenty percent. Right there you've already got 120% of what my entire ship and cargo are worth. The Combine would sell its own mother to make a profit, but your contracts forbid you to incur a penny's loss for revenge. That's listed as a 'Nonproductive expense, never justified,' Article IV, Section 14, Paragraph 141 of the General Contractual Regulations. Give up. You lose. I win. Admit it."

Sussaine's face reddened. "You're not going scot-free..."

"Stand aside, Herb." Rector pushed ahead of the PR man and looked wearily at Ed. "It'll be a long time before we trust an Earthman again. Yes, you've won. The course you're following is optimal to several decimal places, and you did it in your head. You will get to Iron Republic space hours before we can do anything about it. We lose, and I'm in trouble. It won't happen again." Ed saw Rector begin reaching to terminate the connection. Herb Sussaine caught his arm and pushed back in front of the video pickup.

"Graczyk, you don't have any arms! How in hell do you expect to fly a tanker all the way to Mars?"

Ed chuckled. "Ask Rector," he said, and switched the screen off with his big toe.

Ed sighed and spun his chair around with his other foot. The centrifuge was turning again, more slowly, but enough to keep him comfortable in the long weeks ahead. His stumps were beginning to hurt and his tongue still felt twice its size, but *Lear*'s medconsole would keep him alive long enough to reach Republic space.

His course was perfect. Now there was nothing to do but kill time following it. Ed would be doing a lot of painting before he reached Mars. He slouched in his chair and picked up a brush with his toes. With his other foot he squeezed a bright orange worm of paint onto his palette.

On his easel was the canvas he intended to present to the President of the Iron Republic of Mars upon his investiture as a citizen: A study of Venus de Milo in a space helmet.

Ed Graczyk got to work.   ■

Afterword: Cold Hands

Like several other stories I eventually sold into professional markets, "Cold Hands" had its beginnings at the Clarion Science Fiction Workshop, which I attended in the summer of 1973 at Michigan State University in East Lansing. Like today's National Novel Writing Month (NaNoWriMo) the emphasis there was getting things down on paper in completed form, if not necessarily polished and editor-ready. It took several years, a couple of heavy revisions, and a lot of wadded-up paper, but I finally sold the story to George Scithers at *Asimov's,* where it appeared in 1980.

The story's reception surprised me a little. It had given me a lot of trouble and I've never been entirely happy with it, but it garnered a pile of fan mail from people I had never met—and eventually landed on the final Hugo ballot in 1981, in tandem with my AI story "Guardian," which you can find in my other collection, *Souls in Silicon.*

"Cold Hands" takes place against the background of the Tripartisan Economic Combine, a future history I had been concocting since high school. Other Combine stories that made it into the professional press were "The Steel Sonnets" and "Borovsky's Hollow Woman," while still others have languished in my trunk to this day. Future history is a tricky business, and without saying a great deal more about the problem, I'll admit that by the late 1980s I no longer believed in the framework I had worked so hard on since I'd been 17. Once I noticed that I had begun making fun of my own future history (as you'll see when I publish my humorous novella "Firejammer!" next year) I knew it was time to reboot.

I've told other writers down the years, and I'll say it again: When your subconscious starts to giggle, it's trying to tell you something. Pay attention!

Our Lady
of the Endless Sky

1974

OUR LADY OF THE ENDLESS SKY

I

U nder a transparent dome made invisible by the lunar night, the Mother of God stretched out her arms to embrace the stone horizon. Beyond the tips of her marble fingers rock and steel lay ash-gray under a waxing Earth. Above her peaceful white brow, the stars stood guard in a sky so deep it had no bottom.

In front of the native granite pedestal in the nearly finished church, Father Thomas Bernberger knelt and prayed.

Let them see what I see now, Mother, and they would run to you.

A faint crunching vibration entered his knees from the dusty floor, newly inlaid with pastel blue tile. Bernberger looked up. Bright light flashes off metal dazzled his eyes. The polished aluminum boom of a crane hove into view and wobbled slowly out of sight beyond the wall that supported the transparent dome. They were driving it to the construction site, where a third of the station personnel were planting new machines in the lunar soil.

Bernberger went back to his personal miseries at the feet of the statue. Not an hour before, Monsignor Garif had spoken to him on the S-band from Houston. As twice in the past, the news was of the rising number of American churches closing their doors permanently. Not due to a lack of funds; the Interfaith Council assured each pastor a living and attempted to keep the buildings standing. It seemed pointless, however, to preach the Gospel to empty pews.

They've lost their horizons. They can't tell the sky from the concrete.

Unlimited energy had put food into even the poorest of mouths in the First World continent. Physical suffering through disease and hunger were becoming rare. Where, then, were the multitudes who should have been giving thanks?

Earth hovered permanently over Mary's white shoulder. *Help them look up, Mother.*

He felt another vibration through the floor. It was slower than before, an wavered in frequency. No crane boom showed itself above the walls. Bernberger rose from his knees, curious, and climbed the first four steps of a light metal ladder the electricians had left behind.

Beyond the reach of the station's huge blue-white night lamps, the landscape was shadowy and unreal. Grinding its way down the gravel-paved road outside the dome was a huge ten-wheeled flatbed truck, its bulbous tires flattening under the weight of its large blockish load. Still more junk for the construction site. Bernberger wasn't quite sure what they were building there. The site at the end of the makeshift road was near Cluster A of glittering Garden domes, each dome itself a cluster of warm yellow stars, each star an artificial sun above a section of the dome's hydroponic garden. The project had something to do with the generation of power for the Garden complex. Station Commander Andreas Kreski always demanded more expansion, more new construction, perpetually twisting the arms of his Earthside contacts in business and government for additional funding. His vision was self-sufficiency for Station Grissom, and every new dome, every new corridor snaking across the dust of Sinus Iridum brought that vision closer to reality.

Two small beetle-like trucks were following the large flatbed toward the site. Bernberger shook his head and climbed down the ladder. He dusted the grout from his knees. As always, more machines. On wheels, on treads, under domes, and beneath the lunar soil the machines proliferated. Still, only seven new people had been added to the station staff in the past four months. The priest wondered why they didn't just send the men home and let the machines spread themselves solidly across the Moon's surface.

Father Bernberger picked up his clipboard and continued sketching out his report on the progress of the Moon's only church. The main altar was almost finished. The great slab of white maple, the first of its kind in human history to rise above the smoky pall of Earth's atmosphere, would soon bear the re-enactment of the Supper. It had been set on its rough-hewn lunar granite pillar, and would be consecrated within the month. The rotator for the large, two-sided cross had been set discreetly beneath the floor behind the altar. A lectern of woodlike synthetic stood to the altar's right. Bernberger mentioned them and made note of his satisfaction with them on the multiple forms.

Only a little remained unfinished: painting, some electrical work, the pews for the faithful and the large dual cross itself, Corpus on one side and plain bare gold on the other.

Bernberger turned to the statue. Crafted on Earth of Italian marble, it towered more than two meters high on its pedestal of lunar rock. The stars shone on her undimmed. He could not look at her and not feel a cool shiver of wonder down his spine. *How many kilos of propellant brought you out of Earth's arms to this place, my Lady?* Kreski kept telling him, over and over, but Bernberger had made it a point not to remember. Kreski loved to speculate on the riches of the Church spent to build a church on the Moon as millions starved in the enslaved East.

But the poor will always be with you. He had said that, the Christ. And the power of the Church could not always reach past the walls of oppression. God would care for His poor when His ministers were barred from them. Yes. The Lord would care for them. Kreski would nod, and nod, and walk away, still nodding.

At those times Father Bernberger felt very small, and false somehow. Kreski was a huge man, brilliant and cold in his understanding of machines and Moon-science. Thomas Bernberger, third son of an Indianapolis housewife, dark and short, mouse-quick and mouse-quiet in all he did, was no match for the station commander and shrank from Kreski's sharp challenges. What was a priest doing on the Moon when there was work to be done on Earth? Bernberger glanced around at the incomplete church, and thought of the machines and thrumming activity further beyond. Man was running for the stars. God's administrators, such as Monsignor Garif, had decided that the Gospel must follow. Thomas Bernberger had been the first to go. Garif assured him that he would be the first of many. There were lots of men like Kreski on the moon. It would be difficult.

Give us your strength, Mother. The worst obstacles here are not the rocks and the vacuum.

The Mother of God smiled down at Father Bernberger, as though to say, *That is your problem, my son. I'll handle my angle, you handle yours.* Bernberger had to grin. What a face the sculptor had given her! She had the face of a card shark. Ten aces up each flowing sleeve, and a dozen secrets behind each ace.

Bernberger stiffened. The Mother of God had nodded. Then he realized that the floor had shifted sharply under his feet at the same time. It had been a quick twitch, sudden, single, sharp. Moonquakes happened infrequently in that area. Moonquakes, however, were slow, languorous rearrangements of the crust that seldom effected solidly based structures. Explosion! But where was the sound?

Bernberger glanced up at the Earth. Man had left sounds behind him. He hurried out of the almost-finished church. On the outside of the thick steel door the words were etched into a copper plate: *Our Lady of the Endless Sky.*

God have mercy on them, he prayed. The decompression sirens were already beginning their nightmare wail.

Kreski hovered like a mad vulture over Lock Six. The lock monitor screens showed men galomphing about outside, weird figures swimwalking in the ocean of one-sixth G. The silver hood of a light crane glinted for a moment under the night lamps. It crawled past the unreal gray vista of the screen and was gone. Other men followed, other machines with them.

In the strange light the men and machines looked related, first cousins removed by a double layer of fiberglass and jointed stainless steel. Bernberger's eyes drifted to the painted sign hanging above one of the monitor consoles, reading in black Roman: *We are all in this together.* He could never quite fathom it, never quite decide what its real portent was. Somehow it seemed to him that the machines were saying it. *We are all brothers under the sheet metal.* It disgusted him. For the last half of the twentieth century Man had been at war with his machines. Now, in the first half of the twenty-first, he was becoming one of them.

The oily smell of machines was very plain in his nostrils. Was this the first skirmish in a new war?

Kreski was punching buttons by the door of the lock. An embarrassed gleep announced the outer door opening. Kreski caught a glimpse of Bernberger out of the corner of his eye and whipped around.

"Bernberger, are you deaf? Go back to your cubbyhole and turn on the air!"

The priest noticed then that, save for the helmet, Kreski was fully suited. The sirens remained in the background, not quite real. His ears had not popped.

"But if there are injuries..."

"Damn!" Kreski reddened in anger. "On the moon you're alive or you're dead. I'd sooner you be alive. Mind those sirens, man!"

Bernberger, cowed somewhat by the huge man's rage, turned and reentered the main corridor. The lock was cycling double-time emergency, air screaming protest at the furious pumps. The priest tried to shut out the noise.

Around the corner stood the Reverend Arthur Chamblen, the other half of the Interfaith Council Lunar Mission. Graying, sixtyish. He was tall and lean, proud of the fact that he had been certified physically able to withstand the rigors of space travel, proud of the degree in astronomy, which allowed him to work on the small base telescope backing up the four hundred incher seventy kilometers away. Bernberger, whose contribution to the station was limited to being caretaker of the numerous laboratory animals, envied Chamblen at times. The man spoke confidently about many things. He had a sharp mind and had no qualms about laying criticism where he thought it belonged.

"He's right about that, you know. Alive or dead. Not much in between." The voice was cold, unmoved. Less the voice of a minister than a physicist. The eyes were much the same, pale blue, ice blue, certain.

"Then why aren't you locked in your room like a good boy?" Bernberger was sweating.

"I was looking for you. When the sirens began, everyone came running. But you."

"My ears haven't popped."

"The sirens are for a reason. Let's go."

With a weird whining snap the inner lock door yielded and hissed into its sheath. Both men stopped. Among the confused noises from Lock Six was the sound of a man in pain.

Bernberger's breath left him in a short sigh. He turned and ran back around the corner to the lock. Chamblen said nothing, merely continued to walk, slowly but not hesitantly, hack toward the tiny cubicle to which the sirens called him.

Three men had been brought in. Dusty anonymous suited figures milled around them, tearing at resistant half-metal suit cloth with fingers and knives and sheet metal shears. Even as Bernberger was about to reach them several men in clean pressure suits pushed by him pulling two surgical carts. They had the red cross on the white band around their arms. He flattened himself against the wall to let them pass, then continued to press forward.

Kreski was shrieking orders and shouting into a wireless microphone. Disembodied voices crackled reply from speakers in the walls. Father Bernberger elbowed his way between two of the dusty-suited men and looked down on the first body.

It was in several pieces, crusted with melting blood-slush. Bernberger glanced away, then steeled himself and looked again. The medics were roughly piling the fragments into an opaque bag. The head and shoulders and one arm were still intact, although blackened and the faceplate opaque. Bernberger was regretfully glad of that.

Eternal rest grant unto him...

The other two were at least mostly intact. Both had been brought back inside emergency pressure bags for suit-puncture accidents, and both were still alive. One, his name Monahan, the priest had met briefly at the first Mass held in his little room. Monahan's left leg below the knee was a bloody ruin, his foot nearly sheared off at the ankle. He moaned softly. The other man was not familiar to Bernberger, and was breathing noisily and spitting up blood. His eyes were closed and he did not move his limbs.

The speakers began to shout the story for the benefit of the rest of the station. "Hydrogen leak in feed tubes to unfinished fusion plant leading to explosion Garden Four destroyed Gardens Two and Three damaged slightly H-culture team injured no nuclear materials involved repeat no nuclear materials involved..."

That seemed to be what separated a minor disaster from a major one: whether nuclear materials were involved. Human life didn't seem to enter into it. Bernberger watched the medics lift Monahan onto one of the carts, bereft of his suit and all but tatters of his blue longjohns. A tourniquet had been crudely twisted around his left leg above the knee. He continued to emit low sounds of pain and occasional muttered obscenities. Blood was everywhere, on the hands of the medics, soaking into the padding of the cart, still oozing from the ruin of his leg. Bernberger pressed forward, reached out and put his hand on the man's forehead.

God, Father; Son, and Spirit; he was a good man. He came to Mass once. He worked hard. I know him. He worked... hard.

The Sacrament was in his cubicle. Time, time, that was all he needed. He started making the sign of the cross on Monahan's forehead when Kreski grabbed him by the shoulder and roughly pulled him back.

"Get that man to surgery. Bernberger, stand back or I'll club you." The station commander held a heavy sheet-metal shears in one hand. Bernberger stepped back while the medics pulled the muttering man away.

Kreski tossed his shears to the floor next to his discarded helmet. He faced the priest, sweat-drops dotting his thin sideburns. "What the hell's the matter with you?"

The ruddy face was furious, the man still breathing deeply and quickly. It was not an easy face to confront. Bernberger licked his lips. "I'm a priest. These men are my spiritual responsibility. If they feel depressed, I encourage them. If they feel guilty, I hear their confession. If they're about to die, I give them the last sacraments. That's my job. This is my parish."

It did not seem the right thing to say at all, somehow, but Bernberger could not harden before Kreski's sweating fury. Kreski turned away for a moment, wiped some of the grime from his face and turned back, his anger dampened.

"You want to make mumbo-jumbo over Odhner, go ahead. He won't hear you, but it might make you feel better." Kreski pointed with a gloved hand to the other injured man, still lying on a makeshift pallet on the floor. The medics had thrown a sheet over him. Bernberger, flushed with a sinking dread, bent down over the body and pulled the sheet back. The face was ashen, the mouth closed. Dried and drying blood discolored the cheeks and neck. The chest held no pulse. "A ten-ton heat exchanger fell on him. Slowly. His insides are smashed to pulp."

"But…" Bernberger pulled the sheet farther back. He felt like a ghoul at an opened grave. The body was whole. It had not seemed very damaged, was not twisted or torn out of shape. But where the skin showed through the ripped material of the longjohns, the flesh was purple and black. Crushed. The priest pulled the sheet forward quickly as though to replace it over the head, then paused. He looked up at Kreski. The name was circling like a hawk in his mind. Odhner…Odhner…Odhner.

It did not seem Jewish, nor conspicuously Catholic, nor conspicuously anything. It was only a name and a pain-whitened face attached to a crushed body. "What was he?" Bernberger asked the commander.

Kreski glared at the question. "A human being." He pulled off his large gray gloves and tucked them under his wide pressure suit belt. "That, and a damned good farmer. That's all I know about him."

The priest dropped his eyes to the corpse. He moistened his thumb and forefinger in his mouth and made the sign of the cross on the gray forehead.

"I baptize you in the Name of the Father, the Son and the Holy Spirit." *Father, find a place for your son Odhner. He was a damned good farmer.*

II.

"He can't do it."

Chamblen shifted and looked at the floor. "He can. I'm sorry, Tom, but he can."

Bernberger leaned against the railing protecting the statue of the Mother of God, and looked angrily around the church. There were no pews, but the pews were to have come almost last. All of the statues were in place, at that moment unhidden by the discreet curtains which would at the push of a button bring the church into concordance with the Protestant theology on icons. There was the lectern, stern and simple. Only the pews and the large cross still remained in the storage dome, soon to be uncrated and put in their places.

Mary looked down at the priest and minister, card-shark smile warm and strange.

"This isn't his. It was paid for out of church pockets. Your church and my church, and a lot of other churches. What about the other ministers who were to come after us when all this was finished? What gives him the right?"

The Reverend Arthur Chamblen blinked, and made a gesture of obviousness. "Clause 70. That's all he needs."

Thomas Bernberger tightened inside, glanced up past Mary's outstretched arms to infinity. He was caught in a corner a third million kilometers deep and as high as the endless sky. He held the directive in his hand.

TO: INTERFAITH COUNCIL LUNAR MISSION, REVS. CHAMBLEN & BERNBERGER

FROM: THE OFFICE OF THE COMMANDER

OFFICIAL: AS OF NINETEEN MAY 2029 INVOKING CLAUSE 70 REINSTATING GARDEN FOUR INDEFINITELY AT AREA EW9D. REMOVE ALL NONSTRUCTURAL ITEMS IMMEDIATELY.

"He didn't even give me my own 'Rev.' Nuts."

Chamblen took the outthrust directive, folded it neatly and tucked it away very calmly in an inside pocket. Bernberger did not want to catch his eyes. They were, as always, too blue, too level, too at peace with the inevitable.

Bernberger felt like fighting. "This was no minor disaster. Men were killed. Why doesn't he take the best interest of this place to heart and send home for another dome?"

Chamblen grinned. "That would cost two hundred million dollars out of taxpayers' pockets. It would have to he legislated. Legislation takes time. Months."

Bernberger broke away from Chamblen's ever-logical hammerlock, strolled eyes-down toward the lectern. Halfway there he turned back. "So we'll wait. Are we going to die? They fixed the other two. Does one dome out of commission mean instant destruction? I thought they would have designed this place a little better than that."

Chamblen nodded. "They did. We're not going to die."

"Then why can't I have my church?" Bernberger tried to sound as firm and certain as Chamblen, Kreski and all the others always did. But a ghost behind the eyes of the tall minister returned every time to haunt him and knock the sticks out from under his feeble protests. Chamblen always had an answer. Kreski always had an answer. Everyone always had an answer. All but Thomas Bernberger, who was only a priest.

Chamblen leaned back on the railing and brought one hand up, to place a finger lightly against one cheek, as though anticipating an itch should the itch come. "I'm sure you know more or less what goes on in those domes. They grow a certain plant there in intense light on a glut of nutrients. That plant is genetically engineered to be what I would call hyperthyroid. They grow like crazy, soak up nutrients like crazy and photosynthesize like crazy. Their rate of CO_2-O_2 conversion is unbelievable. They're also fairly tasty." Chamblen grinned. "You know, those army-green 'bugger biscuits.' It's the same stuff."

The itch came. Chamblen scratched it. The hand returned to the railing. Bernberger was running the process hazily through his mind, trying to recall the dynamics of a system he was hardly equipped to understand. "There are ten domes. Nine, now. Does ten percent make that much of a difference?"

"Depends, Tom, depends. We could leave things as they are now and continue on nine domes. It might get a shade stuffier and we might eat a little less. But the next time a dome goes down we'd all be in bad, bad trouble."

"This has never happened before." Bernberger was adamant, and hoped he looked it. "I don't think it will happen again."

The minister shook his head. "Always count on the unexpected. It can kill you. You know, Tom, I'm not selling out. It's a blow, I know. But we're no worse off than we were before. Honestly, do you know why they built this church here and sent you to staff it?"

The words came easily. "To allow the Gospel to follow Man as he conquers the universe."

Chamblen clucked. "Right out of one of Monsignor Garif's pamphlets. I know Garif. He's a shrewd politician. He's the one who pushed like crazy for a church up here, and he pushed you through as Catholic chaplain. You're one of his best students and most loyal supporters."

"Yes, but still…"

"And that line is pure PR. The truth is, the Catholic Church is fighting a losing battle on Earth, and Garif wants to plant a pocket of orthodoxy here as precedent for future extension of the Church once we branch out beyond the Earth-Moon system. You're as orthodox as they come, and you think highly of Garif. What would you have expected him to do?"

Bernberger, for once, allowed himself a smile. "You're being a little cynical for a minister of the Lord."

"No. I'm adapting to the environment. This is a no-nonsense place, peopled by no-nonsense men. There's no room for the extraneous. After having thought about it quite a bit, I'm still not convinced we need a church up here at all."

"I'm surprised you don't declare yourself extraneous and jump out an airlock. You do believe in God, I hope."

"I do." Chamblen nodded. "God to me is a loving Father who once cared very carefully for His newborn sons, but now, the sons having grown out of their cradle, expects them to get along more on their own."

Bernberger refused to look at the minister. "I'm sorry we don't see God the same way."

Chamblen stood up and began to walk toward the door. He had gotten most of the way there when he stopped in the starlight, and tugged on the lapels of his black clerical shirt, which was opened at the collar and dampened deeper black under the arms. "Tom, see it this way. You never wanted to spend the last dime in your penny loafers, did you?"

Bernberger said nothing.

"Well, you're asking Kreski to spend our last dime up here. I'm sorry, terribly sorry, but I'm on his side this time." He walked the rest of the way into shadow and grasped the door handle. "I'll remove our nonstructural items. You take it easy for a while."

The door closed with solemn slowness behind him. Alone again with the Mother of God, Bernberger continued to glare at the walls, not wanting to catch her smile and feel the pain of not knowing what it was he didn't know.

What is your ace, Mother? Play it, please.

III.

Father Bernberger stood to the left of the cast-wide doors, watching. He watched the men rip the pastel blue tiles from the floor, their grout barely dry. He watched them hammer ragged craters in the new concrete and draw forth from the ruin snaking cables and twisting tubes, carrying electricity and water to feed the strange sorceries he had never found the desire to study. He watched them rip his lectern from the floor, and plant in its place a blinking, multikeyed computer terminal, which drew the same power that would have illuminated the Gospel at some future celebration of the Mass.

He kept nodding to himself. They were efficient. They worked like madmen, around the clock, never pausing. They used every sliver of space in the church. Every square inch under the dome was mapped and assigned to some subtle and obviously necessary purpose.

It seemed to him that every time he glanced at the door beside him a forklift was rumbling in, heaped with crates and bundles of copper pipe and spools of spaghetti wiring. In moments the lift was emptied and gone, only to return in a matter of minutes bearing more trash to be laid at the feet of the Blessed Mother.

Who is their God, Mary? What force drives them like this?

Even Kreski was there, his hands in the chaos up to his elbows. Often he paused to give orders, but when there were no more orders to give he was back down on his knees, brazing copper fittings to a pipeline running down what should have been the main aisle. The flame hissed softly, cleanly. Drips of molten lead hit the floor and froze. In that hard face there was a tension, an urgency almost frightening. Kreski was running ahead of something greater than himself, when every impression he had ever given Bernberger stated in solid certainty that nothing on the Moon was greater than he.

Other men were bolting together skeletal tables of perforated magnesium, upon which were being laid the hydroponic garden units. When the forklift arrived carrying one of the long, narrow, coffinlike black bins sprouting with tiny green newborn shoots, work stopped. Four men lined up along the unit, positioned their hands carefully beneath it and lifted with a machinelike precision. They carried it levelly, almost reverently, and when they approached, all the other workers stood back. Only when the unit was positioned on its table and firmly bolted down did the welders take up their torches and the electricians their pliers. Row after row of garden units filled the church from front to rear, separated by the pipe-tangled main aisle.

Men crawled like animals beneath the rat's nest of magnesium beams, pulling plastic tubing and multicolored wires. The clink and scratch and scrape and tap of wire and tube faded into a rushed and uneasy whisper filling the dome and echoing past Bernberger's ears until he wanted to cry out against it. The stink of sweat and ammonium flux made tangible the blasphemy, which otherwise would only come half-clear. He would look outside the dome for solace to the calm sterile wastes, but there the crawling cranes and leaping figures in metal suits were raising the new power lines and settling a new fusion plant into its yesterday-poured foundations. Blasphemy was everywhere. They were forcing him to wallow in it, and he was drowning.

Along the walls they were hanging the narrow aluminum ducts, through which the station's air would soon pass, driven by pumps laid beneath the floor. It all went together so quickly, so logically. It seemed as though the men in the dome were merely throwing the beams and ducts together. Everything fit so well, so quickly, and always the first time. There seemed to be no effort to it. And yet Bernberger could see and smell the grimy sweat streaming from their faces. He saw the concentrating grimaces, the set jawlines.

This work … is important to them. Bless their labors, Mary.

In time, only one space remained where a garden unit might be placed, and the tubes and wires were everywhere nearby. Bernberger left hastily, not wanting to see the altar of God plugged into the clicking machines.

The funeral of Odhner and Beckwith was held in Lock One, the largest lock and single area large enough for all station personnel to gather. Monahan was there, on a surgical cart plugged into the medical monitors. Soon after, the lunar shuttle took Odhner back to the arms of Earth, and Beckwith, as his wife requested, was laid beneath the lunar soil. Bernberger watched the coffin vanish beneath the dust through a port, and then fled through the iron hallways of Station Grissom, past the bulletin boards and the graffitti, around the ubiquitous machines, to the only place where he might find shelter.

They had removed the plaque from the door. Inside was nothing but the continuous mechanical purr of automatic activity; the H-culture team was lingering by the lock. Bernberger recoiled at the sight of the completed garden, yet quickly slipped between the black coffins full of sprouting vigorous life, working his way toward the now-oddly beckoning arms of the Mother of God. Men live, and men die. The priest mediates between death and life. Life comes from God, and goes back to God. Something in him burned to think of bending that path around and feeding life with death, growth with waste, breath with suffocation. Where could God fit into such a closed circle? He touched one of the brilliant green leaves. He could not understand. If God could not fit, no priest could either, except by selling himself to the machines and tending their needs while the circle of life ate its own tail.

"Blessed Mother evicted by a radish patch. God help us." He wanted to look up at the Virgin, to draw strength from her, but could not.

Bernberger bent down over one garden unit and sniffed directly above the carpet of close-planted leaves. The air seemed fresher there. Or was it just a memory?

Pushing himself away from the garden units, he made his way to where the lectern had been. The computer terminal made a soft thrumming sound as it monitored the pressures and pulses of the machines all around. Bernberger chuckled bitterly. They have uprooted me and planted a machine in my place, he thought. In this place, with such a congregation, perhaps it was just as well. He laid his hands on either side of the terminal keyboard, tears coming that he refused to fight, and thumbed the loveworn pages of his memory.

"The Gospel According to St. Luke," he said, looking out at the silent rows of green. "Listen to the word of the Lord, damn you radishes!"

For two days Father Bernberger avoided Chamblen and remained alone with his thoughts. The dilemma ran through his mind again and again while he cleaned the endless rows of rat cages and talked to the sad-eyed dogs wagging at him through the close-mesh screening. He wanted to fight, and place his banner on the side of Life; but cast about as he might, he could not distinguish the lines of battle. Men walked the empty wastes with body-function monitors tattling continually to the machines, and felt safer by it. It was hard for him to believe. The poor dogs he cared for he understood. They were too stupid to comprehend the electrodes taped to their skulls and flanks. They wagged whenever he offered his hands to them, whether or not those hands bore another plate of bugger biscuits. He watched men brag about how sensitive their monitors were, and how completely the machines guarded their welfare. He wondered without praying if men would ever again be able to live without them. Nothing in any of his books gave any hint at an answer, nor even so much as admitted the question.

Not long after B-shift dinner call on the second day, the buzzer roused Bernberger from an uneasy sleep. He put his cot in order and shoved the door handle down. Outside the airtight portal was a man in a wheelchair, smiling.

"Sorry I can't come in, Father," Monahan said. "My wheels won't make it through your door. But I wanted to come over and thank you anyway."

Bernberger smiled. His eyes burned a little. "Are you sure you should be up and around like that?"

Monahan laughed, and lightly thumped the blanket-covered stump that ended just above his left knee. "Takes more than a little leg missing to lay *me* low. People heal pretty quick in one-sixth G. I should be on crutches next week, if I'm lucky."

The smiling face peering up at him through a castwide airtight door moved him terribly for one long moment. "I don't know why you should want to thank me."

"Kreski told me you tried to give me the last sacraments."

"I see."

"It takes guts to tangle with that old monkey wrench."

"He had your best interests in mind."

"Yeah." Monahan grinned sourly. "He's hell to get along with, but he knows his business. Like I said, thanks. Also because I think you're good luck."

"Oh?" Bernberger was startled.

"Sure. Me and the other guys from H-culture have it figured out. Reverend Chamblen was here for six months before you were, and nobody talked much about a church. But when you get here they start building one right away, and as soon as it's finished, but not finished so that it would be all sacred and everything, that's the time when my Garden blows up. The church was ready and waiting for us to move in.

"But..." Bernberger was astonished. The man spoke as though the destruction of a church were a blessing sent by God.

"Sixty hours, from total destruction to full operation, in a dome that was never designed for life-support machinery. I call that pretty close to a miracle. It'll be something to tell my kids about."

"But I don't see why..."

"It wasn't easy," Monahan said, his tone gone more serious. "Take it from me, it was a bitch."

Amen.

"No, honestly, Father, me and the guys got to thinking about it, and found you were pretty lucky for us. If they hadn't had a dome, we would have had no emergency margin. Houston wouldn't have liked that. They might have issued a Directive Five."

Directive Five. Evacuate Immediately. The end of Station Grissom. Bernberger shook his head in wonderment. "I never knew it had been that serious."

Monahan whistled. "Not anymore, but for a while there it was really touch and go. And if it had turned out to be go, it would really have broken my heart. That trip home would have been a one-way trip for me. One-legged men aren't popular as flight or station crew. So things didn't turn out too bad. Except for you, I guess."

"Well, I..."

"You probably feel like a dog that got kicked out of his dog-house so that it could be used as a chicken coop. That must hurt a little, but I figure God forgives more easily than nature. Anyway, it wasn't really fair for you to get shoved out into the cold without someplace to go, so I leaned on Kreski a little hit, and demanded the space in the storage dome where all the spare parts for the new Garden came from. There's quite a hole in there now. So the rest of the H-culture guys got together off-shift, uncrated the crucifix and a couple of pews, and we made you a church."

"Kreski let you do that." It was a statement of disbelief.

"Heh. We threatened to dye the bugger biscuits purple. They're his favorite food and that's the color he hates the most. And we're the guys who make them. We got our way."

"It's not you who has to say thanks. It's me. I mean..."

"No. Just say Mass. For us. We want to let God know how we feel. When do I tell them?"

Bernberger paused, mouth open. *We made you a church.* These were his people. How could he ever have doubted them? "Tomorrow morning. 0900."

"Thanks, Father. You got some real grit, you know that'"

Bernberger shook his head. "No. But I'll take your word for it. Take care of yourself." The door swung closed as the man rolled away.

IV.

The Mother of God stretched out her arms to embrace the barren lands. Over her white shoulder had been thrown a sheaf of electric cables. Glued to her crown was a photoelectric sensor.

Sunlight, earthgleam. Life must have its light.

"In the Name of the Father, and of the Son, and of the Holy Spirit..."

Between shadow-cast crates and ranks of stacked barrels, seven human beings clustered around a slab of scrap synthetic. Over it had been laid a fine linen cloth. One one side of the cloth was the golden cup. On the other, a small golden plate of dark green biscuits.

Mary stretched out her arms. In each hand, fastened with strap-iron, was a cluster of sodium-mercury lights. Other pseudo-suns grew on stalks all around. The dome sang with light.

I saw a woman, clothed with the sun, and the Moon under her feet, and on her head a crown of twelve stars.

Twelve stars. Twelve hundred stars. Twelve thousand stars.

Twelve *trillion* stars.

Mother, they are yours. We will make them yours.

"Lord have mercy. Christ have mercy. Lord have mercy." Seven persons paused, silently, and recalled their faults. Every five seconds each took a breath. Life was at work there, in their lungs, in their blood, in every cell. Oxygen to carbon dioxide. Energy. Life. God forgive us.

The machines hummed with their own life. About Mary's shoulders the ducts wound, thrumming with their own purpose, speaking their own language. Molecules of gas wafted over tiny shafts of green. A moment ago, a breath. The breath of a priest, of man, of woman, of Catholic and Protestant and Atheist. The breath of six dogs and three hundred white rats.

The last breath of a human being. Someday, if all went well, the ducts would carry the first breath of a moonborn infant.

Life from life, breath from breath. Death is only a waystation. Mary stretches out her arms to embrace the tiny fields of green, growing in chemical baths under forty artificial suns. Tiny shoots of green taking the bad air apart with sunlit crowbars, giving back their breath, giving up their food. The new air enters the ducts once more.

The circle is unbroken.

We are all in this together.

"This is my body...."

Mary stretches out her arms to embrace life. All life. Green life, animal life, life that walks on two legs and one leg. She embraces the false life, the buzzing circuits and leaping rockets.

"Give us this day our daily bread..."

For these things are necessary. Man lives not by bread alone. He must have his ecosphere.

"Go, the Mass is ended." Yes, but our days are beginning, just beginning.

Thank you, Mother. Help me to understand these things.

On her head a crown of twelve trillion stars.   ■

Afterword: Our Lady of the Endless Sky

I'm a Catholic. (You could tell, right?) And while I'm not precisely a *Roman* Catholic, that's another tale for another time; look up "Old Catholicism" on the Web and you'll get a sense for my precise affiliation. But setting organizational differences aside, the Catholic *idea* is a tremendously powerful one, an idea little understood in this secular era. Catholic faith is not something imprisoned by mere words. It reaches out and embraces all that is good, sometimes before we who are Catholics completely understand the nature of the good that confronts us. Those who see modern history as technology pitted against God have it completely wrong.

This was the first story I ever sold into the professional market, and it appeared in Harry Harrison's original anthology *Nova 4* in November 1974. I was only 21 when I wrote it, back at the Clarion SF workshop in 1973, and I took a lot of razzing back then for not being stylishly cynical and atheistic. Guilty, guilty! Cynicism is simple cowardice, and I'll have none of it. Atheism, well—what can I say? I'm a Catholic. We don't explain faith. We feel it, we live it, sometimes we rage at it, and every so often it explodes within us, showing us universes of the human heart that we had never suspected could exist. But I could not, without lying to myself, ever claim that there's nothing to it.

INEVITABILITY SPHERE

1978

INEVITABILITY SPHERE

That's my ship up there," said the young captain with undisguised bitterness.

Old Tom Hoyt tugged thoughtfully at his beard, and looked up. A brilliant silver point was crawling across the sky, dimmed and sometimes hidden by a scramble of late summer clouds crawling in from the east. The alien air was sharp with its own hint of thunderstorms. Evening's smoky yellows and pinks still hung in the west, but the gray east held flashes of distant lightning.

The captain went on. "The orbit won't decay for another sixty-two thousand years. The computer told me that as though it mattered."

"Somebody will come after it, sooner or later."

"Not me. The junkman maybe. I've got a desk job now."

"When the next Earth-normal world turns up, your ship will fly again," Hoyt said.

"Only until they poke another Low Road through."

The simple truth, that. Hoyt had nothing more to say. They stood beside his torchwing, which glinted silver in the cold blue light of the airstrip marker lamps. Aerodynamically, it was ancient. The fuselage was thicker, the wings stubbier than those of the twentieth century jet aircraft that had spawned it. The basic lines were the same.

Inside the silver skin was very little but torch and ignition capacitor. The airborne fusion tube had been born with the third millennium A.D., and Hoyt knew of little that would change it in the future.

The captain squeezed in through the tiny hatch, Hoyt climbing after. Hoyt settled both of them into their webs, then pulled a tight fitting helmet over his head. The captain began to don his own helmet, emblazoned with the silver galaxy of Earth's Star Service. Hoyt stopped him. "Cover your ears with your hands. They don't build Star Service helmets nearly sound-proof enough for torch work."

Hoyt started the torch sequence. The torchwing's wings were tanks filled with heavy hydrogen. For half a minute the turbine burned the hydrogen in air, turning a generator with ever-increasing speed. The resultant shreik was painful, even through Hoyt's own helmet. The captain was hunched over, thumbs pressed hard into his ears. When the turbine had charged the capacitor bank to capacity, the capacitors fed their entire accumulated charge to the ignition laser, for one star-hot pulse—

Wham!

For the thousandth time, Hoyt felt as though it would shake his teeth loose. The turbine sank back to a dull whine, now feeding hot deuterium to the rising burble of the fusion torch. The noise faded from painful to merely maddening.

"How old is this thing?" the captain called over the racket.

"Hundred and forty years."

"They should have scrapped it a hundred and thirty nine years ago."

Hoyt shrugged. "It's what I've got."

They taxied to the edge of the airstrip, waited for clearance, and let the torch go. They left the strip at two Gs. Graveltown was lost beneath the thickening clouds before they ever saw its tiny scattering of lights. Hoyt punched in a familiar course on the autopilot and turned to look at the young captain. His uniform, crisp and spotless, was hung with brass and ribbons. His face was Celtic and a touch craggy, and very proud. His eyes were humorless and intelligent. Hoyt was troubled by the bitterness and anger he sensed. "You were about to say that this is the crudest thing you ever rode in," observed Hoyt.

"It is."

"Do you know what a tailgunner is, son?"

The captain nodded. "A suicide who shot steel slugs at other suicides in some twentieth century war. I saw one in a video years ago."

"You're looking at another."

The captain's eyebrows rose. "So when did they stop your clock, old man?"

"1996. I'll be seventy-two forever. Time gives you perspective; crude is what's ten years older than what you're used to. I've known men who fought on horseback. But they did it well. That's what counts."

The captain remained silent. Hoyt looked ahead toward the advancing thunderstorm. True Grit's atmopshere was thinner than Earth's, but much deeper. The squall line was a churning black wall rolling out of the east, easily five miles high. Hoyt leveled off at twenty thousand feet and recovered control from the autopilot. That high, the sun had not quite set. The storm flashed purple from within.

The captain was peering ahead, suddenly interested. "I tried to spot it from space. Thought it would be easy. But the weather's been lousy."

Hoyt grunted.

"You fly like you've been a pilot for a long time."

Hoyt felt the younger man groping for a reason to respect him. "Quarter of a millennium. More."

"So why didn't you ever get into space?"

Hoyt shrugged. "I'm too old—and too dumb. When I was young space was a kid's dream. Flying a wing is nothing like flying a starship. That takes real brains. Lots of things to keep straight, all at one time, but it goes slowly enough to let you stop and think. A supersonic wing you have to fly with your reflexes. There's no time to sit back and ask a computer questions. Old habits are hard to break. I never developed space brains."

"Ahhhh!"

Hoyt looked where the captain pointed. True Grit's end of the Low Road had just burst through the face of the nearest thunderhead. The Road darted erratically along the squall line for a mile or so, then shot straight up and was lost to sight. It was a thousand-foot sphere of velvet blackness, without feature or reflection.

Moments later it returned from their left, jigging and jogging and doubling back on its path. Hoyt watched the captain's eyes darting back and forth, trying to follow it. It would slow for a heartbeat, jitter almost in place, then dart off in mile-long straight lines too quickly to see at all. The captain shook his head.

"Nothing can move that fast!"

"Right. And nothing is just what it is. It occupies the same space as the air molecules it seems to cover. There is no interaction between it and the atmosphere, or anything else massing less than fifty pounds in one lump."

"So how in hell do you expect to catch it?"

"Instinct," Hoyt said, and grinned. "I've got *good* instincts."

Hoyt was swinging the torchwing in a wide arc, keeping the bounding sphere below and to their left. Instantaneous star travel indeed! It was easy enough to anchor one end of the Low Road a mile over the Mohave Desert. But the other end—Hoyt thought of holding a twelve-foot fiberglass fishing rod in one hand and trying to follow a fly creeping randomly across the opposite wall with its tip. Then he imagined a fishing pole twelve light years long, and put it out of his head.

It wasn't entirely random motion, though it seemed random enough to him. The Low Road was slightly flexible in ways that gave Hoyt headaches to think about. Noise in the control circuits, changing solar wind pressures on the Earth, even minor temblors a thousand miles from the Mojave were multiplied by a seventy trillion mile lever. A man who followed that darting black ball could develop a feel for its wanderings; not enough to predict it exactly, but enough to improve his odds at catching it. Improving those odds was what Tom Hoyt did for a living.

Hoyt kept his eyes on the sphere. At last he chose to play his hunch, and without warning threw the torchwing into a power dive toward a point just ahead of advancing clouds. The Road hurtled toward the spot, jumped back, and came on again. The captain pressed himself back into his seat and cringed when the wing missed the black sphere by a few hundred feet. Then it was gone, into the clouds, and moments later the storm closed around them.

Hoyt swore under his breath. The torchwing bucked in the storm's rough air. Hoyt glanced aside and saw the young captain breathing rapidly.

"Things seldom happen...this fast...in space," he said.

"Relax. They usually don't happen this fast dirtside either. That's most of the problem. It's also the only reason I got this job. I have a reputation as a fast flier."

The young man laughed bitterly. "So do I. My ship is a premium speed courier. Too small for cargo, and rather spartan for passengers. I handled all government traffic in documents, credit transfers, and important people. The government never trusted the Low Road with things like that—until now. They want me back on Earth in a bad way. So bad my own ship isn't even fast enough. You have my job now, old man."

Hoyt began wishing for a change of subject. He made a badly planned dive and missed the sphere by several miles. The captain watched it plummet into the clouds and vanish. Lightning glared around them.

"What happens if it hits the ground?" the captain asked.

"The Road tries to suck the whole planet through to Earth. It doesn't get too far before the breakers blow and the Road vanishes. It takes three months of calculation and a billion kilowatts of power to poke it through again. They're careful. Believe me."

"They should have kept it in space."

Hoyt was searching the dark clouds for the Road. It was getting very dark. "It *had* to be in space, back when the damned thing wandered through a volume of space a million miles in diameter. Graveltown came through loaded in one-shot re-entry vehicles made of foam lined with brick. One of the unmanned ones burned up in the atmosphere with a fortune in farm machinery aboard. Entering a planetary atmosphere from orbit is *dangerous*.

"Control systems improved over the months. The volume of space in which the Road wanders is called its 'probability sphere.' Finding the thing when it was out in space was like finding an electron in an orbital. They knew it couldn't be in space forever, but they couldn't bring it down until they got the probability sphere tighter than ten miles. It's down to about three now, and getting a little tighter every week."

"It's crazy," the young captain said.

"It took me to the stars," Hoyt said, "and I was the first man ever to ride it back to Earth again."

"Look!"

Night had fallen completely now. The front had passed, and the bulk of the storm was retreating into the west, beyond them. The sphere had risen from the writhing clouds below, black and invisible. In an instant it flickered and had ignited to a warm yellow-green.

"I'm glad they can do that," Hoyt said. "I don't like chasing black cats through coal bins at midnight. After dark it's just me and that big green ball, and no distractions to make things difficult."

Twice more Hoyt dove at the glowing green sphere. Each time, he missed by almost a mile. Each time, the captain went pale from the acceleration and the sudden, gut-wrenching turns and dives.

"This is worse than crazy," he said at last while Hoyt circled, resting. "We've been up here for two hours now and gone nowhere but around in circles."

"What was your fastest geodesic through paraspace from tau Ceti to Earth?" Hoyt asked.

"Eleven days."

"Then my slowest trip is still ten days faster than your best. It's inevitable, son."

"Then it's mighty sloppy engineering, to have to chase your hyperspace tube around the sky like a feather blown in a windstorm."

Hoyt shrugged. "The tiniest noise pulse we can measure sends the thing skittering across a thousand feet of sky. Then there's the little matter of matching velocities between two planets rotating on skew axes while revolving around stars moving in two very different directions. No easy job."

"But the same job one good starship captain can do without half trying."

The captain sounded frightened, despite his arrogant words. Hoyt looked closely at the shiny buttons and medals. He saw the youth, pale and naked, beneath the awesome uniform. "What sort of job did they find for you? Civilian?"

"Yes." The captain kept his eyes straight forward. "Plotting geodesics in paraspace involves solving systems of equations of a large number of variables. They said jobs for starship captains were 'uncertain'…but that I could have a solid future as senior analyst for the sociometric department of a very large processed food distributor. My first assignment is waiting for me: I am to solve the system of equations that should yield the parameters for selling the most breakfast cereal to the largest number of North American eight-year-olds."

Hoyt understood. He dropped the subject, and there was silence in the cabin of the wing for some time.

It was a bad night. Ten more times Tom Hoyt dove for where he thought his course might intersect that of the Low Road. Each time the sphere chose to move in the opposite direction. Hoyt knew his job was as much a matter of luck as anything else, but knowing what his passenger was leaving behind and knowing what he was going toward kept Hoyt from concentrating.

"Give up, Hoyt," the captain said after they had been aloft for nearly four hours.

Hoyt frowned. "Give up? Think of where I've been, son. When I was born space travel was fiction, children's fiction. I had a little telescope and I wanted to go to the stars, but I took what I could get. I tailgunned in the War and learned flying when it was over. After retiring from soldiering I flew a cargo jet for an air express company until *they* made me retire. I was middle aged when we landed on the Moon for the first time. I was old by the time MIT let slip that it had a twenty-year-old hamster—which ate its millionth sunflower seed last year, by the way—and I was almost dead when I volunteered to undergo a clock stopping. I knew damned well that the process killed two people for every one it made immortal, but I had damned little to lose. Funny that it takes a suicide to become immortal. But it does. And I did.

"So I waited it out. And when space travel arrived in a big way, I couldn't get in because of my physiological age. So I did what I've always done: I flew. One day a friend of mine got me a rather odd job with the Low Road project. It took me two hundred eighty-eight years to get to the stars, but I'm here. I never give up. And nobody's *ever* going to take the stars away from me!" Hoyt deliberately turned his last statement into a challenge and threw it in the younger man's face.

"Don't preach at me. I'm through. You finished me. Now leave me alone."

Hoyt bit his lip and dove once more at the dancing luminous sphere. He missed by a hundred feet. The captain choked off a cry of surprise as the mammoth ball lit the cabin with a sickly green light. Angry now, Hoyt threw the wing into a tight turn and followed. It went high. Hoyt went after it, straight up, and broke soundspeed with a dull thump. The sphere bounced like a child's ball for a second, and plummeted. Hoyt cursed and followed in a power dive that took them nearly to Mach three. The ball darted to one side and disappeared. Hoyt pulled out of the dive and began to circle idly again. The captain looked nauseated from the constant furious changes in speed and direction. It was Hoyt's worst night. Perhaps the captain would get one more starship ride.

"Okay. We'll try again tomorrow. The weather..."

Crump!

The captain swore in surprise. They were plunging straight down at the mottled barrenness of the Mojave Desert at seven hundred miles per hour. Hoyt's reflexes took over, and he jerked the stick back. The wing pulled out a thousand feet above the ground.

"What happened?"

Hoyt shrugged. "Dumb luck. The ball hit *us*. We went through. Never happened before."

It was a brilliant cloudless afternoon over California. Fixed a mile high above the ground was solid ink-black ball a thousand feet in diameter. It was quite immobile.

For no apparent reason, the captain began to laugh. "You're an ass, Hoyt. The three-mile-wide volume of space with that big green ball bouncing through it isn't a probability sphere. It's an *inevitability* sphere. Sit still in it long enough, and the ball *has* to hit you. You'd save a lot of time and hydrogen in the long run sitting in the basket of a hot air balloon and just waiting for it."

Hoyt grinned, and threw the challenge back. "I'll bet we could. I think we might be able to ship cargo that way, with a tethered balloon and some patience...and I'd be glad to have you as a partner in the venture. *Balloons to the stars!* Jules Verne would have loved it!"

Hoyt turned the torchwing toward the Low Road airfield. They flew wide around a huge ring of slender concrete towers rising hundreds of feet above the desert rock. Each was surrounded by an...aura? Not precisely, Hoyt thought. More a distortion. Light did not travel in straight lines around those towers.

The captain laughed again, more bitterly than before. "Forget it, old man. You're finished too. Give them another year. They're going to shrink that probability sphere more and more, until the True Grit end just sits there and shivers a little. Hell, they'll make it stand stock still! They'll pull it all the way down to the ground. They'll build an approach, like a bridge approach without a bridge, and there'll be a stinking super-highway that starts out in California and ends up on Tau Ceti. Then you'll be out of a job too. How will you get to the stars then, old man?"

*Ahh, the stars, the stars, may they soon belong to all, not only proud young soldiers and strange old men...*Hoyt smiled.

"I'm not above driving a truck, son. Are you?"   ■

AFTERWORD: INEVITABILITY SPHERE

I can't always recall the precise moment that a story concept occurs to me, but this time I can: It was on the trip back from SunCon, the World Science Fiction Convention, which took place in Miami over Labor Day weekend, 1977. I was peering out the jetliner window at the landscape below, when the plane suddenly banked such that the land swung away and the bright sun flashed in my eyes. For twenty minutes afterward a dark purple ball darted around my vision, as the temporary scorch the sun had made on my retinas slowly faded. I recall being amused by my futile efforts to "catch" the ball as the motions of my eyes made it dart around the sky. Now, what if there were a twelve-lightyear-long hyperspace tube anchored to Earth and constantly steered to follow the motions of a distant planet...

This was the first story that I ever sold to a magazine, in the September/October 1978 issue of *Isaac Asimov's Science Fiction Magazine*. Editor George Scithers liked my work and pestered me to send him more of it, and he protected my reputation by rejecting the inevitable crap I sent him at his request. Still, both stories I placed on the Hugo ballot in 1981 came out of his magazine and his encouragements, and I owe him seriously for helping me believe that I really could do this stuff.

WHALE MEAT

1977

WHALE MEAT

SITTING ON A COLD CHICAGO BUS-BENCH at night-west I wished I had never been born a witch. I had just killed a man and Mara wanted whale meat. But I am on the canvas. I am not the painter. Creator forgive me. We had to stay somewhere. It would have been in the park with the ice if Lennie had not looked in my eyes in the public library and half-snerfed my pain.

There is no word for Lennie now. Years ago he would have been a hippie. Longer ago, a beatnik. Further back into time's fog, a bohemian. Head. Weirdo. I don't know what people call them now. Freak, perhaps. But he knew we were tired and homeless, and told us to stay with him.

His apartment was a filthy hole. I was too exhausted to snerf him. He gave us hot coffee and a blanket and we slept on ragged foam rubber with the roaches. My dreams floated in hunger, tormented by Mara's request for whale meat. She told me without words. I snerfed the picture in her head, a gray sea-mountain blowing steam from its nostril above moonlit swells.

I woke from restless dreams in a sweat of fear and anger. Some part of me never sleeps, and knew Mara was in danger. In yellow candlelight Lennie was bending over Mara, knife in his hand above her belly swollen with James. His eyes were slits and he chanted a language I never learned. I snerfed him. Some bad acid (is it still called acid?) was eating away at him and leaving only insanity in its wake. Snerfing him gave me a grim glimpse of the future: He would kill Mara and James in seconds. The knife began to circle for its last time, like a live thing in his shaking hands.

I had to time-opt. The universe ground to a slow halt around us while I dug up power from my heart-place, and zotted him.

Lennie's poor head shorted out like power lines blown away in a windstorm, with sparks and shrieks of inner agony.

I gathered Mara up and with the blanket we left. Lennie's heaviness will be with me always. To take life you must give of your own. And Lennie came so close, *so* close to being able, though of course he could never make it. He hurt too, almost knowing where he almost was. Now he won't hurt anymore.

But my family was safe. Chicago is cold as hell in March's slow night-morning. The icy wind stirred my head, let me think. We needed food. Me especially; it is hard to stop the whole universe but yourself, even if only for an instant.

Mara felt my hunger and echoed it, and there was a frightening edge of desperation beneath it. "Whale meat, Yonnie. Please get me whale meat."

I nodded, and soothed her with the fingers that extend beyond my fingertips, not thinking about her strange demand. "In the morning. Right now we have to eat." We have no money; it is hard to come by in the usual way and dangerous to have sometimes. We keep a type set of coins and Mara dulps. It was easier a century ago, when a single gold coin would feed us for a month. Metal is more obedient than paper and ink: Whoever now prints money for the government has met a witch, I suspect. I took out the type set and pulled Eisenhower from his slot. "Dulp us four. Four should be enough for breakfast."

Mara pulled the blanket tighter around herself and James. Her slender fingers placed Eisenhower on the bus-bench. She shivered, and tightened inside. She put both her hands together, thumbs linked, little fingers pointing down. I felt her humming the dulp-song while she lowered her fingers to the bench, fingertips far enough apart to embrace five Eisenhowers: one from the type set plus four-to-be.

Mara swallowed hard. One Eisenhower dulped instantly. The second dulped in a few seconds, and I could sense her effort waged against fatigue. The third dulped more slowly, faded once or twice, then finally came back solid. The fourth appeared slowly, very slowly, flickered uncertainly, and took a long time hardening. At last Mara let out a deep breath and smiled. I picked up the Eisenhowers and looked at them. The first three were good. The fourth was thin, dull, blurred. It seemed wrong somehow. I looked once more. Eisenhower was backwards, facing the right. Funny in a way, but it would hurt Mara.

"Three out of four," I told her, smiled gently, and tossed the backwards Eisenhower in a sewer.

Chicago is hard on witches. I think sometimes that we should go to California. It might be easier for us there. There are lots of strange people in California. They would barely notice us. But California is near the ocean, and that is bad for witches. The ocean lies at the center of the Circle of Great Life, and its pull on life is strong. People who are not able can sometimes snerf when they are near the ocean. We must keep our secret. Salem was near the ocean.

In Chicago our secret is safe, except for the freaks. Freaks live in all ages and go by different names. But they are always the same: sensitive, smart, and very close to able. This is not bad in itself, but too often an almost-able knows he is almost-able by a means that is not snerfing but almost-snerfing. This hurts him, because he knows he is very close to something ancient and transcendent, and wants to get there very badly. So freaks put all sorts of stuff into their heads and it warps them out completely until they get like Lennie. Mara and I have wept for centuries, snerfing the freaks groping around us, groping for something inside they know is there yet will never get. It just isn't fair somehow.

Still, we live with them. We must. They live, as always, on society's fringes, anonymous in their pain. They are the poets and ghetto-artists who live and die forgotten. We hide from a society jealous of immortality in their rags, changing the rags with the decades but always wearing rags. These days it is even more important, now that James is coming. He will be coming for another two years. We must wander always, and never let anyone know us longer than a week or two, a month perhaps. People would wonder, seeing a girl pregnant for seven years.

Our rags for these strange sullen times are working people's clothes, old denim and boots and flannel shirts. If people knew, I am sure they would laugh. Witches wear funny pointed hats and ride brooms.

It is better this way.

The restaurant was not fancy and not filthy, as ordinary and tired and stained as Clark Street itself. I made sure there were no freaks around. Freaks can get snerf-flashes around food. Life's sources draw the able toward knowledge that not-ables cannot share.

But it was empty except for us. The waitress sat in a booth near the front, working a puzzle in a book. She was dumpy and faded, blond but old. I snerfed her loneliness, loneliness recalling happier years now lost. The kid at the register behind the counter was a college-type, clean-cut. He was leaning on the counter doing something out of books on paper. College homework, I snerfed. His head was full of numbers. He looked Greek. It made me shiver, since Greeks eat unusual foods. Perhaps…

"Yes, can I help you?" he asked.

"Early breakfast," I said, and tried to smile. "Uh…do you have whale meat?"

He smiled and shook his head, which was still full of numbers. He wasn't paying us much attention. We took the menus he handed us and scanned the smudged food-lists. Hamburgers, as usual. The prices, of course, meant nothing to me. My number-spot never grew. Perhaps it never was. I cannot count past seven, life's number.

"We want two hamburgers. This is all the money we have right now. Is it enough?" I put the three Eisenhowers on the counter.

He started to say something, then looked at us, and caught his words. I snerfed empathy shoving the numbers aside. He wanted to help us, wasn't sure how. I snerfed a decision being made about the numbers.

"Sure, that's plenty." He picked up the three Eisenhowers, and just then noticed that Mara was pregnant. The numbers in his head vanished. I thought for a moment that he was snerfing my hunger and pain; but no, he wasn't able, not at all. He was just a kind person who knew the look of hunger and hopelessness. I am sure that Clark Street can teach you *that.* "You want something to drink with it?"

"If the money is enough."

"Sure thing. How about hot chocolate?"

Mara's eyes cried out for joy.

"Thank you, friend."

"Call me Tommy."

"Thank you, Tommy."

Tommy turned and yelled loud back toward the end of the counter. A beat-up old man in a t-shirt and an apron stuck his head out from behind a door. The kid told him to hurry up with the hamburgers; the little lady at the counter was eating for two.

Mara reached out under the counter and grasped my hand. At once she filled my mindseye-present with a picture of Tommy, question-mist spinning around him. She painted his eyes deep and full of reaching: *I want to help you. Let me touch you.* She snerfed him well. I feared the numbers in his head but she looked beyond the numbers to his true self. Yes, I answered her. Inside he wanted to help us. We would help him help us.

When the hamburgers came he poured our chocolate and then went back to his books. Mara just ate. She was hungry and James was too. But I snerfed the kid while I ate. Witches snerf their companions over food to learn more of one another. It is a deep and necessary act of friendship. Tommy knew nothing of that, of course. But I wanted to know him badly.

So I snerfed him deeply, and there were the numbers again: big numbers, frightening numbers, numbers not sitting still but stretching, changing, jumping and leaping, getting bigger, smaller, higher, lower. It frightened me but I snerfed more deeply to find the man beneath the numbers. If I am to be his friend I must know from what well spring his thoughts, that I may drink from that same well. The numbers went on, deeper, deeper, so I went deeper too. The life-source in the food around us pushed me on. Sweat sprung out on my hands and face. The numbers grew closer, edge-to-edge, becoming connected. He was thinking hard, too hard for me, perhaps, but by then I could no longer stop. I went down, riding on the swells and plunging into troughs of numbers, numbers now like live things, clustering around me, twisting beyond all recognition as they covered me and tried to drown me. *Strength, strength!* I cried to my heart-place, guarding whatever I had left of myself...but then something broke around me, and the numbers began to dissolve. They disappeared into haze and steam, leaving behind a frame that kept the purpose of the numbers but not their substance, like a honeycomb emptied of honey. The frames changed their shape without moving, as though they could hold many numbers and speak many things with one tongue.

Functions, he called them, and at once a strange word rose up in my mindseye-present reading CALCULUS in capital thoughts. It frightened me a little but fascinated me in spite of that fear, because the frames too were warping and flowing in a peculiar way, though each stood fixed in its place. Drunk with fear and excitement I slipped between the squirming frames, going deeper still until the frames too began to dissolve, leaving behind a single frame of frames that neither moved nor changed, yet in its subtlety of form told the frames how to change, which in their diversity of change told the numbers how to move and then...a blinding snerf-flash roared into my mind, repeating that the whole thing makes sense: *I know what he's doing.*

Next thought Mara was screaming and pulling me from the floor. I felt Tommy's warm strong hands laying me out on a booth-seat, and Mara's hand grasping my own. Love-mist (past, present, future, *forever*) spilled into me from her, and as well as I could I sent the same in return. When Tommy asked me what was wrong, I told him it was epilepsy, and happened every so often. That was a lie of course, but I could not explain how my own flash of understanding had blinded me into unconsciousness.

Tommy gave me cold water and soon I sat back at the counter. He kept looking at me, not knowing what to say, and I could snerf concern and empathy tracing warm circles inside him. I could only think inside myself: *Thank you, Creator, for painting us here together on this cold and difficult night.*

Mara caught my eye and filled my mindseye-present with question-mist but no picture. The question was understood. I tried to picture the frame of frames of numbers but it didn't fit into her mindseye. Mara is better at numbers than I, and can do arithmetic, but strange ideas unrelated to things right here in front of us are difficult for her. I pushed it but she clouded up, thinking; *no Yonnie stop, it hurts…what is it?*

What indeed? That was a hard question. *Alas, my dearest, there are no words, no mists, no pictures for it. It will not hurt us, nor is it of use to witches. Think of James and how he will make the stars weep and the oceans laugh!*

Mara returned to the mother-thoughts that enlivened her. Tommy in the meantime had gone back to his books. I snerfed sparks in him, his desire to help us rubbing against his need to work with his numbers and his frames. I gently helped him forget about us, and tried to guide him to the knowledge he sought.

Spread out before us I saw a problem: A rocket was going from here to there by a certain frame, and by reading that frame he was to predict when it would arrive. I snerfed him trying to read the frame while tripping all over the numbers. It is easier to ignore something that is meaningless to you. So I guided him past the numbers, arranged the frame of frames in his mind so that the numbers disappeared. It stayed there awhile, a tiny flame of revelation that smoked for a moment but finally ignited a brilliant flash of surprise.

Tommy said something out loud that sounded like a cuss word. It must have been Greek because I had never heard it before and freaks use them all.

"You know what?" he said, looking up from his books, "I just figured out calculus. Weirdest thing: It all came in one bang. 'Flash of genius,' maybe? Ha ha."

At once he vanished under his blanket of numbers, armored with new confidence, to do battle with the frames beneath. I snerfed him as he went, and tasted warm nondirected joy. He liked me. He was not sure why, but he liked me. And I liked him.

So I sat back and chewed on memories for awhile. I called up one memory stolen from Tommy from college. It was a big man in front of a blackboard writing a sentence in capital letters: CALCULUS IS THE MATHEMATICS OF CHANGE. I thought about this frame of frames of numbers, calculus. It is a little like time-opt, a little like taking a stopped slice of something moving and changing and looking hard at the slice so that you know where it is going from there. And all the numberlessly thin slices placed side to side fit into the frame-of-frames, which in some way contained the key to it all. Yet when I tried gingerly to fit numbers into their frames I got scared and tripped and fell and lost my grip on the whole thing. It collapsed down atop me like a tall house of cards on a shaken table.

It is sad. I liked this thing calculus, even if I couldn't do anything with it. Calculus without numbers is like a hammer without nails: Nice to have in your hands, nice to swing in the air, but a hammer by itself won't hold a house together.

It was a little past east-southeast on the clock when we finished our burgers. Outside the big front window the street was swarming with winos. All the Clark Street bars close at east-southeast, and the winos spill out and start milling around. Mara and I had to look the other way. It was too easy to snerf them. In a wino you only snerf cold I-am-nobody thoughts that hurt too much to bear.

We knew the worst would happen and soon they began coming into the restaurant. It was only business for Tommy and the waitress, though we cringed. In twos and threes they came in and sat down, talking to one another and laughing to release their wordless pain. Mara took my hand and fled inside my thoughts to get away from them.

She fled into me but I must confront their pain, now as always. I hated snerfing them, but my judgment-spot said, *better do it; remember Lennie.* Yet that night I could not bring myself to snerf them. It was enough just to look.

Most were older men but some few were our age-in-body. All looked shabby. Some had long coats, some short, some only ragged flannel jackets. Some walked quickly, some slowly; all walked differently. Most people walk upwind in life. Winos walk downwind. Their faces were hollow, starved of life's sources. All needed a shave, whiskers bristling gray and patchy under their eyes, which were deep, sunken hollow pools of loneliness. It hurt just to look at them. Snerfing would hurt too much. I told my judgment-spot: *They are defeated creatures. They cannot hurt us.* My judgment-spot answered yet again: *Remember Lennie.*

I did not want to remember.

I sat there and fought with myself, cold and hurting all over. It was some moments before I was fully aware of a new feeling: a tide-wash inside my head, then a flow, a current, a roaring flood, a raging tidal wave. I was wet and washed away and drenched in terror, and I did not know why. Black thunderheads poured into my skull, every spot in my mind screaming *warning!* I jerked and shivered, my thoughts spinning aimlessly. Nothing would come clear. Chaos grew in me with every second until I had to flee inside myself, but Mara was there already, cringing. All I could do was pick her up and run...

Then I saw the wino take a seat at the counter beside me. By reflex I tried to snerf him and bounced back like a ball off a concrete wall. Psycho! The wino was a psycho! I wanted to run down to the floor and melt into the cracks. Psycho sitting next to me! *Creator, help us!* my old, too-little-used prayer-spot yelled. My vision of primordial life overlaid upon James hardened me, and I tried to think.

I have said often that freaks of all beings hurt the worst, but I was not thinking about psychos. Not-ables are human, witches are human, even freaks as warped as they may be are still human. Psychos are different. Everything that is human in them is stillborn the moment they enter the world, and they spend their lives raging beyond the bounds of love or rationality. Their bodies are the same as ours. They even act human most of the time, out of undermind instincts that preserve their bodies from violence and starvation. But inside their heads are clouds and lightning and steam and lava, a jumble of undermind and overmind in one swirling chaos of no-sense no-control. Vast power is in them. But it seethes without direction, rising and falling like the tides. Psychos lack the control given humans by the metamind. They are like houses without fuses. Most people let hatred and anger build up in them until their fuses blow. They weep, or even collapse, and then start again. In psychos raw power flowing from unguarded underminds builds higher and higher until it takes them over and makes them dance, run, slobber, scream, kill.

Witches can't snerf psychos right. We can't zot them, use time-opt, or any other witch-trick. These work only on the metamind, and in psychos the metamind is shriveled up like an old raisin.

I could not organize my body to flee. Mara pressed herself into my shoulder, whimpering in my mind. All my spots were screwed up like a radio next to an electric motor. *Protect Mara and James!* I screamed at myself, and forced my head to turn and see the psycho.

He looked like any other wino: an old man about seventy, gray beard-stubble blotching his face over cheekbones high and gaunt. He wore a dirty coat and floppy work cap, and grinned gap-toothed for no reason. He made me shiver. I could see the burning chaos behind his sunken eyes.

Tommy came back about then. He had been helping the waitress serve the other winos. He sat on his stool and smiled at the psycho.

"Hi, Jock," he said.

"Howdy, Tommy," the psycho replied in a cracked rusty-hinge voice with faraway accents and angles.

"None of your carrying-on tonight," the kid told him. "The young lady here's tired. You just be quiet or I'll kick you out, okay?"

The psycho glanced molten lava at us, then nodded, still smiling. "Dontcha worry, Tommy-me-boy. I'll keep me peace."

I swallowed my fear as best I could. I had been trying to put my mind back in order, but it was like trying to catch a Sunday newspaper blown all over Grant Park. Slowly things fell into place. With eyes closed, I didn't even have to snerf deliberately. All I had to do was open my snerf-spot a little and there he was, a creature of chaos far too vast for the withered body to hold, boiling out into mind-space, a shadow-cloud place where flesh and metal do not go. Mara and I have touched it in the midst of lovemaking at the furthest reach of our joined spirits. But mostly it is beyond us, an endless height or a bottomless pit, unseen and felt only in moments of ecstasy or terror. In that place Jock was a shadow-cloud man miles tall over his cracked and shriveled little body, shadow-cloud hands on shadow-cloud hips, shadow-cloud eyes looking, looking, looking for something. What psychos look for. Even among witches, there is no knowledge of it and no word for it.

"Got any stories to tell us, Jock?" Tommy asked the psycho. I snerfed that the kid was trying to keep him quiet. He had memories of Jock running wild in the restaurant, screaming and spinning between the booths. Tommy didn't know that psychos do their worst stuff with their minds, and can burn an unwary mind to ashes for no reason or any reason at all.

"Sure, Tommy-me-boy. Strangled a six-foot rat last night, I did. With me bare hands. Me specialty's them octo-pussers, y'know, but this ol' bugger crawled out of an open sewer an' started hissin' an' growlin' an' I..."

"Something a little less gruesome, huh, Jock?" Tommy broke in, and winked at me. I cringed. You don't say things like that to a psycho. Priests used to drive devils from madmen long ago. Only witches know that psychos installed the devils. But somehow Tommy was keeping the psycho down, supplying that missing control, if only for a little while. I decided Tommy was safe, and wanted to use the lull in the storm to get Mara and James out of there.

"Thanks a lot Tommy it's been good talking to you," I said all in one breath and got up, herding Mara with my hands so she wouldn't have to look at the psycho. Tommy rose, concerned, and handed back our three Eisenhowers across the counter.

"No," I said. "We...have to pay."

"Do you still want whale meat?"

I stopped short, cold to the middle of my bones. "Y...yes," I answered. Mara tensed under my hands.

"Well, I just thought of something. You take this money, get on the bus going north and get off at Lawrence. A block west of Clark is a little imported food shop. If there's whale meat anywhere in this town it'll be there. If there isn't, maybe the man can tell you where it is. You'll get your whale meat." He lowered his voice and leaned closer. "I know how it is with pregnant women. When my ma was carrying Dimitra she wanted skinned squid every night."

For all my fear, I appreciated his humor.

"Thanks. Thanks a lot, Tommy."

We started to walk toward the door. But then the psycho stood up and looked at me with fire and hot ash in his eyes. I froze, unable to move.

"Whale meat? In the ocean, laddie! Lots o' whale meat in the ocean! Toons of it, I tell ye! *Toons!*"

With the words hanging molten in the air, Jock shut his eyes for some inner pain. The spell broke. I thought nothing, felt nothing, said nothing, simply blundered our way out the door. When the cold wind hit us we began running, bumping into winos and bums and not caring. We ran for blocks before we found another bus bench and sat down.

By that time the sky was getting a little light.

We sat and shivered for a long time. Mara and I had never been so close so long to a psycho before, yet we were alive. I closed myself off from Mara for a second and remembered my snerf-image of the psycho. The psycho was looking for something. I have snerfed that in other psychos glimpsed from afar. I always thought they were looking for their stillborn part, the control-negotiator metamind that is dead and will never grow. But this psycho was looking for something else, a shadow-cloud something like himself, something not-earth not-sky. I recalled his words about a giant rat. I bit off a cold prayer halfway through, let my guards down and let Mara flood into me like a wave of honey. The question-mist did not form, nor any mist at all. It was just us together, as it has been for centuries, and we shivered on the bus bench as the day began.

By morning-west the streets were full of hurrying people, and Mara and I shouldered between them onto the bus. Through the whole ride I snerfed echoes of thoughts in people around us, wondering why we didn't have jobs, wondering why we lived off welfare money, wondering why we were agents of a country on the other side of the world. People think we are many things. It is good that they do not think we are witches.

We were glad to get off the bus. The food store was nearby, with signs in three languages. When we opened the door little bells tinkled and hundreds of smells flew around us, daring us to guess what they were. Food was stacked to the ceiling on narrow shelves, and the wood floor creaked when we walked on it.

The man at the cash register was middle-aged, with black hair and a curly mustache. He had a big pot-belly held in with a stained white apron tied tight around back. I snerfed him hard and carelessly. He twitched as though a third arm had itched and he was wondering what to scratch. Mara warned me to be careful. He was closer to able than most and food was all over the place.

He grinned as we approached.

"What can I do for you?" he asked, with a funny accent echoing down his rain-barrel voice.

"We would like some whale meat."

He smiled, but his smile had gotten a little stiff. "Well." Two sausage-fingers twiddled his mustache. "Squid I got. Octopus I got. Forty kinds of fish I got. Even snake meat I got. But they won't give me whale meat any more."

I felt Mara lean more heavily on my arm. I was beginning to feel that this whale meat matter had gone far enough. "That's a shame," I said. "I know not too many people probably eat whale meat. We can pay you in advance. Maybe you can order some. From San Francisco, or maybe Hawaii?"

He shook his head. "Sorry. Whales is endangered. The government won't let the whalers catch them anymore. Against the law."

"You mean nobody has it anywhere."

"That's right. How about octopus? I got a special on it this week. The only whale meat's on the whales in the sea."

I shivered, thinking of Jock the psycho. I shook my head. "You know how pregnant women are." We walked away without smiling.

Outside Mara sat on a salt box and looked at the sidewalk.

"Yonnie, I'm scared. I need whale meat."

For the first time since the grocery man twitched I opened my snerf-spot and reached out to her. I recoiled in shock. Her snerf-spot was locked in a vise, clamped shut for fear. I put my hands on her head. Fear encased her. "Mara, tell me what this means."

She would not look at me.

"Mara!"

Her eyes would not rise from the sidewalk. I reached into her mind and struck that knot of fear, so hard she gasped and drew back from me. "No. Stop. Please stop."

Her eyes rose to mine. I was born the year bad Pope Urban Prignano ascended the Throne of Peter. I took Mara for my mate and my partner a century later. Since then I have stood by her side. When plague drove us from our farm in Carpathia I carried her by night away from fearful crowds with torches.

In France I zotted the emissary of the Inquisition who would torture us, and in Saxony I stove in a corrupt tax collector's head with a brick. Fear and hunger are a witch's lot, always. We are driven from land to land, across seas, over mountains. Someday they will drive us to the stars, when there are no more places left on Earth to flee. Through it all I have provided for Mara without question, protected her without hesitation. I have seen her face death itself. But never did her eyes display the bottomless despair they did at that moment.

I took a deep breath. "Speak it then. But speak."

"Whale meat." Her mouth was dry. "I know I need whale meat like I know I must breathe, or eat, or drink. And every second I go without it makes it clearer what I will be if I do not get it. Yonnie help me!"

"I am. I will. If you don't speak I can do nothing. You are closed off away from me."

"That's it! That's what I fear beyond death or any pain! Without whale meat James will not come. I will stay on, but my snerf-spot will die, and there will be no more dulping, no more tricks...as you say, I will be closed off from you forever and ever, my mate and partner for all time!"

Her bitter parody of our wedding vow made anger growl up in me. There is no witch-trick to dispel fear. But knowledge can make it subside, and for knowledge I drove into her, ignoring all else but the deepest balances of life's sources. Yes, something was wrong, but the answer lay deeper still: James. I broke through brain curtains and snerfed his growing humanity as only Mara could. She began to scream beneath my touch but I felt it coming and caught it in the air before people could hear. It died in my hands, echoing tinny and cold to the place witches make bad sounds go. And now I knew why Mara needed whale meat.

She did not. James did. Without words, and upon a tapestry of luminous symbol, James told me of how the human mind had been broken into three warring parts and severed from its own spirit by some dire accident millennia past. The great swimmers who rule the oceans and think with unsundered minds knew of our plight, and have been waiting for one among humanity with sufficient power to return the human mind to the wholeness bestowed upon it by the Creator. In the tiny echo of the ocean within Mara's body James swam with them and learned from them. With the gathered power of their great minds they had begun shaping his mind in the image of theirs. Much had been done, but the final reshaping required that he partake of their bodies as well. Only a little of their flesh would be enough, and they offered it freely if only we could find it.

He will be the greatest witch since humanity's dawn, and he will heal the brokenness in humankind that he suggested (with dark hints) the first witches had had a hand in creating. But James also warned me that without whale meat, his new unbroken humanness could not grow to completion, and he would die before he is born, taking with him all that makes Mara able. She will be a prisoner within her own skull, trapped within immortal bone and flesh for the rest of time.

I had to make a horrible decision. There was nothing I could do alone.

"Come on, Mara. We will go back to Tommy. We will tell him what we are and what we need. He will help us. No one else will."

We had no money for the bus. Even all the money in the type set was not enough, and Mara in her fear could not dulp. I thought we could walk, but the cold and the wind made short steps seem like miles. We stopped, and I squeezed Mara's hand in a gesture I had used to beg her trust in dangerous times. I stepped to the curb and put out my thumb.

Many cars passed us. Finally a big car pulled to the curb. The window zipped smoothly down without the driver cranking. A man in a dark blue suit looked at us, frowned, and then the big door swung wide.

Mara looked up at me, her eyes echoing memories of traps we have seen and avoided, and traps we did not avoid and had to fight to escape. But some chances must be taken. We got in.

Immediately I snerfed the man. He was all clouds and rain inside, filled with the fog of guilt and confusion. At the center of his conflict was a boy who looked something like him, only with long shaggy hair and raggy, bright-colored clothes. In the boy's eyes were questions and defiance and poetry and pain. The boy was a beginning freak. It must have been from his mother's side—the man himself was not able at all, even the least little bit.

I also looked at the car. It was bright and new, with soft wrinkled leather seats and buttons beyond my counting. The man was wealthy. Everything in his mind had a price.

"Where you going?" he asked, trying to sound friendly. It was a little forced. The man was trying to figure us out, trying to resolve the conflict in his mind. If he was close to able it would be dangerous.

"Just to Fullerton," I told him.

"Long way to walk in this weather."

"We're a little short this week on bus money," I said.

The remark made him uncomfortable. Morning west-northwest had come and gone and cars moved quickly. He wanted to change the subject. He glanced at Mara's swollen belly. "How long?" he asked.

"Five years," I said without thinking, so lost was I in the puzzle over whale meat. Fear bit me.

"I mean, how long has she been expecting now?"

"Oh. Seven months and a week or two."

"Congratulations. Hope it's a boy." He reached into his suit pocket and pulled out a cigar in a glass tube. "Care for one?"

"No, thank you. We don't smoke."

Smoke. The word rang painfully and angrily in his mind. The snerf-image of his son had changed, now with awful green smoke pouring out of his mouth and nose. The smoke was pot-smoke. The man was angry, and afraid.

Nobody said anything for a while. The traffic lights flashed and changed, cars crept and moved and stopped. The man's mind was full of horror, his son wrapped in smoke, around him bars and lawbooks and the stain of disgrace. I realized that it was fear for the future. There was still time for a solution if he could find it.

Fullerton came and I had to tell him; he was lost in his thoughts. He pulled the car to the curb and stopped, nodding. I grasped the polished silver door handle. He put his hand on my arm, dug in his pocket, and pulled out a paper Jackson. He stuffed it in the pocket of my jacket, and in his face the question was so loud, so full of confusion and anguish, that I could almost hear it with my ears.

I clicked the door open, and the noises of the street roared in on us. I hadn't realized it had been so quiet inside.

"He feels a void within him," I said. "He wants to fill it with smoke and pills. Love will fill it. Put money aside and love him. Just love him."

The man's face went white, his eyes wide. *"You read my mind,"* he whispered. I swung the door open and almost threw Mara out before me. We ran, and ran, like we have run for centuries. There is no escaping the pain of those we try to help.

The paper Jackson bought us chicken in the bucket with the old man's face on it—plus a greasy stack of paper Washingtons; money is so strange!—and we munched past store windows until night west-southwest. Tommy would be at the restaurant then. We hurried down the streets, still holding the empty chicken-bucket. Through the restaurant window we could see Tommy talking to somebody in a booth. We barreled in the door, bubbling over inside our heads Tommy help us we need whale meat…whale meat…whale meat….*whale meat….*

The thought echoed and echoed. We stopped dead in front of the counter. The person in the booth was Jock the Psycho.

Then I noticed something strange. We were still stopped dead in our tracks. So was Tommy. So was the waitress. Mara had dropped the chicken bucket in her excitement; it was still only halfway to the floor.

The whole world had stopped. This was time-opt, time-opt like there had never been before. Mind-minutes ticked past inside us, and nothing moved. In time-opt only able minds move; all else of mind and matter stands still.

Except the psycho.

He sat in a booth, picking his teeth. "Whale meat, Yonnie?" he asked, crooked hand scratching his stubbly old chin. A picture crowded unbidden into my mindseye-present, of a vast gray creature stopped in unmoving water amidst curtains of frozen bubbles, teeth glinting in the narrow jaw. Mara's mind leapt at the sight.

The psycho smiled with crooked holes showing between stained teeth. He raised a gnarled finger into the air.

"Come, Yonnie. This time I'll pay the bus fare, I will. She will have her whale meat, laddie!"

I saw bubbling green lava welling up in the psycho's eyes. It flowed out slowly, roiling and curling to the floor, shimmering into smoke and breaking into flaming tatters around us. It filled all space, devouring reality and making the world go away. Then it was just minds floating in mind-space, lost and drifting amidst endless smoke. Tommy was a hard little ball, closed up and trapped within himself like all not-ables. Mara and I were tiny flickers of thought, clinging and fearful. I felt a plan beginning, a psycho-plan snapping shut like chains around me. I had never imagined that psychos could make plans or anything but destruction. Still, the plan was there, building and rebuilding in the shadow-cloud eyes in the shadow-cloud head of the shadow-cloud man extending from the top of the universe to the bottom. I reached for the plan, to try and understand it, and for a moment I thought it tried to leap from those eyes to me on an ancient whisper of human tenderness, but the psycho-chaos burned me and it was gone.

The shadow-cloud man reached out and touched Tommy's hard little self, and Tommy became a flicker like us. He was able. His mind bounded out of its broken trap, and like a little child he tripped and stumbled and blinked in surprise. Then he steadied, and in him there were words, and numbers, and things far beyond my understanding. If Tommy were a witch, he would be a witch and a half.

The shadow-cloud man reached down, down with his shadow-cloud arm, down toward me. I screamed but there was nowhere to go. The shadow-cloud arm reached down *through* me, deep into my mindseye-present to the frozen world-picture there, with the whale and the bubbles. The shadow-cloud hand gripped the gray behemoth and ripped it from the silent, shattering waves. Upward, outward, *elseward* moved the hand and the whale, faster and faster like a streaking meteor.

Then Tommy and I began snerfing one another deeply without knowing why. Numbers crowded into Tommy's mindseye-present. My mindseye-past grew full of hazy rememberings that flowed, cooled, and hardened into the hand writing in chalk on a blackboard: CALCULUS IS THE MATHEMATICS OF CHANGE. Beneath it rose the frame of frame of numbers lit up in mind-lights too bright to think at.

A frame! Yonnie, give me a frame! a mind cried, Tommy's new mind-voice. The whale was still rising in the shadow-cloud hand, faster and faster, in the grip of the surging, undirected, uncontrolled psycho-power. There was no direction and no caution. Tommy's voice cried louder: *The frame the frame the frame Yonnie* THE FRAME!

I felt that there was nothing left inside me. Fear and worry had sucked me dry. *For Mara!* I thought, and shut down all my spots. I dug deeply into myself, and from a place I had never known I had I drew a frame. Tommy snapped it up instantly and filled it with numbers. He shook it around and the numbers fell into place. The entity tore loose from him like a peal of thunder: CONTROL.

The shadow-cloud hand pulling the whale curved somewhat, moving neither so quickly nor with such rapid acceleration. It followed the plan of the frame according to the commands of the numbers. Tommy called for another frame. I gave him the frame and he filled it with numbers and again the hand curved its hurtling path. It happened again, faster: a frame, numbers, control, frame, numbers, control, the process blending together between us. It grew around us, one single frame of frames that held the psycho-hand in check according to a single definite path through that impossible place.

Then mind-space shook with a scream, a horrible mind-scream that for a moment made the frames falter and pause. I shut it out and tried to think only of the frames. The scream came again, followed by something else, a warbling nonanimal snarl. I kept making frames but turned one tiny bit of my snerf-spot outward.

The shadow-cloud hand was no longer pulling the whale. The shadow-cloud man was far above us, grabbing something huge and black and horribly not-earth not-sky. The shadow-cloud man screamed in pain and fear as the thing ripped at him, and it howled as he tore at it in return.

Above the din I heard a tiny call. Tommy pointed me to it; the whale was falling back to its rightful place in the frozen ocean like a rubber band snapping, faster and faster. Our frames were coming undone, scattering like autumn leaves, no numbers holding them together, no shadow-cloud hand following their plan. In a single flash my mindseye-future saw no whale, no James, Mara shut up inside herself, trapped in the darkness of her skull, unable to share that awful loneliness with me...

Out of that terror a shadow-cloud hand rose to meet the falling whale. The hand was *my* hand, and although clumsy it grasped and pulled the whale back on its former course. I pulled and the hand pulled, moving the whale faster and faster. I tried to control it, but when I did the whale stalled and began moving back. It was move or control, move or control. I was not enough to do both alone. *A frame, Tommy!* I cried. For a long frightening moment there was only emptiness, numbers sloshing around without guidance. Then slipping through the mire came a fragile frame with numbers in it, ready for me. I embraced the frame and again there was control. My shadow-cloud hand curved and slowed, once more on its proper path.

Another frame came, and another, faster and faster in succession, until it was like it had been before.

Only now we were doing it ourselves. Far away beyond us, the battle continued. The shadow-cloud beast was still ripping at the psycho, but it was not nearly as strong. Shadow-cloud fragments were everywhere, dripping hate and ugly sour mind-stuff. Huge shadow-cloud hands slowly encircled the black shadow-cloud throat, tightened, and squeezed. The growls choked off, rising to a single shriek of agony, and ended.

The shadow-cloud man reached down and shoved us back into the real world. We tumbled outward and downward, inside-up back to our bodies. The whale went too, following the command of the last frame. It was a good frame. There came a mind-shock and a world shock, a dull smashing thudding *boom*. I saw that time-opt was over. The chicken bucket hit the floor. Tommy blinked. Outside the restaurant people began screaming, cars screeching their tires. Yes, we had done a good job.

But Jock, old Jock the psycho, was too far gone. In my mind was a shadowy, tumbling roar of great mind-towers falling and crumbling. Not much was left inside the crooked old-man body. The pieces of the shadow-cloud man began drifting apart, separating like clouds in a dying hurricane. Eyes once full of boiling chaos now held only stale confusion and heaps of ashes growing cold.

Yet still some small fire remained. The old-man body suddenly leapt from the booth-seat and grabbed a steak knife from the counter by Tommy. He screamed an old-man scream and ran out the door.

"God! What's going on out there!" the waitress demanded, leaping to her feet.

Tommy was still blinking and rubbing his eyes. His able-ness was gone. Perhaps he would never really understand what had happened to him. "Funny thing. I have to get more sleep. I dozed off just now and had the weirdest dream, you wouldn't believe..."

There was nothing I could say to that. Moments later a crooked figure limped past the window and stumbled in the door. He was covered in gore and grease. In one hand he held a bloody knife, in the other a chunk of raw meat dripping blood. He threw the meat down on the counter and leapt up on a booth table. Old Jock the Psycho looked up at the ceiling, screamed something not-earth not-sky, and stuck the knife in his heart.

The waitress screamed again. Tommy swore in Greek and jumped up, but I put my hand on his shoulder and picked up the chunk of meat. "Tommy, please cook this for us. You are my friend, help me."

Our eyes hit solid and locked together for one long mind-second, and you could almost see the spark. For that one second he was again able, and something deep inside him understood what I had asked.

Tommy turned from me and headed for the back room, meat in his hands.

Outside on Clark Street ambulances were coming, their sirens yowling in the night. Men in uniforms ran back and forth. The waitress ran into the street, yelling something about a dead man. More lights lit up the inside of the restaurant.

A little later cops and ambulance men came back with the waitress. They saw Jock, covered in blood, a knife up to its handle in his chest, knobby old-man hand still gripping it. They looked at his face, which smiled in the peace of triumph. They looked at us. Mara was eating a steak, rare, with parsley.

They shook their heads. "This man killed himself."

Tommy nodded. "He was a little psycho, I think."

The cop grunted. "Damn. That's a mess. Gonna need a bag. Nobody leave. We'll be back."

When they had gone I wiped the blood and grease from Jock's face and made the Circle of Great Life on his forehead, smoothing the creases from his sun-beaten brow. Inwardly I commended him to our Creator, who alone knows where suffering comes from, or what good may come of it.

Mara took my hand and squeezed tight. Two more years would see James enter the world, and be the biggest witch the world ever had. Witches take a long time coming because they must learn everything their parents know before they are born. When James comes he will know how to snerf, to dulp, to zot. He will know how to make frames for frames of numbers, this thing calculus. He will be able to extend shadow-cloud hands to where his body cannot reach. He will know what it is that psychos look for with shadow-cloud eyes, and how they have protected broken humankind from bodiless evil since time beyond knowing.

But far beyond that, James will heal us of that brokenness, if we can only bring ourselves to hope that it can be done.

Jock will not hurt anymore, and that is good. Tommy is puzzled but he'll get over it. Somebody is going to have a hell of a time getting that dead whale off the corner of Fullerton and Clark Streets, though.   ■

AFTERWORD: WHALE MEAT

This is the only fantasy story that I have ever sold, though there are people who argue that calculus cannot appear in a fantasy story. Perhaps. But the idea came out of the tension between my love for the *idea* of calculus and my miserable lack of facility with arithmetic. Higher math, to me, has always been pure magic. Harry Potter has nothing on differential equations.

I wrote "Whale Meat" in the cold winter of 1974, after hanging out with my two high-school friends Tom and George at the small restaurant on Clark Street that Tom's family owned. Tom worked there all night, often studying for college exams, and George and I came by regularly to keep him company—and awake. We watched some very strange people wander in and out of the restaurant, sometimes stopping for coffee, sometimes only glancing around with haunted looks before leaving again. White-bread suburbanite that I was, I wondered if there were more going on here than met the eye, and the story itself unfolded from that.

A shorter and much cruder version of the story first appeared in Ohio State University's *Starwind Magazine* in 1977. I rewrote it heavily before publishing it as a standalone ebook in 2007, and that's the version you see here.

BORN AGAIN, WITH WATER

2008

Born Again, With Water

1

Hailmaryfulgrptz...Hailmulyfir...Hailmaryfullofgraaz—glmph. Hailmaryflgz..no use. Maybe I am still a sinner. For days and days of bothsuns I have tried to say my prayers. Ever since Jacobthehermit found me in the desert and brought me to the mission Sistermaria would hold my head in her hands and make me speak the Stickmister words slowly with her. But always, my tongues trip and wrestle and stop. I am sorry, Motherofgod. I asked Sistermaria if you would be cross. She laughed and said you love little children no matter how many tongues they have and that if I came by your grotto and told you in my own words how hard I was trying, you would hear me and understand. I will come every day. I will say my prayers. You wait and see!

2

Hailmaryfull—that is some—fullofgracethelord—yes! Thelordiswitheebless—that is more!—theeblessedis-the—oh.

I have forgotten the rest. I am sorry. It has been a day for grieving, not remembering. Jacobthehermit came again to the mission today, dragging his sledge through the big gates with a bundle wrapped in rags. Sistermaria, Sisterangela, and Fatherbrian ran out with me and watched while Jacobthehermit unwrapped the rags. Under the rags were my parents, twisted and still. I ran to my father and entwined a toucher with one of his, but his toucher was stiff and cracked off, and dust ran from the broken end. I cried out, and Sistermaria held my head away.

I cannot repeat all the Stickmister words they said, but Fatherbrian agreed that they were my parents. Jacobthehermit said he found them in a cave with no water or food, near where he had found me wandering and crying out. My father's right rear leg had been gnawed by a grund, he said, so father could not have walked to safety. Fatherbrian bent down and looked in my eye and ran his fingers through my fur and said, yes, he is clean, he is healthy, he may stay with us. From now on I will be a childofchrist (which I think means a child whose parents have died) and I will sweep sand from the mission halls and sleep under the stairs.

Later that day Jacobthehermit took his sledge and went into the village where other people like me live. I followed him, trying to stay behind him so he would not see me. He fetched one of the shaman-elders to ask what to do with the bodies. The shaman-elder snorted when he saw the bundle in which my parents lay and said, in my words, "Two lost souls—ahya, their meat has spoilt. Do not trouble me about them." And he turned away.

Now my mother and father lie under the sand outside the mission gate, with two crosses of Stickmister metal to mark the place. Teach me, Motherofgod, to be a good childofchrist, and help me to say my prayers for you!

3

Hailmaryfullofgracethelordiswitheebless—No! I cannot stop now—sedarthouamong—what next? Oh, more, more—amongwomenandblessedisthe—the—no, I cannot. I have tried, Motherofgod. My tongues stop and lie flat when I look at your face. Perhaps it is because I have seen water today—and I am not sure I should do that.

Today was a Water Day. There is a Water Day every seven bothsunups. I have counted three Water Days with stones under the stairs since coming to the mission. There is a Stickmister machine at the far end of the courtyard with metal handles and wheels: it is the water machine. When one of the Stickmisters touches it, the wheels turn and squeak—and it makes water.

Water has a taste and smell like nothing else. The taste is in food, the smell often in the air. I always thought the smell only meant: parents are watching, food is close by, and if it goes away, there is trouble! But there is more, Motherofgod. It is strange to stand by the wood trough under the water machine and *see* it in the bottom, all silvery and full of the sky-color. It feels good in a way that nothing else feels good. I love to stand there and see my face and fur and the tops of all my legs down in the bottom of the trough. It makes me want to look and look until I am not sure if I am standing there looking down or if I am lying in the bottom of the trough looking up. I start to get feelings as though my insides were on my outsides and my outsides inside. I get a little afraid but it feels *so* good.

None of the other children like me who come in from the village for missionschool will look into the wood trough. I tried to show them once but when the smell of water grew strong at the end of the yard, they ran away, giggling. One said water was bad, and after that no one would talk to me.

Water *can't* be bad. Sistermaria works the water machine, and she pours water on the funny flowers in the grotto all around you. If it is close to you, it must be good.

4

I woke up early today under the stairs and put my blankets in order as Sistermaria taught me. Right away I heard her walking nearby, singing her own prayers. Down in the courtyard I saw her with two buckets of water walking away from the water machine. I watched her take the buckets down the hall and through a door I have never gone through before. Soon she came out with empty buckets, went to the water machine, and filled them again. I watched while the water rushed out, white and smooth and strange. It almost looks like a toucher reaching into the bottom of the bucket, and whispering. Sistermaria smiled at me and called goodmorning. Then she picked up the buckets and they went sloshing with her down the hall through the big door. All the time she had been singing. I waited but she didn't come out again.

It was so clear and the sun so warm that I wanted to sit beside her and hear her sing again. I also wanted to see the sun glitter on the water, and hear it slosh. So I went down the hall, following the water-splashes on the flagstones, and saw the big closed door. I heard her singing faintly behind it.

All the drips by the door were together in one big drip that all four of my paws stood in. It made them tingle. I touched the door with my nose, but it did not move. I brought my left toucher up and pushed harder. The door swung in a little, showing me a big square room with no roof and lots of sunshine and Sistermaria standing next to a huge bucket that was bigger than she was. I called goodmorning (that much is short and easy, even in Stickmister words) and wanted to ask if I could look at the water with her. But when she saw me she made a squeaky noise and said, "Thomas, please, you should not be here."

I felt sneaky and bad. I knew I was a sinner then. Maybe it is a sin for people like me to talk about water, or to see it instead of just taste it in food. If I could say my prayers I would not be a sinner. Help me, please.

Sistermaria closed the door and made clicky noises behind it and told me to sweep the stairs. I told her I would but I stood there by the door with my paws tingling, and listened to the water slosh for a long time.

5

Ourfath—Ourf—Ourfatherwhoart—if I were not a sinner it wouldn't be so hard! All the other children at missionschool know your prayer now and are working on a new one for Jesusourlord in the chapel. I tried too but every time I look up at Jesusourlord my tongues fall asleep and can't move. I wish he would smile like you.

I should be happy but I am sad and I hurt. Sistermaria told us about baptism today. She said we are all sinners but baptism washes it away. It is done with water. So that is what water is for!

All the other children giggled and poked each other until Sistermaria scolded them. She told us that Jesusourlord said we must be born again to enter heaven, and baptism is the way we are born again. Heaven is where you are. I asked Sistermaria once and she pointed at the stars, where the Stickmisters came from. I know you are there somewhere. Your coat is blue like the sky, when it is only just bothsunset.

Sistermaria said that as soon as she had word from Monsignormichael in Rome we could all be baptized and not be sinners anymore. The children said nothing. But they did not look happy like me.

Just then the bell rang and the other children trotted out the mission gate to go home. I was so happy that I trotted out after them, and I asked Ypp-Nee if he was glad he wasn't going to be a sinner anymore.

"What's it to you, To-Moz?" he asked me, and snarled. Ypp-Nee snarls a lot.

I told him I was excited that we were all going to be baptized. Ypp-Nee scrunched up his eye and bared his teeth. I kept smiling. "Filthy turd!" He said, and curled his right toucher into a ball and hit me on my nose. Then he ran away.

I stood there and watched little violet drops hit the sand from my nose. It is not good to lose blood, my father told me, and it always hurts. I wanted to wail in sadness. Then I remembered that Jesusourlord also had blood drops on him (which were red like flowers, not deep violet) and he died. Now I have crusty blue stuff on my nose and my fur and my legs and touchers. If Sistermaria sees me she will punish me.

The big gate will not close until after bothsunset and the stars come out. You are up there in heaven and you will watch me while I go to the village to get my nose and fur clean. I heard Ypp-Nee talk about it once that when he fights and gets his nose bloody an old person cleans him so that his family will not punish him for fighting.

I want to be clean too. When bothsuns are down I will go and find him.

6

Hailmaryfullofgracethelordiswiththeeblessedartthoua-
mongwomenandblessesisthefruitof—of—I will remember!—blessedisthefruitof—ofthywombjesus—here is where
we all take a breath—holymarymotherofgod—god—that
much I always remember because it sounds like you, Motherofgod. I am tired. The rest is not there. I will practice more, and I
will say it all someday.

Last night after bothsunset I rumpled my blankets under
the stairs, so Sistermaria would not think I was gone, only out
by the necessaries, and I went through the big gate. There were
stars in your heaven and stars across the sand in the village. I
went there.

It was frightening, Motherofgod. At the mission there are
only four Stickmisters. They walk slowly, singing their prayers
almost without breath, and they pat my head when they pass
me. In the village hundreds of people like me were running and
yelling and wailing songs I do not understand. All the houses
were made of burned clay and logs and rope and crumply
metal sheets from the starships that brought the Stickmisters
down from heaven. I felt lost and scared.

I tried not to look at the adults because they would see my
nose and scold—especially mothers with big bellies. I looked
for children but saw none of my friends. The only children I
saw were walking quietly and quickly, or gathered around fires
talking to each other and to the adults. They looked stern and
unhappy.

Finally I came to a small fire and saw a child even smaller
than me who was staring into the flames and mumbling. He
held a big flat book in his touchers. I asked him where I could
find the old person who would clean my nose from blood.

His eye closed and opened again. He seemed tired. But he
nodded and pointed down a dark lane between garbage piles
and said, "Yes, old Tikk used to do that when I knew him, but
that was before I…" He stopped and leaned forward, looking at
me carefully. "You're a newchild," he said, and turned away.

I did not understand, but I was scared and ran down the lane by the garbage piles. I saw low doors and high doors, some open, some shut with sheets of Stickmister metal. On some doors names were written but none that I knew. Only a little light came from smoky fires inside the houses and my eye burned. The lane ended in a huge garbage pile. I had to turn around and come back. I wished I could call for Sistermaria to come but I knew she could not help me.

Then I saw a metal door closed that had been open before. The door had TIKK painted on it in big runes. I pushed the door with my touchers because my nose hurt too much. It swung in squeakily. I was scared but I went in.

"I smell another bloodied nose," someone said, in a rumbling voice that frightened me. I could not see in the house, it was so dark and smoky.

I said, "Yes, please help me. Sistermaria will punish me."

My eye got used to the dark, and the smell of the food of my people was strong, especially the deeproots, from which (as my father said) all water comes. I saw a very old person sitting on his haunches on a plank raised above the dirt floor on bricks. All around him were books and stone carvings and strange things that I had never seen before, lit by pale flames flickering above small clay bowls. The old person had a flat belly so he was not a she. But he had a stern face and looked like he would scold.

He did not. He smiled. "Come here, newchild," he said.

I went to him. He stroked my nose with touchers so old the fur was worn away and the scales beneath were polished like glass. He looked in my eye and said, "Fighting is for fools. Why have you been fighting?" It sounded like he was scolding, but he still smiled as he spoke.

I scuffed at the dirt with my paws. "I was talking to Ypp-Nee about baptism."

He made a clucking noise. "Indeed," he said. "That is a funny sort of word. Tell me what it means."

"It means being born again, with water."

He nodded. "So that's what you young bucks are calling it these days. Slang does come and go. Ypp-Nee likes to fight, the young fool. His father is halfchief of the village, and the arrogance of power is in him, newchild though he may be. I'm surprised he didn't wring your neck for talking dirty to His Royal Highness."

I said, "I do not understand."

"Haven't your parents explained the facts of life?"

"They died in the desert months ago."

"Ahhh, the desert. Not to speak ill of lost souls, they say, but to be lost you must be unlucky or a fool. Your parents chose the desert, away from the village's deeproots. They were fools."

"No." I remembered my father in our desert cave, thinking and writing, while my mother groomed me. "They liked the quiet. My father said it helped him think. A grund attacked him and ate part of his leg."

"I see. An unlucky fool, at that. Thinking too much is foolish. And they left you, newchild, unprepared for a very complicated sort of world."

I got scared and told Tikk I only wanted the blood off my nose and fur. I said it twice, and my voice became unsteady.

Tikk leaned down and looked in my ears, and felt my belly with his touchers. "Old Tikk doesn't do this for nothing," he mumbled. "You're still very young—yet I think you've achieved puberty, or will very soon. The ears are right. The belly is right. The smell is right. Yes… Well, then, newchild, I will clean your nose and your fur. But I must tell you a few things first."

I told him I would listen.

He then began to speak without looking at me. It was something like a wail of my people, high and rhythmic, as though he had repeated it many times. "Every thinker eventually asks himself this question: What is the purpose of life? The purpose of life is to cheat death. We cheat death two ways: by creating new life, and by preserving old life. You, newchild, are new life. As a newchild you are vastly outnumbered by oldchildren— surely you see them, you see them everywhere, learning to walk and talk and use their bodies, for they already know how to use their minds. Oldchildren become adults. So will you. Adults grow old and eventually become oldchildren again. So will you."

"How?"

"Why, you used the word yourself, though it is a word new to me: baptism. Being born again, with water. Death claims some. Your parents. They chose to live in the desert, a long walk away from the deeproots, in defiance of the counsel of the shaman-elders, away from the Cauldron of Life. They might have denied it, but they chose death. Others lose too much blood too quickly, before they can be baptized, or they wander alone and are eaten by grunds or golliks. Still others become ill and die too suddenly to be baptized. So one tenth of every generation are newchildren. They replace the fools and the unlucky who die and are lost. Thus we cheat death. It nibbles at our flanks, but nine tenths of every generation are saved, because of baptism." He paused, and took a long, noisy breath. "Yes, baptism. That is a good word. I like it."

He nodded, and paused again, and nodded again, his eye closed. I think he was in pain. But then he opened his eye again, and said: "Old Tikk has been baptized many times. He has wailed many songs. He thought he was wise. Ah, I saw the dangers in these walking sticks from the skies. They bring metal, which we all want—and worse things: ideas, obsessions, plants and creatures that do not belong here. I told the halfchiefs and the shaman-elders that we should simply kill them with their own metal and burn their bodies, before the things they have brought can kill us more slowly.

"I have seen a strange web growing on the undersides of the leaves of some of the deeproots. I have never seen anything like that in my many years. What if something came with the Stickmisters that eats the deeproots? The deeproots raise water for our food. They raise water for the Cauldron. Without them we are *all* lost souls.

"The halfchiefs are slaves to the metal the Stickmisters bring, and the shaman-elders are slaves to the halfchiefs. They called me traitor. They demanded that I unsay what I said, but I would not. So the shaman-elders told me, Old Tikk, when you reach your time, *we will not baptize you.*"

He bent down close to me, and whispered, in breath that smelled dry and ill: "I will not unsay what I said. But the village will not be rid of me. I am old, and wealthy. It takes two adults to bring forth a newchild, but it takes only one to baptize an old man. One adult...and water."

He took a wheezy breath. I was getting scared again, but I kept listening. He said: "Old Tikk gets water. Here, there, I get a leaf more than I need to eat, and I squeeze the water from it. I have a glass vessel, made by the ancients, in which I can put gollik hatchlings and force the water from them by holding it over a fire. A drop here, a drop there...it is enough. And my time is near. So I will clean your nose with my precious water. But you must promise me something. You must promise me that when you hear a rumor, that Old Tikk has fallen ill, or that he is hurt, or that his time has come, you must return here. You must baptize me. I will tell you where the water is, and how to baptize me, when that time comes. Many children with blood-ied noses have made me this promise. How many will remember? How many will keep it? The more children who make me this promise, the better chance I have to be baptized.

"So...do you promise, newchild?"

I gave him my promise, and entwined both my touchers with both of his, as I did with my parents when I promised them I would always love and obey them.

He said nothing more. I could hear his old joints creak as he left his plank and went behind some skin curtains. I listened, and I heard the clunk of metal and the sweet slosh of water. Then Old Tikk returned with a skin that was dark with water. He held my snout in one toucher while he cleaned the blood away. It felt so good, Motherofgod! The water seeped into my mouth and nose and made my head buzz. I wanted him to do it again, and again, and never stop, but soon he told me: "Your nose and your fur are clean. Now go, and remember your promise!"

I ran all the way back to the mission in the dark and buried myself in the sand until Fatherbrian opened the gate in the morning, and I sneaked in when he wasn't looking.

So I am back and my nose is clean. It is bad to lose blood. Sistermaria would have scolded me. I wish I could ask her to explain what Old Tikk told me. There is so much I do not understand. But I cannot tell her I was fighting.

7

What has happened? I wish someone would tell me! Oh—the prayer! Hailmaryfullofgracethe-lordiswiththeeblessedartthouamongwomenandblessed Isthefruitofthywombjesus—a breath, quickly!—holymary-motherofgodprayforussinnersnowandatthehourofourdeaths!

There, Motherofgod, there! I have said your prayer, all of it. I see you smiling and your face is still kind, not like Jesusourlord who looks sad and hurt, or Saintjoseph who holds his club and looks angry.

Do you still love me? Can you help me understand what has happened?

Today was not supposed to be a water-day. Water-days come only every seven bothsunups. But Sistermaria told us in class yesterday that there was a surprise in store: A starship was coming from Rome, and Monsignormichael himself would be here to baptize us.

I was so happy. At last I would not be a sinner!

This morning when I woke up I heard Sistermaria singing a new prayer, and I heard the creak and groan of the water machine. I thought about baptism and began feeling all warm and buzzy inside. I wanted to ask Sistermaria about Old Tikk. Maybe Monsignormichael could baptize him too!

By the time I followed her water-splashes to the big door, it was already closed. I heard her inside, singing her prayer softly and making the water slosh. She had told me that I shouldn't be there, and when I went to listen I always felt like a sinner. But today it didn't seem to matter. It was a special day, and I wanted to share the sunshine in the roofless room with her and feel her pat my head. I wanted to ask her if Old Tikk could be baptized with the rest of us. I wanted to know so many things, and I wanted to feel her touch me.

My nose still hurt a little. So I pushed with one toucher, and could not make it move. Even with both touchers it would not open. So I leaned back on my hind legs and put my front paws against the wood. It swung back quickly and struck the bricks with a thud.

"Thomas!" she said. "I told you not to do that!"

Sistermaria had taken all of her skins off and she was in the huge bucket full of water. She was not all white anymore but pink, and on her head was pale yellow fur like Fatherbrian's.

"Today is a special day!" I said. "I am going to be baptized and I want to be near you!"

She laughed. "All right then. But close the door!"

I closed the door and looked at the big bucket. It was funny to see Sistermaria with all her folds and skins off. She had one little skin, and was rubbing water all over herself. It was just like what Old Tikk had done to get the blood off my nose and fur. And that had felt so good! I wanted her to rub me with it too.

So I trotted over to the big bucket, put my front feet on the edge, and I jumped in! The water was soft and cold and hit my belly hard but it didn't hurt like it would to hit the ground that hard. Sistermaria laughed for a long time, and rubbed my neck with the skin. "What am I ever going to do with you?" she said, laughing. I could hardly hear her after awhile for the buzzing in my head and the sloshing of the water in my nose and ears.

The funny feeling I got when looking into the water trough came back, only much more strongly. I could not feel anymore where my fur left off and the air began, because there was no air around me, only water. I began to feel bigger and bigger, bigger than the big bucket I was in, bigger than the mission, so big that all the world and the stars were folded in a little bundle in my belly.

I thought about you, Motherofgod.

I could see myself as though far away, trying to speak. "I said the maryprayer today!" I tried to say to Sistermaria, but the words got all tangled. My tongues were heavy with the buzz the water gave them. It was getting hard for me to see. All the whole everything of everything was just a speck in my belly, rolling and turning inside me. I felt I was opening, empty, waiting.

Sistermaria took my head and cradled it in her stiff small touchers. "My little tongue-tied saint. Little orphan Thomas. Jesus and Mary love you very much…though I'm not sure you should be taking a bath with me…"

I don't remember hearing her after that. The buzzing in my head was a rolling roar, smashing from side to side. *The sea, the sea!* a weird thought kept rising higher. *To the sea, cauldron and continuance of all unfallen life!* Memories that I never had the first time of endless rolling, smashing water filled my head. My head was under the water, my eye closed, my belly tightening and loosening. I was rising, I was the sea, I contained the sea, I was the place where life had once begun and where life could always begin again.

The sea was in me, and my front paws were over her shoulders, my touchers wrapping tight around her neck, pulling her forward and downward toward the water. The sea was in me and I poured it out onto her, squeezing to release the life in her, and with the salty-sour sea-taste of blood everywhere I saw inside my head the little tattered wisp blowing over the sea to be lost within me, crying *Jesu, Jesu, mercy!*

Then the sea (what is a sea?) vanished and the roaring went away. Sistermaria was under the water and would not come up. I pulled her head from the water with my touchers, and blood was dripping from her mouth. It is not good to lose so much blood. Fatherbrian will scold her.

I am confused, Motherofgod. I ran away and hid under the stairs until the water dried. Now Fatherbrian and Sisterangela and Brotherjames and running around and shouting.

Am I still a sinner? Was that a sin?

8

Hailmary. Fullofgrace. I can speak the Stickmister words better if I say them slowly. Thelordiswith—thee. Also if I rest in places, and let my tongues speak some in the language of my own people, like this.

Blessedartthou. A big starship came down on its tail of fire today, all the way from Rome, in Heaven, and made the sky pale with its light. A lot of new Stickmisters are here at the mission. A big Stickmister in a dark blue coat and skins with gold and silver on them looked at me, and then said to Fatherbrian: "No, it couldn't have been him. He's still a child. Too small to have reached sexual maturity. We'll have to search the village. Jesus Christ, what we'll do to that devil when we find him!"

Amongwomenandblessed. I thought Jesusourlord put the devil in Hell a long time ago. Maybe he got out. Isthefruit. The water has all gone but my belly is still twitching. I guess I'm going to be a she now. I wonder what the other children will think. Ofthywombjesus.

Motherofgod, did you scold Jesusourlord for losing so much blood? Did you baptize him?

Do you remember the Sea?

Holymarymotherofgod. The Stickmisters put Sistermaria in a metal box lined with shiny skins. The box is in the chapel, with candles all around it. Prayforussinners. Fatherbrian gathered all the children from missionschool together and told us that Sistermaria has died, but she is in Heaven with you, and happy. Brotherjames will be our teacher now, and there will be Stickmister guards at the mission gate.

There is still so much I don't understand. But I do know some things:

She didn't die. I baptized her. And she *will* be born again.

Now. Andatthehourofourdeaths.

Amen.   ■

AFTERWORD: BORN AGAIN, WITH WATER

I don't write a lot of fiction about aliens, and never have. Part of it is an aversion to hokey TV aliens: Producers slap a few ounces of latex on the forehead of a pretty girl and say she's from Tau Ceti V. Aliens that are essentially ugly humans are not that interesting to me, and I don't write them. The other, greater part of it is an appreciation of the challenge: Assuming that there is intelligent life elsewhere in the universe (of which I'm not entirely convinced; see Fermi's Paradox) it is likely to be *so* alien that there may not be much that we can all talk about. Somewhere in the middle lie rich opportunities for yarnspinning, where the aliens are understandable but poorly understood, where we can live beside them for lifetimes without having the foggiest idea what they're really about, especially if we never bother to try.

So it is with "Born Again with Water," which appears here for the first time. A friend of mine called it "low-key horror" and if true, it's the only horror story I've ever written. If it sounds a little Fifties, that at least was deliberate: I wrote it after my most recent reading of Walter M. Miller's short-story collection, *The Best of Walter M. Miller*. It was a half-deliberate tribute to a favorite writer who did most of his work when I was a toddler, during the era of Triumphal Catholicism.

If there is horror here, it comes out of unwarranted dogmatism, and the universal human pitfall that things are never *quite* as simple as they seem.

The Gaians Saga

and

The Drumlins World

In the summer of 1997, I got restless about SF again, after doing very little for almost ten years. I wanted a universe to play in. And being the contrarian that I am, I started playing with notions that my fellow SF writers would find misguided: Suppose there were no aliens after all; suppose that zero-point energy could be harnessed. Suppose—gasp!—that there is sufficient richness to the physical universe to support a form of consciousness after the death of the physical brain. What themes could one spin out in a universe like that?

Sitting with my feet in the pool one Arizona August evening, my brain fairly *boiled*, and it wasn't the Scottsdale heat. At once I had not only a universe but a situation, a set of large themes to explore, and an entire cosmology in which to explore them.

You see, the things that really matter are part of the cosmology, and if your cosmology is rich enough, there's no limit to what you can do with it. The big error in most SF these days is thinking too small. I deliberately went as big as I could go, and with any luck at all I'll be working within this fictional framework, which I call the Gaians Saga, for the rest of my life.

In the universe of the Gaians Saga, humanity emerges from the grim middle of the 21st century (a period called "Bad 50") humbled but invigorated, and hits upon a mechanism to tap into the energy of quantum pair creation, what most people today call "zero-point energy." A few years later, it is discovered that the same mechanism, pushed a little harder, can provide instantaneous transportation to any point in the universe. With the Hilbert Generator and the Hilbert Drive in hand, humanity sets out to meet the other intelligent inhabitants of the cosmos.

Except that there's nobody there.

This is peculiar, because in searching for other intelligent life, humanity discovers that around every Sun-like star is an Earthlike planet, complete with ecosphere and living things genetically identical to those on Earth. Although some worlds are farther along than others (and quite a few are still in the equivalent of the Mesozoic period) the only living things completely lacking are primates—and, of course, *homo sapiens*. Those exist only on Earth.

It sure looks like a setup. Earth assumes that somewhere, some unthinkably powerful cadre of intelligent beings is pushing buttons to make our universe amenable to creatures like us. The authors of this insanely expanded Anthropic Principle are nowhere to be found, but a term is coined to describe them: the Gaians, because of the obvious preference they have for Earthlike planets.

As the decades roll past into centuries, some odd little hints are discovered, but the Gaians hide well. And against this backdrop, I have any number of tales to tell.

The first of these to be written was my novel *The Cunning Blood*, of which I'll say more (and from which I'll present an excerpted chapter) a little later. After I completed the novel in 2000, I began work on another, mostly independent concept: the Drumlins world.

The scenario: in 2162, the Hilbert drive of a starship bound for Earth's first colony malfunctions, resulting in a "black fold." The drive itself vanishes, and the starship is dumped somewhere else in our galaxy, in an unknown system containing a G5 star and the inevitable Gaian planet. Starship *Origen's* 700 passengers shuttle down to the planet's surface and dig in, assuming that rebuilding the Hilbert drive (which requires half a tonne of *extremely* pure ytterbium) might take decades.

The accidental colonists find the expected Gaian ecosphere, but there's something else, something peculiar but in some ways wonderful: hundreds of thousands of alien machines scattered every ten or fifteen miles across the landscape. The machines appear to be made of some kind of stone, and consist of two pillars in front of a shallow bowl a little over two meters in diameter. The bowl is filled with a fine, cohesive gray dust. A young teen boy discovers that tapping 256 times on the pillars causes something to coalesce in the dust. Different combinations of taps lead to different artifacts forming in the dust, and the same pattern of taps (called a "rhythm") always produces the same artifact. Simple patterns produce simple, useful things: rope, tools, knives, gears and bearings, and so on. More complex patterns produce strange glassy and metallic artifacts with no obvious use.

The artifacts are produced by drumming on the pillars (which respond to each tap with a sound) and come to be called "drumlins." Bogglingly, there are 2^{256} possible drumlins, which is 1.16×10^{77}, or *a million drumlins for every atom in the observable universe.*

The drumlins allow the colonists to survive their first winter, and little by little allow them to build a mostly agrarian society resembling 19th century America. Familiar factions appear: city vs country, those who want to return to Earth vs. those who like where they are. And over time, some very strange drumlins are discovered, some of them what we might call game-changers.

"Drumlin Boiler" appeared in *Isaac Asimov's Science Fiction Magazine* in 2002. "Drumlin Wheel" and "Roddie" appear here for the first time. Three novels about the Drumlins World are planned, as are more short tales. Stay tuned.

Drumlin Boiler

2002

DRUMLIN BOILER

Mike malleted a pin into the coupling, and we watched *Sam'l Borden* chug and puff a cart of rocks down the length of the track, maybe as fast as a man could walk with a gimp leg. Next run, Mike coupled up the second cart of rocks, and *Sam'l* just sat there, blowing steam out of his leaks and damn near screaming. Mike threw his hat in the dirt and stomped on it. Call *Sam'l* a size six loco with a size two boiler, but it was all the iron we had, and it wasn't enough.

We've been here on this planet 252 years now since the *Origen* did a black fold and died, and nobody's yet drummed a boiler up out of a thingmaker. And a boiler is what we needed, Mike and I and *Sam'l Borden*, to get the President to take us serious and let us enter the big loco race. Just about all the rest we found in *Banger's Big Book of Drumlins*, or bought as thingie doorstops from townfolk hereabouts, and as far away as New Scottsdale. Mike was annoyed but he wasn't worried, even as we saddled up and set out for the Capital to put our papers in before October, like the rules said. Trust in God and the thingmakers, that was Mike's way. If one didn't produce, the other would. We had put word out as soon as last February, not that we thought it would help: *Mike Grabacki needs a boiler and will pay big. Get drumming.*

We saw them drumming all the way to Colonna, where the road plays connect-the-dots with the thingmakers as roads do everywhere, towns every so often and the thingmaker in the square, if you can call some dirt and three stone houses a square. They waved at us and sometimes we ate with them, the hopeful drummers with little good-luck thingies and goose bones hanging off them every which way, dancing in place to their own cockeyed rhythms as they hammered on the two pillars, whistling sometimes as though whistling would improve their chances for making the Big Drum. At every thingmaker along the road, Mike pulled back on the reins and handed the drummers the drawing he did of the drumlin we want. Meter wide at least (and perferable two), three-five meters long, and hollow. Two hundred hands unknown, and with the rhythm, ten thousand.

Ten thousand hands! That isn't quite what the Ball of Gold most folks dream of would fetch, (nor a were-wheel, which would fetch even more) but it's a Big Drum anyway. I'd never see that much money in my life, nor would the folks we danced to by torchlight after dinner, drumming on the gold and silver pillars, praying and whistling for something nobody's ever seen but everybody wants, whatever it might be.

Most everybody keeps a good-luck thingie (a thingie being a drumlin for which there's no practical use) hung around their neck or in their pocket, mostly drummed up by themselves at random. A really random thingie is the only one in the world, and only you have it or ever will, especially if you never write down the rhythm.

Mike's is an odd one; it's a drumlin cross he made for Mother Polly Jerusis, Huffer's town priest who's rectored St. James for a lot of years, by carving up a flattish thingie with drumlin drills and drumlin files, all edged with diamond, and gluing precious stones to it with drumlin glue. But Polly gave it back to him, saying the metal is haunted and ungodly, and she cited all the campfire legends of drumlins that squirm and dance and sing back when you sing to them, which ain't natural.

Mike said he'd never seen anything like that himself, and drumlins were his stock in trade and main passion (though I think Polly is his real passion, and keep my mouth shut) but she said Jesus didn't die on no drumlin metal cross and that was that. Me, I say Jesus used what he had on hand to do the job he had to do, and that's Mike too—only drumlins are what he uses, for almost everything.

Third night out, we were at the fire where the road cuts Rad-ley's Ridge and the thingmaker sets right on the ridge saddle with the rocks, up above the valley where the Big Lumpy River winds down to Colonna. There were two farmer families there with their carts and mules, coming back from harvest market, and we shared rumors and stories, played some flipcard-threes in the dirt and drank new wine from diamond bottles.

Mike's what you call a rich man by accident—he wants to win the race not for the purse but to prove his mostly-drumlins loco can outrun a poured iron one—and it both-ers him. So he's good to poor people and gives them money without bruising their pride by buying useless thingies from them that anybody could scuff out of the dirt next to a thing-maker. He was giving whole hands out for these geegaws that looked like squashed metal fish, when a girl about ten named Rosa Louise asked Mike if he would buy a thingie with a song attached.

Mike grinned his killer grin and said, sure—a hand for the song and a hand for the thingie too. We all got in a half-circle around the thingmaker to listen.

She started by touching the sides of both pillars like some folk do: The Sun Pillar on the right, spiky jagged across like you'd draw the sun, colored milky gold like a late winter morn-ing; and the Moon Pillar on the left, round and smooth and dusty silver like the big moon through thin clouds. Once her little hand struck the first low beat from the Sun Pillar, there wasn't any sound left on that ridge but from her and the pillars, one beat per syllable, no fudging, in a little-girl voice that was strong if not too steady:

I love my dog Hank!

The pillars spoke beneath her words, as if they were really drums and not who-knew-what made by God-knows-who:

Boom-Ping-Boom-Boom-Boom!

Sun-Moon-Sun-Sun-Sun. Not a common intro. Mike's eyebrows rose as she went on, listening hard to see if he could remember it. Most folk can't invent anything but the plainest rhythms. Words help add the variety you want, with-out going quite random, and give you a memory to hang the rhythm on:

He was big and warm and he slept in the barn

With the cows and the owls and the mice and the hay

And he worked all day but he still would play

When sun done set and we all had et.

I've seen some kids say poetry and beat out time on the pil-lars, just for fun, alternating pillars with every beat, Sun-Moon-Sun-Moon for all 256 counts, and drum up an axe every time (or Moon-Sun-Moon-Sun, and get a bucksaw) but not Rosa. She made Sun the accents, and Moon the soft words, and never got it wrong even once, and hit not one more beat than the 256 she needed:

Daddy brought him home in a box from town

And his back was white and his butt was brown

And his tail was black. He was made by God

From the parts that were left at the end of the day

From the dogs that He made that were all one way.

God had a spare tail and some good sharp teeth

And a big brown butt at the bottom of a box.

So He made my Hank and he sent him down from heaven

To be mine for awhile, though it wasn't too long.

And I made him this song to remember him by,

When I want to go to sleep and I don't want to cry.

It was a lot of remembering for a girl that small, and the tune wasn't anything much, but she got all the beats just *so*, making it more a chant than a song. Her nose stayed screwed up in con-centration, but she had that good-girl grin on her that'll make a daddy do anything at all.

I love my dog Hank!

Even though he's dead 'cause his blood ran red

When the cat bit down on the road to town.

Daddy came a runnin' but the smilodon was comin'

And he wanted me for dinner so I woulda been a goner

'Cept that Hank sank his teeth in the cat's flank deep

And the cat turned around and he bit Hank's throat.

Daddy shot the cat's head but by then Hank was dead.

Mike's eyes were still closed, trying to get the sense in the pattern. Simple rhythms drum up simple things, complicated rhythms more complicated things. Stupid random hammering, or even a good rhythm with one beat out of place, gets thingies. If we could figure how to make *real* complicated rhythms, we'd get all the stuff they have on Earth, and wouldn't ever have to go back.

You gotta be brave if you're made from a batch

Of loose dog parts that don't all match.

God took him back to heaven where he barks and runs

'Cause dogs that don't match are the very best ones!

When the last two booms from the Sun Pillar echoed away, little Rosa leaned forward, looking wide-eyed-and-all-wonder down at the silver dust in the big black stone bowl behind the pillars. Bigger boy, her brother I think, stuck a torch in the fire and leaned over the bowl, and we watched the dust ripple and boil and make rainbows with the light.

Big drumlins just surface and bob there, held up by the dust that seems alive right then. Small drumlins are different: The dust parted like the Red Sea over something slender and long, and a dust wave picked it up and carried it toward the pillars, and set it down gently on the little shelf at the edge closest to Rosa. Then the dust drew back, and settled flat again with little rings that rippled and died away clean.

Rosa Louise reached between the pillars, and grabbed the shiny metal drumlin from the shelf. She held it up high in torchlight. We cheered, and the grown-ups were all dabbing their eyes on their sleeves from the song.

She ran over to Mike and pressed the drumlin into his hand. Sometimes you can't say if it's a thingie or not, and this was one time. Her drumlin looked like a silver sausage with a big hole on one round end and lots of smaller holes all over it. Mike hunkered down and held it every which way in front of his nose, checking it over. He nodded, and grinned at her, and after digging deep in his big front pocket, pulled out the little leather sack people've been seeing a lot of recently, and dropped the two little golden hands from his fingers into hers.

She leaned forward and kissed his forehead, giggling with delight. "It's a wish-whistle," she said, suddenly grave again. "Least that's what I call it. You blow on it real hard, and if God wants you to have your wish, it'll fersure come to you."

Mike raised the big-hole end to his mouth to blow, but she put her finger on the other end and pushed it down again, her little mouth all pouty. "Now, don't go blowing it without no wish, or a bad one! God gets tired of sayin' No all the time."

Mike stood, and I saw Rosa's daddy nod to him in the proud gratitude of poor people. Mike stuck that drumlin in his chest pocket, then stood off aways and stared at the stars for a real long time. I didn't hear any whistle—but I could almost hear his wish.

When we got to Colonna we left the horses with Mike's cousin Ignaz and shoved our way downtown to the market square, where we found what was like to be a riot. Several hundred farmers and their boys were camped out with their chickens, their fruit, and their potatoes, waiting for the government's damfool poured-iron steam loco to pull out, and it was already two days late.

Mike and me elbowed up to the hunchbacked thing they named *Mazeppa* and saw Quill Nunday standing next to it with iron chips in his beard, screwing clamps on a crack-busted main drive rod. The farmers were eating peaches gone a little too ripe and throwing the pits at him, and there was fire in his eyes. Quill was the seventh son of a rich man, which is supposed to be good luck, but his brothers got all the money when Mel Nunday died, and they 'prenticed young Quill to a smith to get him out from underfoot. He was a reasonable fair mechanic but resented having to make a dirty living, and with a long-handled wrench in one hand everybody was giving him some room.

Didn't look to us like he'd made any progress that day nor maybe the day before, so Mike snuck up behind him and clapped him on one arm to say, "Hey, Quill, looks like you need some help!"

Quill swung the wrench, but anybody with one eye could've seen that coming. Mike ducked back, and the wrench hit *Mazeppa*'s left cylinder with a clang. Quill wanted to swing again, but Mike grabbed the wrench and the two of them danced around, hands on the wrench like a couple of farm wives fighting over a broom, Mike laughing like a drunk and Quill's forehead bright red with his veins sticking all out.

Finally Quill yanked back the wrench and dropped it in the dirt. The fire was gone, and Quill just looked tired now, like a not-quite broken man looks when he knows he'll be broken before his time. "Some help you'll be, Mike Grab-Thingie. Gimme an iron rod and we'd pull before suppertime—but everybody knows you're too lazy to lift iron."

Maybe the insult stung, but Mike had a position and he stuck to it like burrs in doghair, and I hadn't seen him riled since spring before last, or longer. He always won by being true to what he was. I never yet seen him change direction because some yokel told him to. "You can't fix a main push rod with clamps, Quill—what'd old Howie teach you? Let me drum up a thingie like I use on *Sam'l Borden* and we'll pull before lunch!"

The farmers were gathering around now, and spitting their pits on the ground, cheering Mike whatever he said. That got Quill riled again, and he leaned back against Mazeppa's cracked rod and pointed his greasy finger at Mike. "Ain't gonna be no magical alien crap in *Mazeppa*! We gotta build things the Earth way or we'll never get back to Earth!"

I could tell Mike knew how to handle Quill now, from that grin of his, broad as a sea horizon. "Well, I'd venture Earth'll still be there—and these good gentlemen here'll be just as happy getting their peaches to the Capital before they rot. I might lift iron if the Government'd sell me some—but I'd guess before I'm lazy that you're just plain *scared* to drill a hole in a thingie, for fear a little red goblin'll pop out and set your beard on fire! Scared, that's it! Ain't it, Quill? Scared of thingies that any dirt-poor kid'll build a bed out of and sleep in? Scared!"

Quill lunged and got only half a swing in at Mike's jaw before the farmers closed in and grabbed him on all sides. Mike ducked back, yelling "Hold him, boys, and I'll fix this thing in two shakes!" over his shoulder while he grabbed for his carpet bag. I saw some tools and the measure-tape come out onto the dirt, then Mike tossed me his copy of *Banger's Big Book*. "Ike, go drum me up a Cricket-Leg Bar #42, like we use on *Sam'l*! Haul it!"

I hauled. The farmers all pulled back, and I ran for the thingmaker at the center of the square, where some pedlar was hammering out a private drumlin on contract behind a curtain, with five trained dogs howling like banshees to mask the rhythm so nobody could memorize it. The farmers pulled down the curtain, and somebody threw a live squirrel at those dogs, which were halfway past the courthouse in three breaths. They grabbed the pedlar by the neck and hauled him back, and a boy hammered on the Sun Pillar to finish the drumming until the dust boiled up some useless thingie like a flower all made of tiny forks.

Mike's copy of *Banger's Big Book of Drumlins* is the fancy one with the rack and cord tucked inside the spine, done up in tooled blue leather. I pulled out the cord and threw it over my neck and unfolded the rack so it set on my chest and kept the book open. We use cricket-leg bars a lot back home and I fol-lowed the grease smudges to the page where #42 was laid out, rhythm and all, and as soon as it set right with the bookspring down I started to drum.

One bad beat can change a drumlin to a thingie (though one man's thingie is Mike Grabacki's drumlin, most times) and #42 was weird one, with no real pattern. Facing the page where Hermann Banger's son Henry drew the drumlin were the rows of symbols to drum it up, yellow suns and blue moons, in thirty-two rows of eight. Mostly you drum a row, take a breath, drum another row, take another breath, and on until you're done. I found myself holding my breath for three rows straight until I figured I was purple, and was glad the farmers were still holding that pedlar, kicking and screaming as he was.

But I didn't really start holding my breath until I hit the last beat, and stared at the bowl while the dust boiled. Something broke surface and kept coming, a long skinny something in that strange blue-glint silver metal that most all drumlins are made of. It rose arrow-straight vertical out of the dust, first one leg, then the kink, and then the rest of it. The dust holds it up until somebody grabs it, then it lets go and you've got your drumlin. Three farm boys took it out of the bowl, even though one could do it with only a little puffing, three meters long and then some, with a ten-degree kink almost in the middle, the shorter leg a little fatter than the longer one.

Two farm boys galloped behind me with the cricket leg between them, all the way back to *Mazeppa*, where Mike had his sketchpad full of sketch, and a big drumlin diamond drill in his brace and bit. Mike knelt over the cricket leg and did his magic with the measure tape and diamond scribe, and I leaned into the brace and drilled four holes where he'd marked them. Drumlin metal doesn't scribe with anything but diamond, and the drumlin drills sort of eat into it, as if the metal knows it's being chawed by one of its own, and just gives way.

It took some work to get it mounted right, but with Quill Nunday watching from behind five tall farm boys you wouldn't want to mix with, Mike Grabacki and me got that cricket leg in place on the bearings and bolted in hard. Then they turned

Quill loose, and he looked the cricket leg over like you'd look over a skunk that's been dead in the road for three days. "You cain't tell me that skinny bent thing won't break three puffs after we pull."

Mike shook his head, wiping his hands on an old red towel like he always does after a job. "Not only won't it break, you won't even see it flex. And if it does break, I'll hand you the rest of my daddy's fortune so you can be the idler you want to be, and chase skinny women around inside mansions. I stand by my work, Quill."

Quill'd like to take another poke at Mike for that, but those farm boys were still there, each hitting one fist into the other palm, and Quill thought twice. "We're steaming up!" he yelled instead, so everyone would get back away from *Mazeppa*—and out of his hair.

Mike and me only laughed, and threw our carpet bags up into the last car, with the peaches and the chickens and the potatoes they've been waiting on for three days up at the Capital.

Iron was *the* problem. Mike and I talked about iron a lot on our way to the Capital. Three days, two nights, eight short stops for water and coal, riding in an open car under mostly the best September weather I've seen. Mike sat on a barrel with his boots up atop a chicken pen, tossing cracked corn in to the chickens through the slats. I just laid back on a big bin of barley with a blanket tossed down, arms crossed behind my head, watching clouds go by while we talked, *Mazeppa* puffing away sixteen cars up.

Iron is expensive, for all the work to mine it and haul it, so what doesn't go into the railroads mostly goes to small things like horseshoes and wagon parts, which are used over and over until they're gone. Mike works iron in his forge, but he can never get it when he wants it, and we bought all the horseshoes people dared sell us to make Sam'l's teeny little boiler. That's why everything Mike can make out of drumlins, he does.

Some drumlins aren't metal at all—the diamond bottles, lenses, and window panes, the hanks of rope, the little pillows full of glue, and all sorts of weird thingies with no use that look like globs of melted glass. Everything else is drumlin metal, which you can drill with drumlin drills and turn with drumlin bits, but no one has ever seen melt. Government science people with their microscopes insist that the thingmakers are for the sake of the unknown people—called Gaians after the type of planet we all favor—who built them. Mike says the Gaians saw us coming, and that the thingmakers were for us from the start, so we could get a foothold on this planet with simple tools that come of simple rhythms and work our way up to their level, where we could understand what every weird thingie in *Banger's Big Book* is actually for. He's a believer, in God and angels and the whole Old Catholic religion, and a lady named Julian who God told up front and in her face that everything will turn out all right in the end. Me, I got some problems with God, like why He let my daddy beat me bloody all the time when I was little, but Mike's the boss and I don't argue with him about questions with no answers.

The government wants iron—*lots* of iron—and wanted people to mine it and smelt it, but there were no takers. Farming's a good life, and if one axe breaks you drum up a new one. Who'd want to crawl on their belly in a hole, dragging up rocks all day? Almost nobody, so the government started its own mines, and made prisoners do the digging. Crime rate fell real good after that, and there's only so much iron coming up. So the government is kind of pouty and won't sell the iron to anybody but people that say all the same stupid things they do: That the only thing we all ought to care about is fixing old *Origen*, that you can see most nights like a star crawling against the sky, and then high-tailing it back to Earth.

There's not even a million of us here in Drumland. The government wants iron mines and copper mines and aluminum mines and microsphere fabrication plants and above all Ytterbium (whatever that is) to fix *Origen*. Trouble is, food doesn't come out of thingmakers, and most people like being farmers, so the government gets mostly rich people and no-accounts like Quill Nunday on its side.

Mike and I want to buy enough iron to forge *Sam'l Borden* a respectable boiler, but the government says that all the iron is spoken for, mostly by the government's pet horseshoe smiths and Luke Gorman, the main railroad man. Mike just grins when he says that, and peeks over one shoulder when we go around a curve, to watch that drumlin cricket leg pump and pump on *Mazeppa*'s main wheels.

Quill dropped our sixteen cars in the yard behind the Capital roundhouse, where Mike and I jumped off, with Quill bumbling after.

Behind the roundhouse are the offices of the Valinor and New Scottsdale Railroad—those being the two cities farthest apart—and that's where we went. We strolled right in the door, waving to the ladies and the messenger boys, and back to where the V & NS mechanics were at their tables drawing bigger and more iron-hungry locos. There, at a monster oak table you could build a dance hall on, was the railroad's big man, Luke Gorman himself, looking over the shoulder of the only bigger man there is: Chester A. Arthur Harczak, President of the whole damned government of what city people call Valinor and country people call Drumland.

President Chester is a little short and getting pretty bald, and he's got those big wild hunted eyes like a rabbit in a dead run ahead of a wolf. Luke Gorman stood behind him with his arms crossed, black Irish and a head taller than any man present, lean and well-carved in the face, with green eyes that make women melt, and a charcoal-dust beard that shows up right after lunch even if he shaved at eight AM.

"Mr. President, Mr. Gorman—brought my Race papers in person," Mike said, waving the bundle of forms we filled out months and months before.

The President sneered, which in a big-eyed man is a funny thing to see. "You got yourself a boiler yet?"

Mike shrugged. "Well, we're buying up horseshoes as we can get 'em, but even half a tonne of pig iron would do the job way quicker."

Chester rose up hard, knuckles down on the table, like an ape. "I will *not* sell scarce iron to be built into any machine stitched together out of alien artifacts."

Another voice came up from behind us. "Mr. Gorman, I'm back, and I have to apologize for the breakdown. It was *Mazeppa's* left main tie rod. Compression crack, couldn't pull… until…until…"

"Until *what*, Quill?" Gorman's voice was as deep as the man was tall.

"Until I stitched in one of them alien artifacts and made it go," Mike said. "Quill woulda sat there until the farmers hung him if we hadn't drummed up a new tie rod."

"It was *you* incited the riot, Grabacki!" Quill's forehead veins were sticking out again.

Gorman came up behind his man and put a hand on Quill's shoulder. "Take it down a notch, Quill. Mr. Grabacki, the V & NS thanks you for helping us get perishable cargo to its destination. Send us an invoice for your time and effort, and your 'prentice's too."

Mike shook his head. "I'll take my fee in iron."

"You will do no such thing!" President Chester said. "I own the iron, and even the V & NS is on allocation. And you can take your papers and burn them, because the Race is for native technology, not alien technology! I told you that last year when we announced the Race. I am not going to change my mind."

Mike pursed his lips and nodded. He dug into his carpet bag and pulled out the sheaf of papers on which the Rules were printed. He spun them across the big oak table until they stopped at Chester's knuckles. "Show me where it says, Mr. President."

"Says *what*?"

"That the Race is limited to native technology."

The President spun the papers back toward Mike, but his fingers were shaking and the papers flipped into the air off the table's edge. "*I say so.*"

Mike shook his head, all solemn now, which for Mike means about what it means when a rattler starts to rattle. "Contests are regulated, Mr. President, and I'm not all entirely sure the courts would agree that the Rules isn't a binding contract—on the Government. And you know as well as I do that the Rules make no statement at all about what kind of technology a loco can use."

Mike locked eyes with the President for a long time, and nobody seemed fit to budge. About then Mike finally revealed his trump card, in a voice so low it was almost like the voice you use to a girl in your bed. "I heard seventh-hand, by the way, that nobody else even started a loco to enter. It's your *Star of Valinor* against my *Sam'l Borden*, and without *Sam'l*, there's no contest. And no way to show off your pride and joy. No way to prove that drumlins don't stack up to poured iron."

The President looked his big buggy eyes over at Mike, then up to Luke Gorman, and back to Mike, then up to Gorman again. Gorman nodded.

Beaten, the President growled something you couldn't understand, then looked back over at Mike. "Enter, then—but if you're so damned sure your alien geegaws work better than iron, make your machine out of geegaws. *All* geegaws. No wood, no iron, no copper, *nothing*. Everything comes out of thingmaker dust—or nothing at all. And Mr. Grabacki, I don't think you're mechanic enough to do it."

That was always the wrong thing to say to Mike Grabacki— not that Mike never oversteps himself a little on a dare. He was talking loud now. "Not only am I mechanic enough to make *Sam'l* run with nothing but drumlins, he'll beat *Star of Valinor* by your own rules, *and break one hundred klicks an hour doing it.*"

Silence fell for a moment. The mechanics at their tables were watching now, pencils tucked over their ears, not moving a whisker. One hundred klicks an hour!

Luke Gorman crossed his arms again, his lips pressed together. His deep voice stayed soft, coated with that purely murderous confidence rich people are born with, even if it sometimes kills them. "One hundred twenty. *Star* will do one hundred twenty."

Mike licked his lips. I knew what was coming next. I wanted to crawl under the table.

"One hundred fifty!"

"Then do it, Mr. Grabacki!" Gorman rumbled, his green eyes fierce. "April 1. Be here. And take what fool's grace you can from the day!"

Mike nodded. He turned on his heel and I turned behind him, the rules papers crunching under his boots as we left.

Empty but for some sewing machines and bolts of wool cloth, *Mazurka* took us back to Colonna, it being *Mazeppa's* twin and just as ugly, with a young mechanic named Jack Hrypich driving that Mike didn't know. Jack wasn't angry all the time like Quill and we sat up front with him a lot, and listened to him babble out all the nonsense the Government had poured into his ears at the Bitspace Institute. Earth was a wonder and he couldn't wait to get there, to see a place with four billion people in it, the sky full of airplanes, and electricity living behind holes drilled in every wall, not just in Government labs. At night he'd share his diamond bottle of corn whiskey with us, him tossing back more than he should, and when he went back behind the tender to sleep we heard him crying into his hands from some private pain no young man should suffer.

I long since stopped wondering if Earth is worth all that pain, and I'm sure by now it isn't. Airplanes be damned—on Earth a man is born with nothing, and has to work like a slave just to buy an axe and a plow to get started, if there's any land to plow or even sit down on after four billion folk claim their places. Here in Drumland a clever man with a copy of *Banger's Big Book* can step up to a thingmaker and drum up the framework of a good life in an afternoon, just adding a wife, some seeds, a mule, and a few new-hatched chicks to make it all happen. If Earth has anything to beat that I haven't heard it yet.

The ride back to Huffer from Colonna was lonelier than the ride out. Mike was deep in thought most of the time, and the couple of drummers we stopped and talked with had most already gotten Mike's paper with the boiler sketched on it.

When he did talk, he talked about how we might make a boiler out of a cluster of that big Hollow Ball, #6, connected with drumlin pipes and hanging like silver grapes over a fire. He said not word one about the boiler he was wishing for, and I knew why: He never really expected to get it, even now that we needed it worse than ever. The Intro to *Banger's Big Book* says plain and simple that there are one point one six times ten to the seventy-seventh power different drumlins to be had out of the thingmakers. The number doesn't mean much to me (we didn't get to powers before I left school) but *Banger's* goes on to say that that's one million different drumlins for every atom in the universe, and if you pull one at random and don't write it down, the world'll never see another one like it no matter how many times people try to drum it up again. So while drumming random rhythms may sometimes give you something you can use, it'll never but *never* give you exactly what you want, no matter how hard and how long you wish and drum.

Still, when we got to the thingmaker overlooking the Big Lumpy River, there was nobody there, and it was dusk, when all the best wishes are made. Mike sat high in the saddle looking down into the valley, and pulled out Rosa Louise's wishing-whistle drumlin. He put it to his mouth and blew hard. There was something come out of it, a complex something so high I could barely make out that it was music, ranked together in harmony like a church choir reaching up to blend with the angels. His old horse Coolie is a little deaf and didn't twitch, but my Granite reared up and wanted to run, so I almost missed about the strangest thing that's ever happened to me up 'til then:

Inside my shirt and hanging on its chain, my good luck piece, which is just dead drumlin metal like all of them, was fluttering like a caught bird against my breastbone, trying to sing or fly or both, all the while that Mike's whistle sounded until it died away in echoes against the smoky purple sky.

And when we got back to Huffer three days later, there in the dirt by the forge's front gate was a drumlin boiler.

Mike believes in God but he never seemed superstitious, and for days he went around muttering, "Well, it's not like we never told nobody what we wanted." Mrs. Luchetti, who rents the cottage across from the forge gate and cooks for us most days, said that an old brown man and two boys brought it on a big mule cart, dumped it in the dirt, and went right back west toward Bushville. Stuffed into a pipe hole on one end was a length of sheep gut with some paper rolled up in it, and a note in block writing, unsteady like an old man would do it:

> HEARD FROM FOLKS THAT YOU NEEDED
> ONE OF THESE. DON'T WANT THE TEN
> THOUSAND HANDS BUT A GOOD BOY LIKE
> YOU COULD PUT NEW ROOFS ON A LOT OF
> OLD HOUSES WITH IT. REMEMBER, AINT
> ANY OF IT OURS, JUST BORROWED.
>
> +C RODDIE, WHO DRUMS

After that was the thirty-two rows of rhythm that tells how to drum it up, in the shorthand that most folk use, a cross for Sun and a little arc for Moon. Mike yipped and danced when he saw that, and folded it up carefully and put it in the pocket inside the back cover of his *Banger's Big Book*.

Who this Roddie was we didn't know from Adam. There is a story people tell and swear by, though, that there's a drummer goes from town to town at the edges of where people live (like

Huffer was only thirty years ago) who can drum up anything people ask for, as though he knew the whole drumlin mystery by heart, all those millions of drumlins for every atom in the whole whatever—and never ask a knuckle from the people who want them. The government's gone looking for him more than once, but he seems to know the land better than they do, and the town people always point toward the nearest swamp when government people ask after him.

That was good enough for Mike, and made his wish a coincidence of some drummer's skill and not a miracle. But when I asked Mike to blow Rosa's whistle again while we watched my good luck piece to see if it would dance, he only smiled and said, "Having got a wish as big as that, Ike, I think I'll stop wishing for a while." And when I turned away and he thought I wasn't watching, I caught him from the corner of my eye making the Sign of the Cross.

We didn't waste time after that, it being October 1 and people starting to light fires at night. *Sam'l*'s shot all through with native stuff like wood and horseshoe iron. Me and three hired boys from town winched him up on oak beams and took him apart bolt by bolt. Mike all the while was bent over his table, drawing on paper what the new *Sam'l Borden* would be, starting right with that new drumlin boiler, and working out from there.

The boiler was longer and skinnier than we sketched (not that that mattered a knuckle) and bulged out like a sausage on one end, but bulged *in* for the same measure on the other end. It had small holes here and there, and two big ones at the center of each end. And like most big thingies, it had tabs and barbs and bumps all over it, which were handy for mounting it to the frame and for mounting pipes and other stuff onto it.

The old frame was oak reinforced with thin tie bars of horseshoe iron—what iron we had we mostly put into that pitiful little boiler—and Mike junked it whole. He sketched a brand-new frame made from drumlin cricket legs and long forks, of which we had stacks out behind the forge, in all the sizes

Banger's lists, plus a few odd ones that people drug in over the years. Drumlin metal, light as it is, is stiffer and stronger than anything, and when we bolted together the frame in Mike's new plan, all triangle-braced with the long forks gripping the cricket legs between their tines, ten kids from town and their big brothers could jump on it and nothing even squeaked.

The forge burned all winter, though we didn't forge a thing but a broken wagon part now and then that a farmer brought us. Mike wanted our hands warm and supple while we worked, not half-frozen as we usually did. Both cylinders were made of horseshoe iron, and had to go as well. There are drumlin-metal thingies shaped like cylinders but they're mighty thin, and Mike needed to be sure they wouldn't blow up under pressure. So a lot of the winter we spent hooking up drumlin pipes to drumlin fittings, and stoked fires in the new firebox made of bolted together thingies under the drumlin boiler while watching the pressure on Mike's hand-made gauge. Pressure that bordered on fantastical, that pegged the gauge and would have split *Sam'l's* old boiler like a cleaned fish, didn't faze the cylinder drumlins.

February was mostly gone when me and the hired boys stood back and watched *Sam'l* set on blocks with wheels off the floor, steamed up and howling, while Mike stood on the deck and pulled the throttle. The four big Wheel #34s, meter and a half wide and the biggest wheels ever found in the thingmakers, spun good, the cylinders spitting their spent steam to either side with that fine weird smell of grease and drumlin metal. He pulled it more, and the big wheels spun faster, the cricket-leg beams walking so fast you couldn't but see a blur. I edged the dynamometer under one big wheel, and touched its little wheel to the edge of the big one, my hair whipping in its draft, and read the dial up to Mike in a dead shout:

"One-hundred sixty-one klicks per hour!"

Mike howled and hooted, and we broke out a rare old bottle of wine that night, and even gave the young boys some. *Sam'l Borden* was done and reborn, and not a thing was in him that didn't come out of a thingmaker's dust.

Mike waited until after Breakwinter Festival to leave for the Capital. The square was all mud but we danced by torches anyway, with *Sam'l* at the center of the square beside the thingmaker, enthroned on a four-mule cart, with spare drumlins and the tender on a second cart.

Mike promised he would dance with every woman in town and he did, and nobody got riled, everybody knowing that Mike's only love was Mother Polly, who lost her man twenty years ago and swore she wouldn't never take another husband. She danced with all the men, and the women didn't get riled for the same reason. When finally she danced a wild reel with Mike, and her long gray hair flew out like a dust flame from her black habit, you knew there was a fire inside them both that wanted to burn in the same grate but couldn't, and if there's anything sad in Mike it's only that.

Then the St. James church choir sang "St. Patrick's Breastplate" while Mother Polly walked all around *Sam'l* and blessed him with the holy water wand, and if Mike took it hard (that being a prayer against evil spirits, after all) he gave no sign. Love sometimes just means seeing the good in things as best you can, and she kissed Mike on the forehead while he knelt by her in the mud to ask her blessing on his own head too. And next morning we hooked up the eight mules and headed off down the muddy road for the Capital.

I woke up before dawn on April 1, hearing the clink of tools. The big door on the shed they gave us to use was open, and the night had a frost on it. Outside the shed door I could see Mike up on the catwalk beside *Sam'l*'s drumlin boiler, black against a pink sky streaked yellow.

I hauled up on the cricket-leg frame and stood beside him. He was tightening in a new pipe to one of the holes in the side of the boiler that we had plugged back in Huffer. On top of the pipe was Rosa Louise's wish whistle, mounted to a drumlin cross-lever valve.

"Wasn't sure I wanted to do this 'til this morning, Ike," he said, scratching his head above one ear. "I don't much like talk of magic, and metal's just metal, drumlin or not, and it can't dance by magic nor listen to whistles."

"My good-luck piece sure liked to have flown right out of my shirt when you blew that thing!" I said, like I'd told him too many times by then.

He nodded but didn't say anything for a long time, drumlin wrench in his hand. "Yup. And the cross I made for Mother Polly, the one she wouldn't take 'cause it was drumlin metal and ungodly, tried to crawl out of my pocket like a bug. Sometimes I wonder if Polly's right, and the Government too. We don't own this world. We're just borrowin' it, like the old man wrote. And maybe doing what we do with the thingmakers is like giving an eight-year-old the run of the forge. Maybe he'll build something—but maybe he'll burn himself to death, or lose an eye."

I pointed at the wish-whistle. "That tells me you can't be too 'fraid, or it'd still be in your pocket."

Mike grinned, and he stuck the wrench back in the toolbox. "I got one more wish, Ike, and one only. Polly don't much like drumlins, but she knows the people need them, and she still blessed *Sam'l* back in Huffer—and me too. There's a balance somewhere, a place where things work and do what you tell 'em, and finding that place is what mechanics do. If I was afraid I'd be like Quill, and there's no future in that. A thingie is a drumlin that we don't know what it's for yet. This whistle is a drumlin. I intend to find out what it's for."

The Valinor and New Scottsdale Railroad had set up grandstands five klicks outside of town, by the stretch of twin track that heads northeast to New Boston on the seacoast, and come noon the rich folk had filled them. Ordinary people stood along the tracks behind the rope, eating roasted pine nuts and gaping at the locos sitting side by side, steaming up.

Luke Gorman's mechanics had swarmed over *Sam'l* that morning, looking for contraband iron or wood, and went away slapping Mike on the back and wishing him luck. The government's Bitspace men came by too, mighty interested in drumlins for all that they tell people not to use them. They asked Mike if they could have the rhythm for the boiler, and Mike told them straight out that it was a private drumlin, and the price was fifty tonnes of pig iron. One told Mike they'd get it sooner or later, and not by hammering the pillars at random. Mike doesn't convince easy, and he doesn't threaten easy either, but he made me check every bolt on *Sam'l* another time and then again.

Star of Valinor was on the east track, and all morning *Sam'l* had sat in its shadow. Luke Gorman's new loco was huge compared to *Sam'l*, all iron except for some wood in the cab. The design was from an old book that came from Earth in *Origen*: Four big two-meter wheels with horizontal cylinders, and a leading bogie to support the front of the boiler and help take curves. Its tender alone was bigger than *Sam'l*, heaped high with hard coal from the new mine at Hemingway.

It was supposed to be a stopwatch race, to see who could cross ten klicks in the least time, but with two tracks and only two locos entered, Luke Gorman decided it would be a horse race to cross a finish line a klick past the Dohe River bridge, and whoever got there first won.

President Chester made a speech that was all his usual wind, though much applauded by the rich folk. He acted like *Sam'l* wasn't even in the race, and just bragged how we were re-creating Earth's technology, and how it wouldn't be no time at all before we'd all cram into *Origen* (ha!) and fly right away home.

We all knew it wouldn't be the poor folk to fly home to Earth, and I got the impression the poor folk weren't exactly pulling out their hankies over it.

Once both locos were steamed up and ready, Mike and I stood between the tracks in front of both *Sam'l Borden* and *Star of Valinor* and gauged our chances. *Star* was huge, and had bigger wheels, but we were sure it weighed ten times what *Sam'l* weighed, with all that iron to move, and would need time to get to speed. *Sam'l*, by comparison, looked like some kind of big bug, wearing its skeleton on the outside without no skin, all crisscrossed cricket-leg bars and forks for a frame and two big walking beams that looked a little like bug-legs themselves. Its wheels had that same strange swirly-curvy art to them that most drumlins have, even though they're perfectly balanced and so round you can't measure any error. I had thought then and before that *Sam'l* almost looked like something you *grew* instead of built, and it wasn't always the kind of thought that you think to help you get to sleep on a bad night.

Finally Mike and I were up on *Sam'l*'s open deck, waving our flag telling the railroad people that we were ready. The V & NS man with the synchronized stopclock stood on the green line they'd painted across the tracks and ballast, only a meter ahead of both locos. He held the clock high in the air for a long ten seconds, until the government man with the two-wheeled cannon touched a brand to the port and fired a blank that thundered and echoed to the south hills.

Mike hauled the throttle back, and I heaved down on the left beam, for luck more than anything else. *Sam'l* lurched forward, as quick as he had on our test runs, and quicker, spitting steam that whipped around and vanished with a sound like a little kid trying to blow out birthday candles, compared to the great deep puffing roars of *Star* venting its cylinders. We were three lengths ahead of *Star of Valinor* before the cannon's echo came back, and the rich folk were standing in the grandstand and yelling.

But we were yelling too, both of us, stamping on the deck and waving, as *Sam'l* pulled ahead of *Star*, and after ten seconds we had a hundred-meter lead. We had no pressure gauge, nor even a water glass—Mike hadn't had time to work them up in drumlins. He had more faith in drumlin metal than I had in boilers, having seen two little iron jobs blow up on us when we first started learning steam years back, and take the track out from under them. So we were running on faith, pure faith, as I shoveled more coal into the firebox, not knowing if the drumlin boiler would hold all that pressure, and knowing we would never know if it didn't until St. Peter told us.

It was all show. Mike had done some math, and he knew that we would need every meter of lead once *Star* got going. Mike says he doesn't like horizontal cylinders, but I knew it was because we couldn't work up a big slide bearing for the side rods out of drumlins. Our biggest fear was that the walking beams would shake loose of their bearings at the speeds we were reaching for.

Star of Valinor seemed to be starting awful slow, and I wondered if Luke Gorman had told his driver to give us a little lead for show, then pull past for drama as we crossed the Dohe River toward the finish line. I kept shoveling, and adjusting the windscoop to feed blast to the fire and keep those coals white-hot.

Mike was watching the walking beams for wobble, pulling back more and more on the throttle as seconds passed. He was feeling for the wheels' grip on the iron-strap rails, knowing that we were mighty light for the power we had, and that if the wheels lost traction and started to slip, we would lose speed we might never make up. *Star of Valinor* was unlikely to lose its grip on the rails for all that iron pressing down, but a few seconds' slip could put us in the big loco's smoke for good.

We might have been almost a klick off the start when it got obvious that *Star* was closing the gap. Mike stopped watching the beams, and had one hand on the cricket-leg frame and one hand on the throttle, pulling forward notch by notch as he felt for traction on the wheels. By then I was sure we were doing seventy klicks an hour, faster than any loco we'd ever built or rode on, and the wind was a coal-stinking roar in my ears. Watching the beams hurl up and down from the shop floor had been scary enough; now they were pumping like fury half a meter from my left shoulder, and one hit would turn my arm to pulp.

Half our lead was gone. *Star of Valinor* was pulling up on us, and we had already passed the four-klick marker. Mike's face was a grimace, and I saw sweat and knew it wasn't from the firebox heat. He hadn't pulled further on the throttle for long seconds, and I knew what he was feeling: *The wheels were slip-*

ping. Down beneath us was an uncertainty expressed in small lurches, but it wasn't any bumps in the new track. *Sam'l* had plenty of power, but didn't have the mass to pull more acceleration from the friction between four drumlin metal wheels and the track's strap-iron rail. The only way to win was to slow down enough to let the wheels grab again, and then try to make up speed.

Mike pushed back on the throttle, and we felt the acceleration back off to nothing. I was getting the sense for the track now that Mike was feeling, and I felt the wheels take hold again. But *Star* was having no such same problems, and it was hurtling up from behind. Mike pulled forward on the throttle again, and we began to build acceleration, more slowly this time, feeling for the wheels through the frame and praying.

Six klicks gone now, and although we still had traction, *Star of Valinor* kept pulling up on us, and was three lengths back, then two, and then, pouring smoke like a black cloud and billowing steam in one continuous roar, it pulled beside us.

It seemed to pause there and I felt like a fly stuck in a molasses jar, seeing *Star's* fireman waving at us and knowing it didn't look good. Luke Gorman was no fool, and no braggart. If he said *Star of Valinor* would do one hundred twenty klicks per, it was because his mechanics had done the math and knew the truth of it. When Mike said so, he was working on faith and a gut sense that had done him proud in his fifty-one years, and he only used math when he had to.

Then *Star of Valinor* pulled ahead. The fireman tugged on his rope, and *Star's* big steam whistle cried out in salute, or maybe insult. It was a warbling, wandering whistle that said sloppy ironwork (or a mechanic that didn't know steam whistles) but what did they care?

I froze, shovel in hand. *My good luck piece had twitched*, once, twice on its chain by my heart, while *Star's* whistle blew. More than that: *Sam'l himself* had twitched, the drumlin metal of the cricket-leg bar I was gripping went to crawling under my sweaty palm like gooseflesh.

I pulled my good-luck piece out of my shirt and threw it away, and wanted to yell for Mike, but just then *Sam'l Borden*'s left walking beam popped its bearing and ripped free, swinging back like a giant's baton over our heads, missing our skulls by half a meter or less, and spun away to bury itself cylinder-end down in the ballast between the tracks. *Sam'l* shuddered when the wheel pivot popped, but he stayed on the track.

Mike howled in anger, and he pulled forward on the throttle until it hit its stops, and I felt the wheels screaming underneath us, trying for traction against the rails and not finding it. *Star of Valinor* was way ahead of us now, and without our left beam we'd be lucky to finish the ten klicks at a crawl.

Mike shoved past me, cursing like he almost never does, and he was grabbing for the drumlin rope-loop that was flapping in the wind, and tied to the cross-handle valve that fed steam to Rosa's wish-whistle. One good curse deserves another, I guess, and besides, I knew what Mike's one wish was. I could see it on his face. I could practically hear it echoing in his skull, with all the fierceness that he never shows to nobody but hot iron gripped in tongs and sometimes me:

Speed. Speed. Speed! *Speed! SPEED!!*

He pulled the rope loop, and Rosa's whistle sang.

It sang like you'd think angels would sing, so high as almost not to hear, but to feel in your bones, not one note and not even one chord, but a song like chords dancing in fours…

Dancing. Under our feet, and under our hands, *Sam'l* was dancing too, dancing in time to the whistle. I looked down, and I dropped the shovel. The bolts were popping out from all over *Sam'l*'s frame, but instead of flying apart, the cricket-leg bars and forks and fifty other types of thingies were softening and stretching and melting together into something that had no bolts and no seams anywhere.

The right beam kept pumping, and somehow we were holding speed.

Mike panicked, and pulled the rope-loop the other way to shut the valve, but he pulled too hard and the rope came free with the whistle still singing. He launched forward onto the catwalk to shut it off by hand, and I stumbled back, grabbing a twisting, throbbing metal bar in one hand before the right beam could brain me.

I wanted to follow Mike, but just then the boiler itself started to stretch and bulge like a sausage pumped too full of meat. The main steam pipe stuck into its back center hole spat free, and a jet of live steam that would have cooked a man in a wink roared out a meter away. I watched for a second and the hole in the boiler end was growing, the steam jet spreading out without getting any less strong.

That was enough for me. I squeezed onto the catwalk between the twitching boiler and the hammering right beam, edging forward just to get away from the failing end of the boiler. I was pushing past the right beam's bearing when it popped too, the beam tearing back and vanishing. Nothing was pumping anymore, and we should have been stopping.

But no: *We were accelerating.* I looked back, and there was a cloud of steam leaving the back end of the boiler like fury, screaming in answer to the whistle's angel chord dance, pushing back hard like steam does when it makes a jet.

I knew about then that we were dead, but I didn't want to watch myself steam-cooked, so I kept crawling forward, hand over hand on the triangle frame, now stiffer and stronger without bolts. I could see Mike's head edging around *Sam'l*'s nose by the cylinders, his gray hair whipping atop his thin spot.

A new sound was rising now. I looked up the wall of the boiler, and saw cracks opening up along its length, spreading into gaps and bulging out into scoops, making the air howl as it was trapped. And no sooner was that done than I felt us picking up even more speed, and fast.

"Ike!" Mike was yelling from *Sam'l*'s nose, and he was waving one arm at me. "Ike! Get ready to jump!"

Jump? I was hanging on just to keep from falling from the acceleration, and from the speed of the trees whipping past beside the track I knew we were getting close to Mike's brag of one hundred fifty klicks per hour. Jump from that and you were pulp…

But Mike was pointing, and it wasn't at *Star of Valinor*, on whom we were gaining fast. Coming up was the Dohe River Bridge.

"Ike! The river!"

A man set to hang will grab any rope that doesn't have a noose on it. I crawled further forward until I was beside Mike, we both gripping the drumlin metal bracket holding the boiler in place. He had one hand free, but holding it like it held a lit firecracker, too dangerous to keep and too fascinating to let go. I looked at his hand, and sticking out between his fingers were the arms of Polly's drumlin metal cross, thrashing and twitching like a creature alive. I understood then what makes Mike crazy sometimes, caught between his God and his thingies and God's woman that he loves but can't never have.

I was watching that cross thrashing in his fingers while we passed *Star of Valinor* in a roar, and then we were out on the bridge and there was only water beneath our feet. Mike let go the bracket, and reached out for one second to squeeze my left shoulder. Then he kicked free, and I watched him arc out over the brown water for only a second before I kicked too. But I twisted around as I went, and I saw *Sam'l Borden* come clean apart on the bridge, his tender rolling twice over in a spray of coal before going into the river, his drumlin boiler ripping free of its frame and taking to the air on a column of steam, howling with a piercing, vibrating scream I'd never heard before and never did again.

Then I was clawing water, cold snowmelt water from the Cobbler Mountains up north, snorting through my nose and getting into a stroke that would bring me to the bank before I got numb and died.

Mike and I were sitting with our backs against a big oak by the riverside, just shivering, when a crowd of men came down the trail from the tracks and surrounded us. Most were V

& NS railroad men, but some were the President's bodyguard. Somebody was pulling Mike to his feet, him shaking his head and still dripping, and sure enough, there was President Chester himself, standing behind his goons and screaming like short men do when they'd be better off looking imperial and making sense.

"Michael Grabacki, you are under arrest for reckless endangerment of people and government property!"

Mike had nothing to say. He reached in his pocket, and I saw the goons going for their guns, but what Mike pulled out was Polly's cross, now just a cross and not some magical metal with a will of its own. He looked at it, nodded, and smiled.

"Do what you want, Chester. I got my last wish."

"Cuff him and drag him back to the track," the President said. One of the goons had handcuffs and was going for Mike when we heard a shot echoing across the river and back.

Up the trail toward the track stood Luke Gorman, with a rifle in one hand, pointed at the sky. The fifteen or so V & NS men then pulled out pistols and held them at ready. "Chester, tell your men to drop their guns."

Chester A. Arthur Harczak's wide eyes looked fit to pop out of his head. "Luke, dammit, don't forget who I am!"

"I couldn't forget who you are no matter how much I'd like to," Gorman said, his rumbling voice stern. "Have them drop their guns. This is my land, and my police have jurisdiction. You're not immune from arrest except on election day, which is a whole year off yet."

Chester looked at his men and nodded, and five pistols hit the dirt. Luke Gorman came down the trail and handed his rifle to one of his police. "Mike, what you thought was a boiler was apparently a dual-mode zerospike booster, something like what makes *Origen*'s shuttle go, only smaller and much more powerful. If you have the rhythm, we need it. Give us that, and you'll get all the iron you want. I'll even say you won the race."

Mike shook his head, and he started to smile, maybe getting a sense like me for who *really* ran Drumland.

"*Sam'l* came apart before we ever hit the finish line. You won it square, Luke, and you've got one miserable fine loco in *Star of Valinor*." Mike pushed some gray wet hair up out of one eye. "And you can have the rhythm for free—I'm a steam mechanic, not a spaceman. Trouble is, the rhythm was writ down on paper in my copy of *Banger's Big Book*, and that was in my carpet bag beside the firebox. Wherever *Sam'l*'s frame and firebox ended up, that's where the rhythm is, and nowhere else."

Gorman's green eyes darted back and forth for a moment. "Simon, Charley, go get boats and ropes and drag the river. Chase anything floating downstream." Half the railroad men left.

Gorman turned back to Mike. "Mike, I must say, that was quite a show. You can have a job at V & NS any time you want one—figuring you've been cured of your desire to build from thingies."

Mike shrugged. "Cured? Not hardly. Just got my mouth watering, in fact. I was just thinking about tracks and how much iron they need, and how it might be better to build steam into steerable vehicles. I have some sketches…"

"Automobiles are illegal in the Capital!" Chester Harczak announced like he was telling us that apples fall out of trees. Luke Gorman owns the Capital's trolley system too, and he isn't big on competition.

"Sure, Mr. President—which is one reason out of a whole heavy cartful that I'd as soon be going back home to Huffer."

We rode back to Colonna in the cab of *Star of Valinor*, and the crew showed Mike how it all worked, with much back-slapping and steam-talk and admiration on all sides. The young fireman offered up a theory two nights out that Rosa's whistle was called a function controller or somesuch, and that when it sounds off drumlins do what the Gaians really designed them to do, and not what we numbskulled Earthmen try to make them do. And sometimes a cracked iron steam whistle, or even a kid's mouth puckered just right can make a sound that means something to a drumlin, but only a real drumlin whistle can turn a loco boiler into a rocket engine.

The government is happy believing that, and Mike and I are glad to nod our heads and not say more. They never found the boiler or whatever it was, and some say it's on the bottom of the western ocean, others that it went clear to space, waved at *Origen* and kept going. Nobody'll ever know, but in truth, there's something a little bit spooky about whistles, and wishes, and drumlins—and if we ever figure out just what, things are going to change around here. Just you watch. ∎

DRUMLIN WHEEL

2010

.

DRUMLIN WHEEL

"What was your name again, boy?" asked the bandit with the drumlin lashup gun trained on Roper's midsection. His younger and slightly brighter partner banged out another line on the thingmaker, one-handed, holding Roper's much-wrinkled brown paper rhythm sheet in the other:

Boom-Ping-Ping-Boom-Boom-Boom-Ping-Boom!

That was the twenty-fifth line, of the full thirty-two counts of eight—and in that time the gunman had asked his name twice. Thinking at gunpoint was tough, Roper thought. Maybe thinking was tough when you were holding the gun, too.

For these two, maybe thinking was just tough, period. A bead of sweat that was only partly the mid-day heat ran down into one eye. "Carroll. Aloysius Carroll." Roper didn't dare use his nickname, nor glance down at his belt. He was still armed, in his way, but the two bandits hadn't relieved him of his three weapons. They pretty clearly hadn't read the same old books from Earth that he had, nor been anywhere near a cattle drive. Northerners, likely. Ditchdiggers, likelier than that.

"Mmmm. So is it Al O'Wishes? Or is it Carol?"

The younger bandit began pounding another line, using his right fist to whack hard on the golden sun pillar and the silver moon pillar, twisting back and forth from one to the other, his tongue stuck out between his yellowed teeth in what (for him) must have been rapt concentration:

Ping-Ping-Ping-Ping-Boom-Boom-Ping-Boom!

"Naw, Carol's a girl's name. Or is that your maw?"

The gray-bearded bandit's constant string of non-sequiturs was even more unnerving than the gun. Roper knew that with his rhythm paper in hand, they didn't need him anymore, and as soon as the thingmaker demonstrated the truth of the rhythm by coughing up a were-wheel, he'd be headed for a shallow grave—or following a sack of rocks to the bottom of the Dohe River.

He glanced down the rock-strewn bank toward the rickety plank bridge they had crossed to reach the thingmaker, and considered the river, which was young this far south, deep, and ran pretty quickly. If he could break free and get into the water, it would carry him north toward Ferric as fast as a man could run, through some hill country that would be slow-going for quarter horses or anything but a seasoned pack mule.

The water was mighty cold, though, and he none too good a swimmer. A rodeo roper didn't have much to do with water, especially down toward New Scottsdale, where a hot bath at a fancy hotel would cost you two gold hands plus a knuckle's tip for the maid and another for the towel.

Then, silence. The drumming was done, the rhythm was entered, and if the hamhanded bandit had pounded even *one* of the two-hundred fifty-six notes wrong, the thingmaker would cough up something completely unlike the were-wheel—and unlike anything else ever seen, either, whether here on the planet people called Drumland, or off on that faraway Earth where Drumland's hapless and unwilling colonists hadn't been in two hundred fifty years.

An alien planet, ungrateful city folk called it, but there weren't any aliens, just thousands of alien machines that worked like miniature tinker shops, that would cobble something together if you pounded out the right pattern on the tops of the two pillars.

Down in the thingmaker's wide, flat bowl, the strange silver dust was boiling, slowly, like clouds in a gathering storm. There were ten to the seventy-seventh power different things that the thingmakers knew how to make, a number (according to poor Sister Eleanor Marie, who had all her long life tried gamely to teach dusty junior cowboys their numbers) that was simply beyond imagining.

Most were useless thingies, weird and twisted chunks of silver metal or shiny unscratchable glassy stuff.

Most—but not all. And every so often, banging randomly on the thingmaker's pillars would dredge up something from that huge bushel basket of possibility that was not only useful, but—heh!—*real* useful.

Like a wheel that turned all by itself.

The storm in the bowl was calming, its waves retreating to its edges, because up from the middle something was rising. At first a circle of dust hove up like a big dinner platter you'd lay the Christmas goose on, but then streams of dust spilled away on all sides, and what lay there floating was a wheel, big across as a tall man's arm from shoulder to fingertips. It wasn't solid, not exactly, not solid like a wheel you'd cut from stone or a slice from a real big log. The three-layer hub connected to the rim in a tangle of twisting cords like old roots in a riverbank, so dense you couldn't see light between 'em, though Roper knew from his earlier experiments dumping a mug of water on those metal cords that the wheel wasn't solid.

The bandit with the rhythm sheet whistled between his crooked teeth. "Well, that there be a wheel, awright. Keep that gun on 'im, Amos, while I pull it out of the bowl."

The younger bandit reached down into the thingmaker bowl with both hands, and gripped the edge of the wheel. Grunting, he heaved it up and out of the bowl, and let it fall onto the scrubby grass.

The older bandit was not pleased. "Dammit, Boze, we been snookered! That wheel ain't turning a-tall! Only the middle part is turning!"

Roper sighed. The inner hub of the wheel was slowly rotating, a little over one go-round a minute, as they all did when he first drummed them up out of the dust. "Um…you put an Axle #14 through the hub of the wheel, and if you hold the axle still, the wheel turns around it. I can drum up an axle if you want me to; I've got *Banger's Big Book* on my cart."

Boze shook his head. "Don't matter none. We kin hire a mechanic to fit out axles and such. But boy, it don't look like a wagon built with these'll be goin' anywhere in a hurry."

Amos was none too bright, but he kept both hands on the lumpy drumlin gun and held it steady as a rock. Roper gulped. "You need a control rope to speed it up, or stop it again. It'll go as fast as you want it to, once you rig it right."

Boze squinted at the wheel. "You got one of these control ropes somewhere?"

Roper nodded, and this time allowed himself to look down at his belt. "I always keep a couple with me, and if you'd've bought the wheel legal and proper instead of putting on gun on me I would have told you about it, and tossed in a spare."

"Well, then dig one out and rig it right, but don't try nuthin'."

Roper nodded again. Lying didn't come easy to him, but it was the only chance he had. He reached down to his belt and pulled the rope coil from its leather snap. Like Amos' pistol it was a drumlin lashup, just a few meters' worth of Rope #4, with a fist-sized Hollow Ball #7 on each end, filled with sand and sealed with a pillow of Glue #2. This one was more for catching dinner than roping cattle, but it worked, and he'd won awards for his skill bringing down calves and sheep at the big Yearsover Cattlefest in New Scottsdale each December. The bandits looked on with interest, and showed no suspicion.

Had they never seen a bolo?

With the were-wheel at his feet, Roper took the bolo rope coil in one hand and one of the balls in the other. "Ok, now. Look close here: You grab the ball on one end like this. Then you grip the rope about a meter down from it." Amos leaned in, his older eyes on the ball, squinting, the gun still aimed at Roper's navel. Boze scratched his head idly, as though taking mental notes. *Then you wrap it around the fool with the gun!*

Years of practice took over: Roper dropped the ball and whipped the rope around hard while releasing it. The ball came up from under both of Amos' arms and spun hard around them, making two quick loops at mid-forearm. Roper ducked to one side as the gun cracked sharply, the slug going into the dirt and tossing up a divot of grass and brown soil.

Amos tried to spin around and get another shot, but Roper was already behind him, and planted one pointed leather boot where the sun don't shine. The older man yelped, and snorted, and without the use of his arms to balance went down hard, the gun falling from his hands.

Boze dove for the gun but Roper got to it first, stumbled as he rose and then spun around, reaching to his belt for another bolo with his left hand while hurling the lashup gun toward the river with his right. Boze's eyes spent a fatal second following the gun, and before any of them heard the splash Roper had the second bolo swinging and spinning around Boze's legs. Boze went down just as Amos rose, shaking his arms trying to dislodge the bolo. Roper's rhythm sheet went fluttering toward the river. Roper's third bolo caught Amos just below the knees, and the gray-bearded bandit went down again, cursing.

Amos hadn't yet hit the dirt when Roper was already on the riverbank, having snatched his rhythm sheet from the grass before it went into the drink. Sheet in hand, he loped for the bridge, peering across the water to make sure the gunshot hadn't spooked his horse Iris. No, the half-lame old paint was still there, still harnessed to Roper's mechanical pedlar cart, looking over her shoulder quizzically as her master scrambled over the swinging twenty-meter span of drumlin rope and rough-hewn pine planks, just a meter above the surging water.

Roper leapt from the end of the bridge and bounded uphill to his cart. He dug under the canvas tarp and retrieved a coil of Rope #4, that smooth, flexible, unbreakable drumlin rope so beloved of cattlemen. He looped one end of the rope over his cart's rear frame hitch, then ran back down the riverbank and threw a quick clove hitch over one of the bridge's two support poles.

Before jumping up to the cart's seat, he quickly undid the harness holding Iris to the harness poles. "Go, girl!" he shouted, then threw back the tarp behind the seat and reached for a lever of drumlin metal, a stout Short Fork #21.

When the old mare was clear, Roper grit his teeth and hauled forward on the lever. He felt the drumlin gears engage, and, hidden within the cart's plank sides, the were-wheel began to turn. The cart lurched forward, faster than Roper had ever dared run it, even on a level road. The rope paid out, and when it went taut the stakes holding the bridge's drumlin ropes yanked out of the riverbank, first on the near side, and then (as the cart ground onward) from the far side as well.

Roper threw the lever back to its home position, and the cart rattled to a halt. He released the rope from the rear hitch, and watched the roiling waters of the Dohe carry the bridge downstream in an untidy tangle of rope and planks. Roper waved to the two bandits, now free of the bolos and screaming obscenities at him. Their horses, unfazed at the scuffle, still champed the grass on the riverbank. Roper walked back to them, rifled their saddlebags, and tossed a spare lashup pistol and a tobacco tin of slugs into the river. At the bottom of one saddlebag were ten gold hands wrapped in a kerchief. Roper considered—after all, they now had their wheel!—then put the money back in the bag. There weren't no comfort in being a crook, as his folks and the nuns at Old St. Francis' School had told him all his young life.

On the other hand, if there was much comfort in being a drumlin pedlar, he sure hadn't found it yet.

It was four days on bad roads back home to Thusly. Iris tramped gamely in front of the cart, but the harness was slack except when she slowed down, and Roper had to tick back the lever a little so as not to be pushing her. Poor Iris was nothing but cover, a horse to lead a cart that didn't need a horse anymore, but people would wonder seeing a cart rolling along a road with nothing pulling it and no smoke nor sound of an engine inside.

Maybe Sadie was right. Maybe a girl who grew up singing for drunks and card sharps in a beer hall (and somehow didn't never get sent upstairs like the other girls, or so she said, anyway) had better skill for people than a cowboy who didn't do nothing but chase steers across the spiky dry land they called Waythehell when they had to call it something. Sadie said that here was the way to do it: Ride the cart into town on Sunday afternoon as fast as you wouldn't fly off, yipping and yeehawing and getting the young boys to grab their paws' britches and say, geepers, pop, I wanna do *that!*

Of course, for any way to look at a question there was another. A boy who slept on the grass with the rattlers better have a nose for danger, and it wasn't but a few minutes after hauling his first wheel out of the dust and seeing the hub turning by itself that the hairs on the back of his neck started to stand up. Roper had spent plenty of nights lying on his back, looking at the stars and imagining things: Being his own boss, having his own spread and his own crew of cowboys to work it, being old enough to be gray and rich but not old enough to drool. And given that caution was just imagining your blood soaking out your shirt or a leg that didn't work anymore, he was quick to get a sense that he had to be careful, without quite knowing how.

He remembered the night years back when he had lain on the ground, bruised and sore from a harder day than most—pulled from his horse and dragged fifty meters by a steer who'd been gelded but must have had a spare—and made a wish on old broken *Origen* as it crawled its way across the stars at quarter to midnight. He'd wished for cattle with shorter legs, or maybe just steaks that grew off trees. He'd wished for a girl who didn't mind the smell of dirt and manure, and would wink back now and then, and maybe even someday marry him. And as the ache in his leg got worse, he'd wished for a drumlin rhythm that would cough up the Big Ball of Gold so he could put his feet up and not get beat half to hell every day to afford a decent meal.

Right then, the starship flashed, suddenly brighter by five, and a wink later was its old self again. Roper knew it wasn't magic. He knew that *Origen* was just dead metal (if for sure a lot of it) spinning along in odd ways through empty space, like a pliers tossed at a rock when a fence wouldn't fix for nothing.

Some parts of it were shinier than others, and like old Mr. Marwick drew on the slate back at school, if the sun caught it just right it would blaze like a hundred stars in a choir.

He didn't think he was an Old Believer in ghosts and devils and signs, but he pulled out his everyday book and pen and let his hand wander free down a page like Old Believers did, jotting lines of crosses and crescents (cross for a thump on the sun pillar, crescent for a whack on the moon pillar) without thinking which should go where. And the next day, when he happened across a thingmaker along the trail back to Holley, he tapped in the rhythm.

And he got the wheel.

It spooked him badly to see the hub turn, slowly, with neither sound nor anything to drive it. It spooked him more when he dragged it to a small mesquite stump and dropped the hub over the stump, after which the wheel turned just as silently. He'd hammered the hub down onto the stump to hold it hard (knowing that hammering a drumlin with a rock wouldn't even scratch it) and then tried to stop it with his hands. The wheel dragged him around for half a circle before the hub ripped the little stump raw and came loose.

He'd made the Sign of the Cross right then, not ever seeing nor hearing about a drumlin that moved by itself, and remembering all the old-woman talk about drumlins being made by evil spirits from the Big Old Dark, and haunted. He backed away from it and even forgot to eat his lunch, and left the wheel turning on the stump while he rode back to town with the steer in tow.

The boss sacked him that night for taking three days to bring the steer back, and Roper moved on. It was more than a year later that he started hearing stories of the were-wheel that pulled a cart without no horse nor engine. After hearing the nineteenth bruised-up cowboy mutter, boy, what I wouldn't pay for that, Roper started thinking about becoming a pedlar. He imagined himself chuckling and replying, Well, cowboy, it just so happens that I have one right here in the back of my wagon...

And unlike whoever it was that found the wheel he'd left turning on the mesquite stump, Roper had the rhythm. After selling the first one, he could sneak off and drum up another, and another, and another. It sounded simple. And firstoff, it was: He got twelve gold hands for a wheel from a rancher near Dutcher Springs, then sold another the very next week, though the sharp who bought it chewed him down to ten, and got annoyed when Roper said it was a private drumlin and wouldn't toss in the rhythm. Word got around, and when a quarryman from somewhere past Windward came by with five shave-headed toughs behind him, Roper got nervous and let the wheel go for seven, then hightailed it away from cattle country. Farmers were honest folk, he thought—then reached up and scratched the scar behind his right ear, from a wild-eyed corn-row hand who'd tried to slit his throat for the rhythm, and missed. Easy money, right. Roper spat off to one side of the cart. Maybe the wheel would be as much of a curse to the two bandits as it had been to him.

Roper set his pack down on an empty table in the inn's great room, which was now mostly dark, and sharp with hickory smoke from the dying fire. It had been a long day's ride from the scrump at the Dohe River, but he was of a mind to sleep on a real bed in a room with a lock. An old farmer was dozing on a cane chair in one corner, a Granger by the shiny pins on his hat, the rest of him barely visible in the gloom. In the opposite corner a man bent over a table, writing on sheets of paper by the light of a drumlin lashup pinlamp. Roper began to lower himself into a nearby chair, but then the writing man took a deep breath and looked up.

A drumlin pinlamp never seemed to fill a room with light, but it more than filled the man's face. It was Henry Banger. Henry Banger *himself.*

Henry Banger, who drew most all of the pictures in *Banger's Big Book of Drumlins,* as well as all the useful little pocket-sized books set out by themes (like *Banger's Little Book of Ranch-Work*

Drumlins, beloved by cowboys like Roper) that had made his father Hermann Banger the richest man on Drumland—or Valinor, as rich folk called it, especially when poor folk were within earshot.

Each spring, Henry Banger set out to ride his circuit, south from the Banger Publishing complex in Valinor City along the Borden River to the ocean, down the coast to New Boston, then westward all the way across the known lands to New Scottsdale, where the Bashed-In Skull Mountains rose like rotted teeth and blocked the way west to anybody but mountain goats and crazymen. Wherever he went, Henry Banger asked people to bring him previously unknown drumlins they had drummed up since last fall, and he would trade brand-new copies of *Banger's Big Book* (which had gotten *mighty* big in the years since Roper had first paged through his father's tattered copy) for the right to publish the rhythm and put their names under it as discoverers.

Henry Banger, whose face was in every Sunday newspaper on Drumland (all eleven of them, at last count) over his column "Drumming Up the Future," which he split between tales of his adventures on the circuit and descriptions of interesting drumlins he had seen. Each column ended with the rhythm of a brand-new drumlin that Henry thought useful, which meant that most every person within a quick trot of a thingmaker had one by Sunday night.

"Mr. Banger!" Roper gasped, with his recent problems propelling the words past his inhibitions as much as his open-mouthed surprise. "Mr. Banger, I'd fersure like to talk to you a bit."

"Whoa, cowboy," old Hawkins called from his desk around the corner. "Mr. Banger asked not to be bothered while he was writin'."

Henry Banger put his pen down quietly and smiled. "It's ok, Hiram," he called back. "He's an old friend."

"Suit yerself," Hawkins called back, "but send him packin' if he gets pesty."

Henry leaned back in his chair and pulled another from an adjacent table, dragging it over next to his and thumping the seat with his other hand. Roper clumped across the room and lowered himself into the chair.

"I didn't mean to put off your writing, Mr. Banger," Roper began. "I mean, we never did meet or anything, and as much as I'd sure like to be your friend…"

"It's Henry," the older man said quietly, the pinlamp glittering off his round crystal spectacles. "And you looked like you saw a ghost when you walked in. I just wanted to be sure the ghost wasn't me."

Roper felt himself blushing, and suspected that he was talking purely the fool. "Nossir. Henry. No, it was…it's, well, it's a problem with drumlins that a friend of mine has, and I figgered if anybody knew anything about drumlins it was you."

Henry Banger cocked an eyebrow and smiled again. "I know something about drumlins, but problems—especially problems people bring me on their friends' behalf, well, I don't know. I have a knack for seeing a use in a drumlin that most people would call a thingie and toss over their shoulder. Sometimes a drumlin looks like it should do something, but actually does something else, or nothing at all. People forget that human beings had nothing to do with what drumlins are nor what they do."

Roper nodded. "Yup and fersure, and I for one don't never want to meet the alien folk that made the thingmakers, tho I am right grateful for a few of the thingies that come out of them. This one, though. I…we…both of us knows what it does, and that's the problem."

Henry Banger smiled encouragingly, and leaned forward. "It is something dangerous, or valuable?"

Roper swallowed hard. "I'm just a cowboy, and I don't know. It seems mighty ordinary to me sometimes. He—my friend, that is—would like to be a pedlar and sell it, but we both just shook some bandits that tried to kill us for it. It's not like I—we—are asking a fortune for it. I just thought I could make enough money to get me a little ranch and few head…"

Henry Banger held up his hand, and Roper shushed. The older man then turned in his chair and reached to the floor for a careworn leather bag. "Let me show you something." He pulled a small item the width of his hand from the bag, and placed it on the table. It was a little wheel on an axle that was perhaps three ticks long. The wheel was solid, but like most drumlins had strange curves and branching lines embossed into it, suggesting storm clouds and rays of brilliant sunlight. Henry grasped the wheel by the axle, and gave it a quick twist before releasing it. The wheel spun on the table like a kid's top, silently and without the slowly widening wobble that meant the top was losing speed and would soon fall.

Both men sat silently, watching the little thingie spin. The minutes crept past. Henry Banger took the stoneware mug on the table beside the pinlamp and raised it to his lips. The wheel continued spinning.

"How long will it go, Mr. Banger?" Roper finally asked, impatience making his rump itch.

"Don't know." Henry Banger reached out and grabbed the little wheel by its rim, and tucked it back in his bag. "There's one up in my room that's been spinning for all the two days I've been here. And the farmer who gave it to me showed me one under a drumlin cup on his mantelpiece that's been spinning since before his youngest was born—and that's been four years now."

"So it could spin forever."

"It could. Or it could spin for longer than any one man might live. The bigger question, though, is this: What's it good for?"

Roper shook his head. "Haven't the faintest."

Henry nodded. "Nor do I. But that's the whole point. Somewhere, some clever mechanic will take one of these, see the hidden truth in it, and make it do a useful job. Once he figures that out, it may become so valuable that people might kill each other to possess the rhythm that makes it. We won't know unless—and until—that happens. That's why it's going to be in my next Sunday column. There's something about it that makes me twitch a little, and I'd rather it belong to everyone than just one man—or a few."

A few. Roper knew what he meant, gulped, and nodded uneasily. Everybody knew—at least, everybody who ever got drunk and sat around a campfire—that the Bitspace Institute in Valinor City had windowless rooms with guards at the doors, rooms full of secret drumlins, drumlins that did strange and maybe dangerous things. The Institute had been studying drumlins since Rant Messick had shuttled down with everybody else after *Origen's* Hilbert drive had caught the hiccups and died. Rant Messick, Earth's fourth-richest man, had gone halfies on the starship, only to have it dump him on the edge of the far whatever with no going back. Most everyone else who landed from *Origen* got married, had kids, and plowed the land. Rant Messick died angry and childless, and gave his money and his half of *Origen* to a secret club that he ordered to get *Origen's* stranded passengers back to Earth, *no matter what it took.*

Mostly, what it would take was a hundred klegs or so of ytterbium, a metal everybody could now pronounce but nobody knew how to find. The thingmakers coughed up the Big Ball of Zinc soon after Drumland's colonists arrived, and a few other Big Balls after that (Gadolinium? Praseodymium? Roper lost track sometimes, and wondered why metals didn't all have simple names like zinc and iron) but in two-hundred-odd years of hammering on their own private thingmakers that they'd built bunkers around, the Bitspace Institute hadn't found the Big Ball of Ytterbium. Still, everybody knew that a lot of other weird stuff had turned up in the process...

...and everybody cannonballing corn whiskey around a campfire knew that people who accidentally drummed up weird stuff from the thingmakers sometimes went missing. Maybe they all rode west looking for cheaper land, or built drumlin boats to see if they could get past the Bashed-In-Skull Mountains by sailing east around the whole big world. Or maybe they were now in shallow graves, or chained to a thingmaker and forced to hammer rhythms for the rest of their lives, for a bite of bread and a slug of water once a day.

Roper shuddered. His sensible side told him the government wouldn't allow such a thing, but the Institute was older than the government, and there was a dose of old dead Rant Messick in the people who ran it: cold, solitary, spooky people who talked in hints before telling you to mind your own damned business.

Roper nodded again, and realized he'd been staring past Henry Banger at the stacked-log wall, thinking about gun-wielding thugs on the riverbank, and a fight behind a corn crib that had almost laid him in a shallow grave four years back. People who lived ordinary lives and didn't have any secrets of their own were always the ones who worried about the Institute. Corn whiskey just made them talk about things they wouldn't never mention in bright sunlight.

But suppose you did have a secret. Just suppose…

Henry Banger had gone back to his writing, leaving Roper feeling like a gape-mouthed fool. He muttered his good-nights to the older man, who looked up solemn-faced and nodded wordlessly before Roper turned and headed for the stairs, and a night's sleep that turned out to be nowhere near as good as he'd wanted.

Roper heard the next morning's hubbub all the way upstairs, and when he came down he saw the inn's great room all packed with folks carrying thingies in their hands, wrapped in old newsprint or just bare, waiting to present them to Henry Banger in hopes of getting into *Banger's Big Book* and scoring their own brand-new copy, with Henry's handwritten personal thanks on the flyleaf.

Roper laid two gold knuckles down on the kitchen window counter for a fried egg on a fresh-baked biscuit, plus a snicker-doodle for later, and leaned on the doorjamb to watch. The line was out the front door of Hawkins' Inn and out into Bushville's main street, with more people wandering into town every minute to join at the end. Back in the great room, Henry Banger was set up at a good-size table, with a tin box of blank paper sheets at his left elbow, a leather-bound copy of his own *Big*

Book at his right elbow, and somebody's thingie on the empty wood in front of him.

Roper thought it might be easy for folks to scam a free copy (of a book that cost ten gold hands in the tooled blue leather binding) by bringing in some useless thingie lump that Henry'd already listed on the backside of page 1,704. Or maybe not: The man knew his own book, and forty-nine times out of fifty just shook his head with a smile. Those sent off were disappointed, but Henry always shook their hands and offered a little 20-page pamphlet on how to fit drumlin pipe as consolation.

Only once in more than an hour did Henry Banger hand out the real prize. A young farmer put a thingie on the table: a round-edged, shapeless lump the size of a newborn's head that looked like nothing so much as wax run down off a candle, with two handles set close together on one end. The farmer had an arm's length of seven-tick drumlin rope in his hand, and while Henry watched, the young man tucked the middle of the rope into a slot on the thingie's side, and then took the thingie up by both handles. With a quick squeeze of the handles the rope fell into two pieces, the ends squared off and shiny like they were polished on a buffer wheel.

Cowboys didn't have much use for seven-tick rope, which was as thick around as a fat man's thumb, and lashed up mostly into cranes and hoists without ever cutting the big hundred-meter coils that came out of the thingmaker bowl. But Roper knew that drumlins didn't cut or shape easily, and when they did it was only with drumlin tools. So he wasn't surprised when Henry Banger announced that Jonah Bitters from out Empty Mug Road would be in the next printing of *Banger's Big Book*, named as the discoverer of the drumlin rope cutter. After much applause from all around, Henry spent ten minutes doing a careful drawing of the drumlin itself, and then copied down Jonah's rhythm sheet to a fresh piece of paper. Only then did Henry Banger reach to the floor behind him and pick up a brand-new leather-bound copy of *Banger's Big Book*, which he signed for thanks and handed to Jonah.

By then it was most of the way to lunchtime, and while people milled around congratulating Jonah Bitters and oohing over his prize, Henry Banger leaned back and stretched. He saw Roper then, and waved him over to the big table. "You said yesterday you were going back to Thusly, and I wondered if you might have room on your cart for a friend of mine. He's been traveling with me this past month, but he's got business out near Windward, and that's a long trot without a horse."

Roper shrugged and nodded. His cart was a lashup, but the front seat was big enough for two—and Roper knew from his tests loading rocks behind the seat that the hidden were-wheel would haul anything that didn't spill out over the rough-cut oak sides. "Would be my pleasure, Mr. Banger."

Henry Banger smiled, and looked to his left, where an old man with dark skin and gray hair in tight short curls sat in a chair, writing in his everyday book. "Roddie, here's your ride," Henry said. The old man looked up, tucking his book away inside a ragged green mackinaw with frayed edges.

He had an odd look about him: a wide, flattened nose that might've seen the wrong side of a board in a brawl, and larger lips than he ever recalled any man having. And his skin…Roper had spent a lot of time with older cowboys who'd lived fifty-odd years out in the sun chasing steers, and their skin was maybe as dark, but it was a different dark, blotchy and toned more toward red. Roddie was lined in the face like they were, but there was nothing blotchy about him, his skin just a smooth warm brown like a few drops of heavy cream in strong coffee.

"Much obliged," the old man said, and stood. Roper was turning to leave when Henry Banger held up his hand again, this time with a heavy paper envelope in it.

"And if you could, would you carry this to Thusly and hand it to Rory at the post office? The rider leaves early here, and by the time I remembered it, the morning sack was already gone. It's my next newspaper column, and if you can get it into Thusly's Friday morning sack my editor will be able to get some sleep come Monday."

Roper took the envelope, and as he led the old man out the back hall toward the stable where Iris and his cart were, Olive in the kitchen handed him a fat paper sack, containing two wrapped lunches and two wrapped dinners. "From Mr. Banger," the old woman said, wiping her hands on a rag. "Paid for. So's you don't have to stop more'n you need to."

Soon afterward, Roper's cart rattled its way out of Bushville down the road toward Thusly, Iris walking gamely in front, with Roper holding the reins and Roddie seated beside him. As they passed the last saloon before the new-plowed and sprouting wheat fields began, a horned owl the size of a madam's cat left its perch in a cottonwood tree and flew alongside the road, landing in another tree further down. When they passed that tree the owl flew again, pacing them, and (as Roper saw each time they approached the next tree) watching them with huge golden eyes that blinked in the late spring sunlight.

Roper had started to think there must've been a pen of chickens in the back of his cart when the old man chuckled. "Don't give him no nevermind," Roddie said. "Where I go he goes, but he goes his own way, at his own pace."

"Are you sure it's you he's watchin'?" Roper asked, wondering what a skinny cowboy looked like to a hungry owl. With a beak and talons like that, an owl wouldn't have to kill him to fetch home a chunk big enough for dinner.

"Sure as day." Roddie raised his hand and made a quick sign in the air. In seconds, the owl left its perch in the next tree along the road, circled around behind the cart, and landed without a whisper on Roddie's shoulder.

Roper eyed the owl warily, and the owl seemed to return the sentiment. Owls were cranky, and always bigger than they looked at a distance. Roper had seen one take a full-grown skunk by the roadside once, and the skunk never knew what hit it. What Roper hadn't ever seen was an owl made to sit on a man's shoulder like a sailor's parrot.

"Do a kindness for one of God's creatures, and ever so often they stay with you," the old man said, without adding what sort of kindness a man could do for an owl, other than maybe keep out of its way.

They spent the first night in a tumbledown cattle shelter a little ways off the road, Roddie, Roper, and Iris all. Roddie had suggested driving through the night, and had a pinlamp with a reflector in his carpet bag to cast light in front of the cart. Roper considered, but knew he needed sleep, and was uneasy at the old brown man's offer to hold the reins while Roper curled up to sleep in the back of the cart.

The next day dawned and stayed steel-gray, and there was little talk on the cart aside from Roper wondering out loud (and a little too often, for lack of other things to mention) if they were in for a storm. Roddie spent hours reading from his everyday book, stopping here and there to add short notes to the already-crowded pages, using a lashup ink pen with its own ink inside. Trying not to be obvious about it, Roper glanced to his right at times to try and catch the gist of what was written there. The writing was small and strange, and he couldn't quite read it nor even make out the letters. Roper wondered if they were prayers, like the ones he had seen in the old books that always lay in state on the nuns' desks at St. Francis School, written in languages he couldn't read, by people dead thousands of years.

But if they were prayers, then what were all the little pen-drawings of the sort of useless drumlin thingies you could find in a pile behind any thingmaker?

It wasn't until they'd made camp beside a stream that Roper realized that the owl had been gone the entire day. When it finally returned, two hours after sunset, Roddie walked off into the gloom with the owl on his shoulder and didn't return until long past midnight.

Just after lunch on the second day out, Roddie dug something from inside his shirt: A drumlin spyglass, by the unmistakable glint of the metal, with a single thin leg that extended with a pull to something close to shoulder height. They were

on the brow of a long hill with a good view back toward Bushville. Roddie stuck the spyglass leg in the dirt and let it go, but
instead of falling over, the leg and spyglass stayed dead vertical
as though rooted in the ground, with the tube pointed the way
they'd come.

The old man then whistled softly: a long, low warble with
a high, rough edge to it, as though the air echoed inside his
mouth and went out past a broken-off tooth. Roper thought he
saw the spyglass tremble for a second. Then it did something
even odder: It moved, smooth as honey, from left to right, then
paused, and dropped its aim a little. Then it moved from right
to left the same distance, all in a heartbeat. Five or six more
times it scanned across the width a man might see in one
glance, until it stopped abruptly.

Roddie hunched his shoulders down and peered through
the spyglass for a long minute. He grunted, and nodded.
"Riders on the road. Not going as fast as might be. Tryin' to
keep to the side of the road with the cottonwoods, so's to stay
out of sight." The old man gripped the spyglass with his right
hand and made one quick, low whistle that sounded more like
a snort. The spyglass tube collapsed to no longer than a hand
span, its leg folding back against the tube.

Roper was about to ask how a spyglass could look through
itself and spot riders fifteen klicks back on a road, but Roddie
raised his hand. "We'd best be keepin' on." Roper peered off
along the road to the spot where he was sure the spyglass had
been pointing, and saw nothing.

The day got grimmer after that. Twice more they stopped
on high ground, more to let Iris rest than anything else, and
Roddie had his spyglass scout out the road behind them. Both
times it found the riders, and both times Roddie pronounced
them closer. People on good horses needing to be in Thusly in
a hurry would have passed them by now with a whoop and a
hey-all-good-luck, but these were trying to stay out of sight.
Roper started to wonder if it was all some kind of trick—after
all, he hadn't looked through the spyglass himself, and was just

taking Roddie's word for it. The second time, as if to answer, Roddie pointed at the spyglass, and Roper put his eye up behind the lens. Sure enough, he saw the hind end of a blue roan between the cottonwood trunks on the river side, another right behind it, and boots with bright spurs in the stirrups. The scary part was that they were now only a klick or two away.

It was pretty obvious to him now: The riders were waiting for nightfall, hoping they hadn't been seen, and would be looking for a campfire just past dusk, when it was harder to take good aim than by light of day. Roper had owned a gun or two in his life but didn't have much talent for them, and driving off rattlesnakes by throwing rocks was easier and cheaper. Everybody knew that robbing a man with empty pockets was pointless, so he'd never felt much need. It was only once he'd become a pedlar that he thought he'd like something on his hip again, but each time the thought hit him he was fifty klicks from a gunshop.

The sun was heading down quick and orange toward the west hills when the road took a sharp turn, and just past the crook they saw a thingmaker in the thick of a cottonwood grove. Roddie raised his hand, and Roper shoved the lever back until the cart stopped.

The old man hopped down from the cart. He stepped up to the thingmaker without a word, and without pulling out a rhythm sheet or his everyday book like most folk would, Roddie began drumming. From the cart Roper could see his face side-on. Roddie wasn't looking down at the bowl, nor at the pillars. He wasn't looking at anything at all: His eyes were closed, and his old brown face was slack and half-smiling, like a pious man kneeling down in church for Benediction.

Roddie drummed *fast*, like the people who drummed without a rhythm sheet just for the sake of the sounds the pillars made, and then threw away whatever shapeless thingies bubbled up from the dust. As seconds passed and the drone of pings and booms continued, Roper felt his skin crawling without immediately knowing why. Something about the pattern was familiar in a strange way, like a solemn old hymn sung much too fast and a couple of octaves high, so that it was over before you realized what it was.

At that speed the whole two-hundred-fifty-six notes were done in less than a minute, and by the time the last beat on the moon pillar died away, Roper was sure he had drummed that rhythm himself. But it was not for another minute that his mouth opened in confusion and panic, as the thingmaker did its work, and the dust flowed off and away from a brand-new drumlin in the bowl.

It was a were-wheel.

Roper leapt off the cart and charged across the dirt track to the thingmaker, his blood pounding in his temples, his mouth gaping and dry. He wanted to scream, and accuse, and ask a whole sackful of questions, but it all tried to come out at once, and what did come out was only a gasp and a groan.

Roddie held up one hand, his eyes open now, his brow wrinkled. "Don't talk. Ain't no time for that. Get back on the cart." Roddie then bent over the thingmaker's bowl, and puffed with exertion as he hauled the new were-wheel out and onto the grass beside the pillars. For an old man he was mighty strong; the were-wheel weighed nearly as much as he did. After a quick breath, he dragged it the three or four meters further to the edge of the road. "They'll stop for that. It's what they want, and it ain't nuthin' you can tuck in a saddlebag. With any luck, if they're as crooked as I'm guessin', they may even fight over whose it's going to be."

Roddie pointed at the cart. Roper turned, and obeyed.

For an hour and more Roper drove the cart toward Thusly as hard as he dared, seeing Iris panting and snorting trying to stay ahead of it. She'd fall back, and the harness cross bar would touch her rump, prompting her to jump a little, as though ready to break into a gallop that might break a bone in a mare her age. In all that time Roddie had said nothing, but only sat with his eyes closed and his hands on his knees. The owl was nowhere to be seen.

There was a sick, sour taste in Roper's mouth that wasn't hunger. He'd known it before, and ever more often in the past four years. The more wheels he sold, the more word got around, and the more he caught himself looking at strangers out of the corner of his eye, and wondering which way to jump if they pulled a knife or a gun. In another year or so, the whole world would know that there was a wheel that turned all by itself, owned by a cowboy pedlar without an army to guard him, and he'd have to hide in a cave.

The sun had set and the light was getting bad. If their pursuers were still on the road, it would be harder and harder to see them. Roper felt like he was going to explode, and the pressure was driving him to feel less courteous than his folks had taught him.

"All right, we shook 'em, and I'm grateful to have my skin. But are you gonna tell me how you got my rhythm without lookin' at the sheet?"

Roddie opened his eyes, and took his hands off his knees. "I been around a long time, and I've drummed a lot more than most folk. I know drumlins nobody else knows."

Roper spat off to the left. He was truly angry now, like he hadn't been since Amos pulled the gun on him back along the Dohe River. "Screw that—I wrote down that rhythm at random, and it's one in a chance of that great big huge number that you'd ever likely pull the same one as me."

Roddie's reply came maybe a little too quick for a hard question like that. "Random's a funny idea, and the human mind an even funnier one."

Roper shut his eyes for a moment and took a deep breath to calm himself. He was now close to fury. "You don't answer questions straight on, do you? I think maybe you're like a county fair conjurer, but real. You can see what I've got in my pocket. And maybe, just maybe, you can see what's inside my head."

Roddie snorted. "Ain't no such thing as conjurors."

Roper spat again. "Don't have to be. If there's a wheel that moves by itself, there can be lots of other thingie stuff that we can't figure nohow. You've got a spyglass that looks through itself and sees riders ten klicks off—who's to say you don't have something else that can read a paper stuffed in my pocket? And since I'm already yelling, I'll tell you what I think: *I think you're one of these Gaeans that built the thingmakers.*"

Roddie remained silent for a long time. Iris was panting hard now. A man hit with a crazy accusation like that should have been surprised, or more likely laugh. Roddie's voice stayed soft and steady as he answered, like it had been for two days, which all by itself was suspicious. "Truth is, ain't never been nobody ever met a Gaean. And I'm just an old man, like I look."

Roper glanced over his shoulder yet again, fear and anger a gnawing worm in the bottom of his guts. "Truth or not, to me you look like an old man put together by somebody who don't quite know what an old man looks like."

Roddie chuckled. "Now *there's* a blame-fool notion if ever was." Roper thought he caught the first hint of annoyance in the old man's voice. "Don't matter what I am nor who put me together—a man, a woman, and God, if you must know, just like you an' everone else."

Without warning, the owl lit on Roddie's shoulder. Roper listened, even though the notion that an owl could talk to a man was crazy stuff. He heard nothing.

Still, Roddie held up one hand. "There's a crossroads up ahead, and a thingmaker. Stop there, and don't talk."

Sure enough, another quarter klick found them at a crossroads, with stone benches and a thingmaker off to one side, its pillars and bowl still glinting wanly in the deepening gloom. Roper pulled back on the reins and Iris stopped. He hopped off the cart and looked her over. She needed water, and rest. Foam dripped from the poor mare's mouth into the dirt.

Roddie came up behind him, and laid one brown hand on his shoulder. "Unhitch her. She's foundered, foundered bad. You've got another hour of light and maybe one more further to get to Thusly, and she'll collapse sooner'n that. I'll look after her."

Roper whipped around. "And what if those riders catch you here? Givin' 'em the wheel just whet their appetites. They want the rhythm. Are you gonna give that to 'em too?" Roper knew he was whining now, like a kid who thought his brother got the bigger piece of the cake.

Roddie looked south, along the road, and then turned back to Roper. "Listen to yourself, boy, and tell me it ain't long past time to let it go. But no, I ain't gonna give them your rhythm. I think I may give them something else, something to keep 'em off your tail. But go, go as fast as that cart of yours can run. I'll be along with Iris by supper tomorrow, or day after that at the latest."

Roper opened his mouth. *Listen to yourself, boy...* Indeed, and fersure. Roper felt ashamed. An old man and an owl were going to face down two robbers for him. Crazy stuff.

But it was all crazy stuff now: the owl, the spyglass, and a man who could read a rhythm sheet folded up and tucked in a secret pocket Sadie had sewn into his pants. Roddie took the pinlamp in its reflector out of his carpet bag and whacked it against the front end of the cart, where it stayed put with no hint of how. Roper unhitched Iris from the cart and handed the reins to the odd-looking old man. He opened his mouth to speak, unsure what to say. Roddie shook his head. Roper nodded.

He climbed back into the cart, stowed the hitch, and ticked the lever forward. The drumlin gears clicked and ground as they took up slack, and the cart rolled off down the road, first as fast as a young man could run, and then faster. The sound of Roddie drumming furiously on the thingmaker followed him into the quiet night until the rattle of the cart on the rutted road was the only thing Roper could hear.

And some time a little later, a sound like a shriek drifted in on the wind, made soft by distance but clearly heard against the crickets and the hiss-whistle of the night breeze. It sounded like a hawk diving for its prey. Roper shuddered. Roddie was ten klicks back now, at least. If what he'd heard was that far off, Roper decided he didn't ever want to know what it had been.

It was most of the way to midnight by the time Roper left the road and turned onto the farm track that led toward old Henderson Busse's barn, which he'd been renting part of to do his work in between trips. There were lights on in the barn, and some horses tied up alongside. A Grange meeting, likely as not. Hen Busse was a fourth-order Granger and maybe more; ask past the Order of Husbandry and the Grangers would laugh, pour you another drink, and change the subject.

He could use a drink about now, and a change of clothes, and some quiet time in a seat that wasn't moving. More than anything else, he had to talk to Sadie. This trip, long as it was, hadn't been good for a single sale, and almost got him killed twice. Sadie'd turned down his proposals three times so far, on Sweetheart's Day for each of the past three years, saying she wouldn't marry a pedlar trying to hawk something that drew murderers like manure piles drew flies. Maybe Roddie was right, and it was time to give it over and just be a cowboy again. Old Hen had told him he'd expand his mostly idle farm if Roper would be his hand, with Sadie staying on as his cook and housekeeper, but if anything, plowing was harder work than driving cattle, and paid even less.

Selling the were-wheel had been a golden dream for awhile, but in six years he'd sold only twenty-two wheels, and for less and less each sale. He was good enough with numbers to know that that wasn't much better pay than being a cowhand all that time—and as he walked past the overgrown manure pile beside the barn, he could almost see the crowd of flies just waiting for the morning.

Roper pushed the side door of the barn open. He expected to hear fiddle music, or maybe the clink of mugs and the noise of a card game, but there was an awful lot of quiet for the amount of lamplight coming through the dirty windows. He kicked the door shut behind him, edged past stacks of rusty pails that hadn't seen milk since before Roper was born, and turned the corner into the cowbarn.

"Whoa, cowboy."

Roper heard a click, and froze. To the right of the door stood a stubble-faced tough sighting down a long-barreled revolver made of blackened steel. Drumlin lashup guns were notoriously unreliable, though no one quite knew why. Roper suspected he might not have taken on Boze and Amos by the river if he'd been looking down a steel barrel. There was campfire talk that drumlin guns didn't *want* to fire straight, and tried their dangdest not to—just as drumlin knives and saws bent sideways and went dull when they touched human flesh. A man toting an iron knife was up to no good, as Roper's throat had learned first-hand back in corn country.

A second tough patted him down, fishing his everyday book out of his coat pocket, along with his Folding Knife #6 from its sheath on his belt, not that a drumlin knife was a threat to anything except dinner.

Across the open space where Hen had pulled out the cow stalls years before, two more toughs sat on haybales, steel revolvers pointed at Henderson Busse and Sadie. Both were seated on the beat-up oak kitchen chairs Hen had been threatening to revarnish and sell since his wife Patty Ann passed away ten years before, he knowing what everybody knew, that staring at an empty chair over breakfast day after day could make even a strong man die before his time.

Sadie had a look on her face that Roper judged somewhere between terror and fury. Henderson Busse, by contrast, reminded him of Roddie. Nothing ever shook old Hen much, and what did he fixed by laughing at it. It was easy to laugh back, at a half-lame old bald man with a gray beard, barefoot in overalls that should've been torn up for rags ten years ago, but Roper knew that if those huge hands ever took hold of your arm in anger, bones would snap.

Hen sat impassive, his burlwood cane across his lap. "Long night, what, Al?"

Sadie glanced briefly to her right and cocked an eyebrow. "Welcome to the manure pile."

The tough who had been waiting for him beside the door waved him toward Sadie and Hen. Roper rounded the pile of hay bales he had placed to block the view through the barn windows, and stopped. Someone had pulled off the old stained tarps from the work he'd done this long cold winter just past. Up on a rack stitched together from scrap lumber, drumlin short forks, and cricket-leg bars was the unlikely machine he had named *Comet*. And down on one knee, looking closely at the works, was an Invicter.

That wasn't a word they used for themselves, and Roper knew that polite and cautious folk referred to them as Directors. The Bitspace Institute was big, and rich, but most of their people were hirelings who did what they were told and went home to supper without asking questions. The ones who pulled the strings were the Directors, and like everybody knew, the one thing you *didn't* say in their presence was the name of their secret club: *Sol Invictus*. It was in some dead language meaning *no one will keep us from returning to Sol*. Well, they'd been trying and failing for nigh on two hundred fifty years, and if they were grumpy Roper figured that was reason enough.

The man rose smoothly and quietly as a cat, turning toward Roper. As he stood, his steel-gray hooded cloak drew up from the floor without a wrinkle, coming down just below the tops of his boots. It was made of some strange drumlin cloth that only the Institute had, and rumor held that it would stop a bullet, though no one had ever gotten crazy enough nor drunk enough to try for proof.

Roper thought it notable, however, that the man did not throw back the cloak's hood until after the Invicter's thugs had searched him.

"Mr. Aloysius Carroll." He was neither tall nor strongly built, with a pale, smooth face and ice-blue eyes under hair long gone gray and starting toward white. "Known informally as 'Roper.'"

"The one." Roper was scanning the barn without trying to be too obvious about it, looking for something to swing if it came to that. When he'd left there'd been wrenches and crowbars and a two-kleg sledge lying around under *Comet*, but barn or not, Sadie just couldn't stop being a housekeeper.

"You are a dangerous man."

Roper resisted the urge to spit, and nodded toward Sadie. "Hurt my girl and you'll damn well see how dangerous I am."

The tough to his right still had the revolver on him, and now the one on the left drew his from a holster.

The cloaked man's lips rose to something just short of a smile. "I know what's in your pockets. Are you willing to guess what might be in mine?"

Roper thought of Roddie's spyglass and realized he was truly out of his league. He shook his head, eyes downcast.

"My name is Wolfram. I am a Senior Director of the Bitspace Institute. For the past thirty years, my job has been to track down dangerous drumlins and neutralize them. This—" He extended his left hand toward *Comet*. "—is the most dangerous thing I've seen in a *very* long time."

Roper's first impulse was to laugh. *Comet* was a big bicycle, with two were-wheels in a lashup drumlin frame. In between the wheels on the frame were two battered leather saddles that he'd gotten fourth-hand from Ira Cogswell. The front wheel was rigged to turn freely, and pivoted like a bicycle's for steering. Down in the thick of the lashup frame was a pedal connected to a linkage that changed the angle between the outer two of the were-wheel's three concentric hubs, which is what controlled the wheel's speed. That mechanism had taken some serious work, and he'd lost his share of hair perfecting it, but a handful of short midnight rides up and down the road had proved it out.

Dangerous? He'd even put stops in the linkage to keep the rear wheel from turning too quickly. To hurt yourself you'd have to rev it hard and steer square at a real big tree.

"Meaning no disrespect, Mr. Wolfram, but I built it so's Sadie could ride it, and she means more to me than anything else here or back on Earth." Roper felt himself blushing. Sadie rolled her eyes. "Once you learn how, it's safer than riding a horse."

Wolfram had begun walking slowly around *Comet*, touching it here and there. "That's one reason the wheel is so dangerous. It's simple. Nay, *elegant*—just as many other drumlins are, especially the truly dangerous ones. It's far too dangerous to leave in the hands of uneducated farmers. We've recovered eighteen wheels of those you've sold so far. Miss Rochtigan told us that you've sold 22, and was gracious enough to show us your ledger. My people are looking for the other four, and with the notations in your ledger will locate them soon. We have your cart, and we've found no other wheels here on Mr. Busse's property. All we need now is the bitmap." One of the toughs handed Roper's everyday book to Wolfram. "The page number, Mr. Carroll?"

Roper gulped. Gracious—with a gun to her head, yeah. He bit back anger and looked hard at Sadie, trying to make his face say, *it's all right* without words. In vain: She was staring between her feet at the cracked stone-and-concrete floor of the barn.

"Not in there. That's where anybody would look."

Wolfram snapped the book closed, running one thin finger along the worn binding. "True. And so where would it be?"

"First tell me what I'm up against if I won't hand it over."

Wolfram turned toward him, his face now hard. "We will offer Miss Rochtigan a position with the Institute, which I suspect she will accept. Alas, the work is far away from here."

In the long quiet seconds that followed, he heard Henderson Busse breathing, more quickly than Roper ever recalled. The old Granger's face was a mask, but the one big vein in his forehead was standing out. Fury was what it was, righteous fury and well-concealed, but fury that would see the old man follow his poor Patty Ann soon if he wasn't careful.

Roper then looked at Sadie, expecting terror on her face, now that his worst fears had been confirmed. Instead, she was looking up toward the cobwebs among the barn's rafters, her lips pursed. He had seen that look before, when he was dawdling or taking longer at anything than she thought necessary. It wasn't fear. *It was impatience.*

It was his move. She was waiting for him to act—just as she had waited these past four years for him to finally grow up and get over his silly fool idea of getting rich by selling a drumlin that everybody wanted to kill him for.

Listen to yourself, boy, and tell me it ain't long past time to let it go. A silly fool idea indeed. Yes, it was long past time to let it go. He should have just nailed the rhythm to a tree in the town square years back, so that everybody could have it, not just one dim-witted cowboy—

—or a few!

Roper nodded, as a far, far sillier fool idea occurred to him. "Ok. You've got the wheels. If I give you the rhythm, will you let her go? And Hen?"

Wolfram nodded. "We will. Of course, we may offer you that job at the Institute instead—especially if we think you have the bitmap committed to memory."

Roper shrugged. "I'll take it. Has to be better work than chasing steers out past Waythehell." He hoped he sounded bitter and defeated. Certainly his hands were shaking as he began unbuttoning his flannel shirt.

The tough beside Sadie moved in closer, until the barrel of his steel revolver was smack against her blonde hair. "You pull a gun and she's gone, cowboy."

Roper shook his head. He dug inside his shirt until he found Henry Banger's envelope. He wriggled one finger under the envelope's flap and broke the wax seal before he drew it out. He worried for a moment about pulling the wrong sheet from the envelope, but Henry had folded the rhythm sheet for his column ink side out. Roper handed the folded sheet to the tough beside him, who relayed it to Wolfram.

The cloaked man unfolded the sheet and scanned the rhythm. "Well. 'The Ever-Turning Wheel.' I wouldn't think a sweaty New Scottsdale cowhand would be that poetic."

Roper seethed at the insult. "Maybe I had more schooling than you think." He nodded toward Sadie and Hen. "Now call your thugs off and let them go."

Wolfram held the sheet back out toward the tough who had taken it from Roper. "We will—as soon as we've verified that this bitmap is the right one. Reggie, take this to the town square and enter it into the thingmaker. Leave the wheel there. We just need to know if the sheet is readable and accurate." Reggie tucked the sheet into a jacket pocket and headed for the door.

Roper's heart sank as he calculated how much time he had. Reggie didn't seem to be in a hurry, and on a night as dark as this he wouldn't be galloping hard into Thusly. The thingmaker wasn't far. Three minutes there on horseback on the outside, three or four minutes to hammer out the rhythm a line at a time by pinlamp, and three minutes back.

Ten minutes or an hour. What did it matter? There was nothing to be done but dig the real rhythm sheet from his secret pocket and admit the bluff. He would have begun reaching for the sheet had Wolfram not interrupted.

"We have a few minutes. Mr. Carroll, I would much appreciate a demonstration of your linkage. There's some cleverness here I don't quite understand." Wolfram was pointing at the lashup mess of odd drumlins by which Roper had connected the pedal to *Comet*'s rear wheel. Roper had the insight that it might *look* clever—but was in fact the first thing he could tack together that worked reliably from Hen's pile of useless thingies. He was no mechanic, and didn't dare hire one.

Roper nodded. *Comet* was suspended a hand's width above the floor by four drumlin gitalongs attached to the lashup workframe. The machine swung a little on the gitalong cables as he put one foot on the frame and swung his other leg up over the saddle, just as he would mount a horse.

"Nothing to it. When the tabs on the outer two hubs are lined up, the wheel is stopped. There's springs to keep the hubs together when nobody's pushing the pedal. Pushing on the pedal makes the linkage spread the angle between the two hubs, and the wheel starts up." Roper pressed the pointed toe of his left boot against the pedal. Without a whisper of sound, the rear wheel began to turn. "Push it down farther so you get more angle between the hubs, and it goes faster." He pressed harder with his left foot, and began to hear the smooth hiss of air disturbed by the wheel as it turned more quickly. "I put a stop on the pedal so it couldn't only make the wheel go so fast. Pull your foot back, and it slows down. Be careful not to take your foot clear off all at once, or the springs'll stop the wheel just like that and you might fly out over the handles." Roper grinned. "Maybe it's more dangerous than I thought."

Wolfram was again on one knee, watching the linkage move as Roper pressed and released the pedal. "It is, Mr. Carroll. Oh, it is. It could end everything we've been hoping for this past quarter millennium."

Roper frowned. "I think it'd be a courtesy to us all for you to explain that."

Wolfram paused for some seconds, obviously considering. Finally he nodded. "Very well. It should be obvious to anyone with any education at all, but for the sake of you here… Technologies don't just happen. Each advance requires and stands atop countless other advances, and we climb a sequence of technologies like a ladder. The climbing is more than simply acquiring knowledge. Tools need tools to make more and better tools. We know how microsphere computation operates from the old books brought from Earth, but creating microspheres requires the use of tools that we do not have. We know what tools are required, but we do not even have the tools to make those tools. A microsphere is a grown sphere of silicon accurate to five nanometers, covered with three layers of solid-state logic only four or five atoms wide and three thick. We understand the physics that govern their functioning. But we do not yet have the materials from which the spheres must be made, nor sufficient accuracy in our tools to make them.

"*Origen* was carrying people and products from Earth to Numenor when its Hilbert drive destroyed itself and we found ourselves here. Most of those products were gene-space—human and domestic animal diversity to ensure that Numenor's ecosphere and noosphere could be self-sustaining and not fail from genetic or cultural narrowing. Well and good; we would be dead from inbreeding if only a handful of humans had been aboard. There were a fair number of computers, but for fundamental physical reasons that I doubt you would understand, electronic devices fail with the passage of too much time, whether they are used or not. At nanoscale, molecules can migrate into semiconductor junctions despite our best efforts...never mind. The computers that *Origen* carried died one by one. With those computers went much of our knowledge, stored in data files that lived only as nanoscale patterns in tiny bricks of silicon. Some we managed to print to paper before the computers died. Most died with the computers. By the time seventy-five years had passed, all were gone.

"There is a starship in orbit around this planet that we cannot yet reach, much less repair. It lies at the top of a ladder, and we stand at the bottom. The only way to reach it is to build the rungs as Earth built them, one at a time and one atop the other. This takes many hands and many years. We now have the critical mass of people that it takes to create a technological society, but something is holding us back. The thingmakers give us artifacts that we do not understand at all. They might as well be occult magic. But they stand in well for artifacts that did *not* come from Earth. They make it less necessary to search for iron, copper, and rare Earth metals. Why build mills to make plows and hammers and gears and pipe when the thingmakers give us all that and whatever else we need, at little cost in time and no cost in energy or materials? The thingmakers have short-circuited whole segments of industrial civilization. We do not need tools to make the artifacts that come out of the thingmakers, and thus we do not have the tools to make the things that do *not* come out of the thingmakers.

"The more powerful the drumlins that people discover in bitspace, the fewer people strive to build the rungs that will take us up to *Origen* again, and then back to Earth. The drumlin you discovered—" Wolfram kicked *Comet's* rear wheel dismissively, "—is not a wheel at all. It's a motor. Once its bitmap is generally known, no more motors will be built. People will not hunt for copper. They will not smelt iron to build more steam engines. They won't have to refine petroleum to fuel internal combustion engines to power aircraft. Rung after rung of tech-nological civilization will never come to be, because people will not feel motivated to solve the problems that those rungs represent. And so we will be trapped here forever, until…"

Wolfram stopped in mid-sentence. Someone was working at the iron latch on the big roll-off doors at the other end of the barn. It had been only a minute or two; there was no possible way that Reggie could have done his work and returned. The three thugs glanced at the barn doors. One began walking in that direction, pistol at ready, staying near to the north wall.

Sadie stood, and bent down to grasp the hem of her green cotton dress in both hands. "I'm really sorry, Mr. Wolfram, but I'm afraid I'm going to have to take my clothes off." She hauled the dress up and over her head, tossing it dismissively to one side.

Roper gasped. Sadie's step-ins were not where he was used to seeing them, nor her corset. The three thugs looked away, like any man would if he'd had any upbringing at all.

In the long strange second that followed, Roper heard more clicking of ironworks, this time from the barn's side door, through which he'd entered minutes before. Then it all made sense: Whoever was outside wasn't opening any doors—*they were locking them.*

After that, as Roper recalled for many years afterwards, everything seemed to happen at once. Sadie kicked off her slip-pers, then stared straight at him and yelled, "Al, stay *put!*" Hen Busse stood, burlwood cane in both hands. Raising one knee, the old man brought the cane down hard against it.

With a sharp crack the cane split in two. Hen had half in each hand, and swung both halves around in a very fast arc. From the broken ends of the cane streamed tiny round nuggets of something white, each the size of whole black peppercorns, which bounced along the stone floor of the barn until every-where seemed thick with them.

The thug who'd been holding the gun on Hen had been looking toward the doors and now swung around to get a bead on the old man, but the moment he lifted his boot and put it down again, he fell to one knee. From his knee he toppled all the way down hard on one side.

And stuck.

Roper gaped: Going down, the thug had dropped his steel pistol. It had hit the floor handle-first and stood there, aimed cockeyed at the wall as though a ghost were holding it.

The two other thugs took single steps, lost their balance as the first had, and fell to the particle-scattered floor. Cursing, they writhed helplessly, their clothes and boots stuck fast to the stone, their pistols dropped and now immobile.

With a laconic grin on his face, Hen Busse walked three steps on bare feet to where the first pistol stood erect, and kicked it with his heel. The pistol did not move so much as a tick.

"Works good," Hen said, more to himself than anyone else. He turned toward Wolfram and chuckled. "Mebbe we should sit and talk for a spell, Mr. Invicter."

The Director's face, for a moment surprised and then distressed, turned grim. Wolfram pulled the cape's hood back over his head and made for the door, silver-gray boots crunching on the white particles but not adhering. Three meters back he stopped, and drew something from inside the cloak that Roper couldn't quite make out.

Holding the device in both hands, Wolfram crouched slightly, and pointed his arms toward the large barn doors. Something somewhere between a rumble and a mule-kick to the guts shook the barn and made Roper's ears hurt. The peeling red doors splintered and burst outward, their ancient wood flying apart into fragments and dust. Wolfram made the door in three strides and vanished into the midnight darkness.

Roper sensed that this hadn't been part of anybody's plan. Jay-bird naked and barefoot, Sadie ran the two meters to the *Comet*, still suspended from its frame, and leapt up onto the machine in front of Roper. She stood astride the front saddle, gripped the steering handles, tipped her head back…and sang.

Or something like singing. It was a high opera note gone bad and split into razor fragments, rough at the bottom but sharpened to fish-hook barbs at the top, and for seconds she held it while Roper wanted to press his hands up over his ears.

The four drumlin gitalongs from which *Comet* hung all let go at once. Sadie's pretty left foot kicked Roper's boot out of the way and mashed down on the pedal. *Comet* threw itself forward, past the dust that hung in the air where the barn's doors had been, and down the cow path more quickly than Roper had ever run it, hitting the ruts so hard he thought his teeth would loosen up.

It wasn't a minute before they were in the middle of the road that ran from Bushville to Thusly. Sadie pulled her foot back from the pedal in one smooth motion. The rear wheel skidded a little on loose earth but *Comet* remained upright. Roper's breath puffed out of him, and then he listened hard for sounds of Wolfram's horse.

Sadie leapt out of the front saddle and bent down to the road until her right ear was against the dirt. "Damn. Can't tell which way he went." She sounded disappointed, and irritated. "Drumlin horseshoes. Has to be." She grunted. "We almost had him."

Roper took several deep breaths and set *Comet* down on its side. Sadie stood again, her large, pale breasts smudged with dirt from the road. Roper looked at her, and she at him, until he figured she could hear his heart pounding. "You…you're not quite what I thought you were."

Sadie's usual beer-hall grin came sneaking back. "Not quite. And not hardly."

He recalled her yanking her dress up off and away, faster than he thought cotton could manage. "That was a good trick," he said, nodding toward her breasts.

Sadie chuckled. "I learned a lot from a tart named Modesty: Best way to throw off a man's aim, she said, is to draw your own weapons."

Roper nodded. "Ain't it, now." There was some sadness in realizing that some things were just too good to be true. "You said you never got sent upstairs."

Sadie sighed, then came over square to his chest and put her arms around him. She wiped her right ear against his shoulder. "Madame Hilary's Place didn't have no upstairs. All the rooms were in back, behind the stage. So I guess it was only half a lie."

Roper couldn't help but smile. "Then you really were a tart, back in New Boston."

She nodded, leaning up on tiptoe up to lay a quick kiss on his lips. "Good one, too." She grabbed his left ear and tweaked it hard enough to make Roper wince. "All right. I'm a tart. And you're a goodhearted fool. So let's make a deal: I'll stop being a tart if you'll stop being a fool."

Roper glanced down at *Comet*. "You mean, peddling."

Sadie tweaked his other ear. "I never meant anything so hard in my whole life."

About then Hen Busse came up the cow path behind them, followed by Gus Ginter and his brother Willy. "Hey, Sadie," Gus said, tossing her a bundle.

"Thanks, Gus," Sadie replied, snagging the bundle from the air one-handed, and shaking the dress out before pulling it over her head. "It'll be nice to have underwear on me again."

Willy raised one hand, waving what Roper recognized as a camera. "Got some nice shots from up in the hay loft. T'ain't legal to put a gun on somebody so's to steal a rhythm." He grinned. "Wonder how useful that might turn out to be someday."

Roper felt like a schoolhouse puppet with five sets of strings. "This whole business—" he nodded toward the barn "—was some kind of plan, right? Your cane, Hen, and the little glue balls, Sadie getting naked so she wouldn't stick to the floor, that strange old man and his magic owl who wanted me out here in the worst way…"

"How about a drink, Al?" the old man said, grinning through his crooked teeth.

"Hey, Hen, he deserves to know more than that." Sadie took a step back from Roper. "We've been watching you all this time that I've been falling in love with you, since you first rode Iris into town and rented Hen's barn to build your cart and then *Comet*. Ain't never been an hour that somebody hasn't been keeping an eye on you since then. And we've been keeping an eye on the Institute too while they were trying to find you, and finally figured it was getting close enough so that we'd better make our move."

"We. Who's we?"

"Us." She waved at the three men behind her. "The Grangers. Here and everywhere else in the west country. What did you think we all were, farmers?"

"Even Henry Banger? And how he showed me…"

"The little spinning top. And his column. Even that—his idea. We have people everywhere. We knew the route you were taking, and Henry made sure he was where you'd be when you'd be there. Al, do I have to knock you over the head and stake you to the ground while I beat it into you?"

Roper reached into his jacket and pulled out Henry Banger's newspaper column in its envelope. Then he reached deep into his pants under his wallet to where Sadie'd sewed him the secret pocket, and pulled out his beat-up rhythm sheet. Holding one in each hand, he looked at Henderson Busse and the Ginter brothers. They nodded solemnly.

"Has to be your decision," Sadie said. "The Grange has its secrets. It also has principles."

"But what about destroying the ladder up to Earth civilization and gettin' stuck here forever…"

Henderson Busse took a step forward, and put both knobby hands on Roper's shoulders. "Look here, Al," he said sharply. *"How many ladders do I have in my barn?"*

Roper's jaw dropped as he got the old man's drift. "So you mean there's another…"

"Join the Grange and make Fourth Order like everbody else." Hen Busse turned and began walking back toward the big house beside the barn. He did just fine without his cane, Roper noticed. The Ginter brothers headed back toward the barn.

"Gonna be cartin' some naked thugs down to the sheriff in a few," Gus called over his shoulder, laughing lightly, "so you'd better be gettin' on back home, Miss."

Sadie made a gesture that Roper wasn't used to seeing girls make.

Roper looked down at his hands, envelope in one, rhythm sheet in the other. Sadie grabbed his wrists and shoved them together. "We got us a deal, lover."

Roper swallowed hard, and nodded. "We do." He tucked his rhythm sheet into Henry Banger's envelope and closed the flap. "I broke the seal, though."

"Seals are easy." Sadie reached up into her blonde hair, dug around, and came back with a tiny white ball, like all those Hen had spilled on the barn floor. She grasped the envelope that Roper offered her, and crushed the white ball against the fragments of wax from the broken seal. "Sticks to everything but human skin and hair—and drumlins." Sadie tucked the sealed envelope into her bodice, then bent down to wrestle *Comet* back up on its wheels. Roper held the awkward machine vertical while she slipped into the front saddle, then climbed on himself. The morning sack would be gone from Thusly's post office by 8 AM. Better to drop it in the mail slot now so as not to risk letting Henry Banger down—or having second thoughts himself, or third.

Roper imagined what would happen the Sunday after next, when the first papers began to thump on people's porches. It wasn't like Henry Banger's usual column, which described useful things that cut glass or sifted coarse sand from fine. Not this time. Roper remembered what Henry had written of the little spinning top he'd found under a cup on a farmer's mantelpiece:

> "No one knows yet what this drumlin will be used for. The world may have to grow into it a little—and there's always the outside chance that, in some future we can't yet imagine, it will have been the single push that made us turn off one road and onto another, better one."

Roads, heh. Henry Banger was in on the joke, and Roper knew there'd be a lot of fingers scratching a lot of heads that Sunday, when dozens, then hundreds, then thousands, then tens of thousands of were-wheels began rising out of the thing-maker dust. For the slightest moment Roper wondered with a wistful grin what all those wheels would be worth, at ten gold hands a pop. No, wrong wonder. What would it be worth to be a fly on the wall when the Bitspace Institute's top people got wind of it? Worth?

Priceless.

Sadie reached over the steering handles and gave the pin-lamp above the front wheel a hard twist to the right, for maximum brilliance. Its sharp circle of light spread out along the road for a hundred meters or more. She gave a whoop and pressed the pedal hard. *Comet* reared up on its back wheel like a stallion until Roper yelled out in terror. Sadie then settled it gently back to the ground with a bump and they rode, silent as a night wind, toward Thusly. ∎

RODDIE

2003

RODDIE

Roddie was a performer, like some of them drummers who do it for the sound—and then toss the drumlin in the dirt—'ceptin that for him the drumlins *were* the show. Not a pedlar, neither—he wore other people's handoff clothes, ate what people handed him, slept where they pointed him, and never asked a knuckle for anything he drummed up out of the Dust. And I ain't never seen nobody drum that fast. You could barely see his hands move, and the pillars sounded out as loud as ever but blurred sometimes so it sounded like they were singing harmony, sun and moon together with no sense that they were one ahead of the other—and which one came first and then after, no one knew nohow, which I was always double-damn sure was the way Roddie wanted it.

He had this tame owl with no name—and don't nobody ask me how he tamed an owl!—that sat on his shoulder while he drummed, looking around with those big golden eyes, looking at everybody in turn who stood around to watch and listen. Each time Roddie completed a Drumming, he looked down at the Dust to see what bubbled up. If it was something big, he pulled it out and laid it on the ground. If it was something small like a teaspoon, that owl would swoop down and grab it right out of the Dust, then fly back up on his shoulder and hold it in that hooked beak, maybe waving it around so it would catch the light. And every so often the owl would stay put but Roddie'd reach down to the Dust and grab what was there and tuck it in his pocket, so fast you couldn't but catch a glint of metal. And while he was doing that, the owl would fly up over the crowd and drop what it was carrying, and people'd all but beat each other senseless for it, even if it was just a teaspoon and they already had a drawer full.

Everybody just watched the owl most of the time, but I never do what everybody else does. I watched old Roddie. I snuck around and watched his face while he drummed, to try and see whether he gave some kind of signal to the owl, or to see if he was looking at the dust like most pedlars do, trying to wish up a were-wheel or a ball of gold, hungry for something that might buy supper or else a farm—or maybe nothing. But Roddie looked straight on until the drumming was done, then closed his eyes for the seconds it took for the Dust to work. And when he opened them, it seemed like he already knew what was there.

And when his time at the thingmaker was over, he did the oddest thing. He'd pick up the first drumlin from the pile beside the bowl and ask the crowd, "Who you think oughter get this? And no fair askin' for yourself." And anybody who said, "Me!" Roddie'd ignore, and the owl would give him the major eyeball. What he wanted was for somebody to say, "Bo Howell just lost his axe in the creek fixin' the bridge and needs a new one!" and for five other people to chime in and say, "Yeah, give it to Bo!" Sometimes there'd be a couple of contenders, each with a party behind them, but Roddie'd just wait and nag 'em all until everybody upped and decided who the axe or the breadbox or the cartwheel should go to.

Now, there was always a couple of these big thingies in the pile, shiny twisted metal that looked like nothing else and didn't seem to have much use. Roddie'd look each one over, then scratch his chin and say, "Y'know, I'd bet old Harry Rankin at the Bitspace Institute in Colonna would pay a few hands for this," or "I recall a guy named Mike down in Huffer who was lookin' for one of these." How he knew who wanted what was a puzzle—all them big thingies looked alike to me—but always somebody would cart the thingies down to old Harry or to Mike, and would come back with a little bag of hands. Before he wandered off to supper with a family or to bed in some-body's barn, he and his owl would look us all in the eye and say, "When you sell these here thingies, bring the money back and spend it on something that everybody here can use." And even

though there wasn't no way he could make us, somehow when
the carts came back from Huffer or Colonna, we always took
the hands his thingies sold for and bought new granite cobbles
for the crossroads or a new iron pump head for the town well.
Don't know why. Same thing with the hands as with those tea-
spoons the owl dropped on the crowd: There was something of
old Roddie on 'em, and maybe it was just a story to tell before
bedtime, or maybe it was something more.

The last time I saw Roddie I was maybe fifteen, and he'd got
white from his gray since his last time through town. I'd seen
my gramps go that way and be buried the next year, so I took
what I figgered was my last chance and followed him the gray
morning he walked out of town, his owl flying like a cat over
the wheat fields looking for rabbits.

And I asked him, "What are all those little thingies you
tucked in your pocket while your owl was droppin' spoons on
people?"

He laughed, and he clapped my shoulder with his strong
dark right hand that could drum so good like nobody else.
"Them's pieces of God," he said with a straight face.

Half the town would go down to Thusly for church on good
Sundays, but if my pop talked to God he did it inside his own
head, and me not at all. "Must take a lot of pieces to make God,"
I said, and it was the only thing I could think of to say, and kind
of dumb at that.

"Takes *all* the pieces," Roddie said, and I thought I could hear
him jangle as he walked on down the road to the next town,
with his pockets full of God and somebody else's clothes on
his back.

EXCERPT FROM
THE CUNNING BLOOD

2005

Introduction

The first story I set in the Gaians universe was the novel I began writing at the end of 1997 and finished mid-1999: *The Cunning Blood*. Getting it into print took over five years (and rejections from all the major SF print publishers) but in November 2005, ISFiC Press outside Chicago launched it in hardcover at the 2005 Windycon SF convention. You can buy it on Amazon or order it through any significant bookstore. (And, in case you're a publisher, the mass-market paperback rights are still for sale.)

The Cunning Blood takes place in 2374, and is about nanotechnology; specifically, of secret societies that have continued to advance nanotechnology after an increasingly reactionary Earth government has banned it from private hands. Most of the Societies have created—or stolen—distributed nanocomputers that hide by living entirely within the human bloodstream. They speak by hammering on the tiny bones of the inner ear. You speak back to them by subvocalizing, which is a learned skill in which the speaker sends signals to mouth, tongue, and throat as though to speak, without actually pushing air. The nanocomputer monitors those muscles very closely, and understands what is intended to be said. Think of it as reading lips from the inside.

Although Earth has suppressed nanotechnology and nanocomputing AI for 200 years at the time the story takes place, it has used nano in earlier times. Perhaps its most fateful use of nanotech was in creating the perfect prison planet. In the 22nd century, Earth took one of the multitude of Gaian (Earthlike) worlds that were known to exist and released a simple, self-replicating nanomachine into its ecosphere. This nano-machine, called the Magnetotropic Geospecific Internment Device (MGID) has little intelligence, but much persistence. It seeks out electrical conductors carrying anything beyond a few microamps of current and destroys them. The prison society on Hell was created to rely on natural gas and coal power, and kept in a sort of eternal Victorian stasis. Without electricity, there can be no computation, and thus no space travel.

Or so Earth thought.

But Earth was wrong.

Excerpt from

The Cunning Blood

Chapter 0. Covert Contact

Hell, July 16, 2372

Starship *Yellowknife*'s shuttlecraft *Greased Pig* screamed toward the low point of its power dive through Zeta Tucanae 2's upper atmosphere. From there, the planet didn't look like Hell at all. To the contrary: Hell was the most Earthlike of any Gaian world yet discovered. Twenty klicks below, a frontal system was moving across the vast scrub grasslands of the planet's single immense continent. The pod would be down long before the front swept through the primitives' camp that they had spotted from orbit.

"You ready, Joop?" J. J. Rafferty asked from the *Pig*'s controls.

"Sure," the Dutchman answered from the pod in the cargo bay. "Open the door and let's do it!"

Rafferty tapped an icon on his command stone. The panels covering the *Pig*'s cargo bay crept backwards into the hull. The thin air tore into the empty space, blowing scraps of paper and lunch bags in dervish dances before tossing them into the deep blue nothingness. The pod's skeletal magnesium frame glinted in the afternoon sun. Joop Verdaam checked everything one last time. Some food, enough oxygen to get him down to the surface, some deadly presents for the natives (including Magic Mikey's crazy chemical laser teletype) six inflation canisters and balloons to carry more reliable messages back to the upper atmosphere, and one bigger canister and balloon to get his own carcass back to power-dive altitude if the plan were to fail.

The *Greased Pig* couldn't land. Earth had infected Hell with a nasty nanobug that ate electrical conductors carrying current. That was why it was Hell—abandon hope and all that. Nothing electrical lasted longer than a few hours—which meant, pretty much, that nothing technological lasted longer than a few hours. Drop prisoners down in one-way lifting-body landers, and they can't get out.

Not yet, at least. Joop grinned. This was going to be fun, if it didn't kill him first—and things like that were generally the most fun of all.

"So to Hell with you, man!" Rafferty called with a grin, and hit the eject switch.

Joop's pod roared out of the bay end of the *Greased Pig* on four solid-fuel ejection rockets. He was a kilometer east before Rafferty pulled back on the stick and let the *Pig*'s four big zerospike engines have their noisy way again. How fast Hell's nanouglies worked was a big unknown—but Rafferty didn't intend for his shuttle's electronics to become a test case. Beyond Hell's magnetopause the nanobugs self-destructed, so he was heading for the magnetopause at just under three Gs. Hell, 4—a guy's only got one life to live.

J OOP FELL FREELY FOR SEVERAL MINUTES. He was lashed into the pod like a cripple into a dogsled, which the pod roughly resembled. In addition to conventional electronic instruments, he had several purely mechanical items made especially for the occasion: An aneroid altimeter, a thermometer, and magnetic compass. Velcroed to the pod wall near his left shoulder was perhaps the most intriguing item of all: An experiment intended to measure the destructive speed of Hell's MGIDs, the Magnetotropic Geospecific Internment Device, a nanotechnological mechanism dispersed in its atmosphere two hundred years before. Pronounce the acronym and you get *maggots*—as good a nickname as any.

So far it was the same as home: The little color screen at his elbow showed him where he was and how high. At ten klicks the altimeter started feeping, so Joop reached up and yanked down hard on the drogue release handle. The drogue chute deployed with a gut-wrenching jerk, slowed and stabilized the pod's free fall, and then pulled out the Rogallo wing.

The fabric wing unfolded and filled as in the test runs over Columbia in the 109 Piscium system. Joop broke loose the mechanical stick—it steered by pulling on the wing with cables, yike!—and banked this way and that to be sure all was well. So far, so good. He snapped the stick into its wide loop position, and sat back to ride out the long, slow spiral to the surface.

Eight klicks now. The MGID experiment on his left was an open wire-frame box the size of a long lunch bucket. Built into the top was a binocular magnifier. He leaned forward and took a look. The leftmost experiment was a simple coil of naked copper wire carrying a current from a battery to a cesium pinlight. Behind it was a stop button tenth-second mechanical timer, its dial whirling. The four other experiments were the same, but had greater and greater degrees of insulation and encapsulation against the maggots. Joop realized somewhat grimly that his avionics were the sixth experiment. So be it: He was an ancient aviator now, flying like they flew before, well, before humanity had invented avionics.

Experiment 1 was indeed active. The copper wire was growing hair! Greenish fuzz was forming on the coil of wire, and a whitish powder could be seen gathering on the battery and the plastic housing of the pinlight. As Joop watched, the wire broke and the pinlight went out. He reached forward and tapped the stop button on Experiment 1's timer. Thirty-eight minutes, thirty-six and six tenths seconds. And that was starting from the high stratosphere! Joop gulped and began watching Experiment 2. Nineteen minutes later, thick flakes of Teflon insulation were falling from the wire, and moments after that, the pinlight went out.

Scarcely ten minutes more elapsed before Experiment 3 failed—and the whole works had been dipped in a mil-spec epoxy coating, which was now cracked and abraded as though it had sat in Saharan sun and wind for fifty years.

The ominous white powder was thick on the ice-cube sized block that contained the wire in Experiment 4. Black dust was blowing off of the block. Those things were chewing the epoxy! It took another sixteen minutes, but after only an hour and change, the little monsters had destroyed the circuit there as well.

Something by his elbow chirruped briefly and was silent. Joop looked up and realized his avionics screen was now dark, the whole works covered by a sinister coating of white powder.

He fought down the dread of a pilot who lived by his instruments. The aneroid altimeter showed him at scarcely five klicks. The dark blotch of the encampment was clearly visible to the unaided eye. Something odd, though: It now seemed a different *shape*.

Don't borrow trouble, Joop told himself. His unpowered rig would be there soon enough. Life's sole mystery lay in staying alive. All the rest was simply entertainment.

He took another look through the wire box's magnifier. Experiment 5 was different: The whole circuit—battery, coil, and pinlight—had been sealed in a thin transparent cylinder of fused quartz. The pinlight still shone, but it was hard to see through the coating of white that seemed to grow thicker by the second. Joop rubbed the quartz vessel with gloved fingers so that he could see the pinlight more clearly—and realized that the quartz was already etched a milky white. Quartz! The little monsters were chewing through quartz to get at the wires!

Three klicks. Now the mystery below was resolving. Smoke! And in the thick of the smoke, flame. A sour taste seeped into his mouth. It had all appeared so serene from orbit through *Yellowknife*'s big scope: just haphazard circles of tents and large animals that looked like elephants.

With every banking circle that took him closer to ground, the situation below came clearer. Out of the indistinct curdle of smoke and flame he could now see motion. Large objects were moving, alone and in loose formation. He held his fingers in front of his ears to keep the breeze from obscuring sounds, and heard the distinct crack of gunfire.

Joop groaned. He was doing a dead-stick glide into the middle of a battle.

It was late afternoon, and the best heat of the day was hours past. On Columbia he had practiced seeking out thermals to keep altitude and allow him to maneuver. Alas, thermals would be unlikely so late in the day.

Delta-v was the better part of twenty-fifth century valor, but lacking that, discretion would have to do. Joop broke out of his circular descent. A light wind was carrying the smoke eastward, making it hard to tell where the combatants were. He set the Rogallo wing straight cross-wind and headed south.

He was now barely a klick above the chaos below, and it was quite possible that the red-and-white Rogallo wing had already been seen. The wind shifted to the northwest. Some of the gunfire was automatic. Machine guns? Those guys were riding elephants! He thought Hell had been frozen in the year 1800. Or was it 1900?

The Missus had warned him: *People in the past were ignorant. People on Hell are handicapped. Neither is a reflection of stupidity.* Duh. And you could turn machine-guns parts on a pedal-driven lathe. Gunpowder predated electricity by a thousand years. Back on *Yellowknife* he remembered thinking with a smirk: *How hard could this be?* Joop cursed his naiveté.

Banking south had been a mistake. If he turned into the wind he would land in the thick of the battle, but the battle seemed to be following the smoke.

Smoke, on the other hand, was cover. Joop slipped his oxygen mask back over his face and flipped down his goggles. He thumbed the levers and felt positive suction adhere them lightly around his eyes. The tank was slung beside one arm, strapped loosely around his waist. He banked east.

Half a klick, and going down fast. If they couldn't see him now they were blind, and he could smell both smoke and gunfire. And something else, a familiar chemical he couldn't place right away…a stink like rot, and eggs, and fertilizer.

Something exploded beneath him. Something big. He saw the raw yellow-white flash and felt the concussion shake the pod's thin frame. The grass and trees were on fire everywhere he looked, and he felt the heat from the flames on the skin of his hands. The familiar stink redoubled. He recognized it now: ethyl mercaptan. Men had added the telltale scent marker to natural gas for four hundred years.

Natural gas?

Smoke had risen high on the force of the flames. He was in the thick of it now, watching men on huge animals casting surreal shadows through the smoke in the near-horizontal rays of the setting sun. Some of the animals ran like elephants. Some were like nothing he had ever seen, leaping and stumbling as on two legs, though he could no longer see clearly enough in the smoke-obscured gloom to be sure.

He had only minutes left in the air, maybe less. Below, a man on an elephant was chasing a thing like a…dinosaur. The dinosaur had a rider too, and live fire was being exchanged. The dinosaur stopped and turned in a strange stiff pirouette, and leaped on two legs toward the elephant. The elephant reared, tusks flashing with an incongruous metallic glint.

The man on the elephant fired something toward the dinosaur, something that rode a dazzle of fire and left behind a line of gray smoke. It looked like a pocket missile. But…could they have missiles? Surely the maggots would prevent them from having missiles…

Quartz. Maybe the maggots couldn't chew through quartz. Maybe Hell encased everything in quartz. Joop stole a quick glance at Experiment 5. The thin quartz vessel had crumbled to round-edged shards.

Not quartz.

The missile reached its target. Almost directly beneath him, the dinosaur exploded.

The concussion knocked Joop forward in the pod. Something ripped through the fabric of the Rogallo wing. The wing was now smoking. Something else clanged against the pod's frame and ricocheted away, tumbling and flashing as it caught the last of the sunlight.

Metal. And the stink of mercaptan was palpable.

Joop yelled. A bolt had given way, and one of the pod's wing-mount arms was flapping free, clanging against the pod's side scant centimeters from his left arm. The wing had collapsed. The pod was plunging to ground.

In those final seconds Joop reached forward, his teeth grit with panic, to grope by his feet for a portion of his peculiar cargo: An ugly, bulbous weapon the size of an assault rifle but thicker, *rounder*.

The pod struck the ground point first, the Rogallo wing pulling it forward like a sail of rags so that it stood almost vertically on its nose, leaning against the broken wing-mount arm. Joop gasped as he was thrown downward against the web holding him in place. He struggled to release the several straps, Magic Mikey's weapon tucked in his left armpit.

The smoke was accelerating the fall of night. Against the constant rattle of gunfire Joop heard the thudding vibration of heavy legs. He turned his head and saw it coming straight at him: A skeletal machine made of tubes and pipes, running on two legs, a stylized face with shark-like teeth painted on its forward end, and behind the face, a man crouched behind a transparent shield. It made a sound like the roar of strong wind overlaid upon a mechanical whine. Something like a turbine…

Turbines. Natural gas. A gas-turbine mechanical dinosaur.

The machine howled, and a jet of flame emerged from between its painted-on jaws. Flamethrower!

Joop brought up Magic Mikey's fluorine-powered whatchamacallit and with shaking hands sighted lamely on the dinosaur's human rider. Not a good shot, but…he squeezed the trigger. The weapon shrieked, and a crack like a lightning bolt made his ears ring. Searing blue-green light flashed from the weapon's blunt muzzle.

The dinosaur thundered past him on heaving legs, its flame-thrower setting quick fire to the flapping shreds of the Rogallo wing.

Its rider's head was gone.

The machine stumbled on without its driver and vanished in the deepening gloom. Joop's hands shook even harder as he tore at the latches on the pod's straps. This wasn't on the program. These guys had been tossed back into the stone age, and he was a warrior serving a new, starfaring nation! Not fair!

More heavy footfalls, and the trumpeting of elephants. Joop screamed as something metallic thrust through the canvas-shrouded body of the pod and heaved it up high in the air.

In the last, blood-red light of the day, Joop looked down on a massive animal that was not quite an elephant. A mastodon! Its great side-curving tusks had been extended with polished steel blades, blades now piercing the pod, having somehow miraculously missed his legs. The animal was draped in a peculiar covering of dark charcoal-gray, knit together from large squares of something like thick felt. A glinting black helmet covered its skull, exposing only its eyes.

Behind the animal's helmeted skull was strapped a huge black saddle in which rode a tall man with a broad-brimmed hat. The man had an assault rifle aimed at Joop's chest.

"Who in Hell are you, boy?" the rider boomed.

Joop pulled down his oxygen mask but otherwise didn't move. Something else exploded far away, and the machine gun chatter continued. A mastodon was trumpeting in agony. "Not…from Hell. From…offworld. I'm here to help you."

The man laughed. "Some help you'll be strapped into your own goddam coffin. Gimme that gun and don't try nuthin'. *Hiyah*, Chowder!"

The last command was evidently for the mastodon, which raised its head further. The pod slid back another half-meter on the animal's tusks, and the rider leaned forward, hand outstretched. Joop slowly gripped the chemical laser rifle by its muzzle and extended it handle-first to the man.

Joop spoke quickly. "You just aim and pull the trigger. It doesn't kick but it makes a piercing noise. And it stinks when it fires. This one has five shots left. I was sent here to…"

"Shut it, son. You got any more of these?"

"Seven more. In the pod. Look, we have to talk. My boss wants to cut a deal…"

From off to the right, a chatter of rifle fire. Joop looked down and saw the bullets strike the drooping squares of feltlike material covering the mastodon's broad side. The mastodon trumpeted and began to run, its head still high in the air.

Joop saw no blood. The animal kept running. Cloth that stopped machine gun fire!

"Goddam saurs!" The mastodon's rider turned in the saddle and aimed the laser rifle across one thick, ruddy-skinned arm. Joop could hear the pounding legs of another of the mechanical dinosaurs. The laser weapon first shrieked, then fired with a single sharp *crack!* Blue-green light made the rider's face look demonic in the shadows.

The saur pursuing them exploded in a ball of fire and the choking reek of mercaptan. Chowder was thrown sideways and down by the concussion, its rider vanishing behind the mastodon's bulk. The final strap holding Joop into the pod broke and Joop fell free, shielding his face with his hands against the searing heat from the fireball.

He struck the mastodon's side and rolled down against the animal's legs, which were flailing against the ground. Joop darted away from the mastodon and hit the ground as live fire again raked the animal's side. He pulled his oxygen mask down again, reset the seals around his eyes, then rose and began to run in no particular direction, his oxygen tank slapping against his side. He stumbled over a corpse in the choking gloom but kept running.

More pounding mechanical footfalls. The deepening dusk had robbed the world of color, and in gray against darker gray Joop saw another stumbling iron monster emerge from the smoke and loom up behind him. He turned to one side and tried to evade it, but the saur's rider had seen him and turned the machine to pursue.

They had a clear shot but didn't take it. Joop realized he was wanted alive and ran more quickly, leaping over another motionless body in the smoldering grass, looking in the fading light for a stand of trees or anything else into which he might slip and lose the saur.

Nothing. He tried to feint and reverse direction, but for something so massive the machine was tremendously agile. The saur heaved up, its turbine screaming, to spin oddly on one of its stiffly held legs.

Joop ran. He had ceased wondering how a walking machine could be controlled without computers and simply wanted to flee. Two more of its stiff leaping steps brought the saur up beside him, and before Joop could change direction again something dropped over his head and shoulders and jerked him back.

The rope lasso pulled him off his feet and Joop fell hard to the ground. The saur was now immobile, leaning back on its steel-pipe tail, its turbine still whining, waves of exhaust heat pouring from vents atop its tail. The machine's rider hauled back on the rope and pulled Joop up the saur's side. Joop was hauled roughly into a small cockpit set into the back of the machine.

The man who looked down on him was smaller than the mastodon rider and naked to the waist, smeared with what looked like brown mud and streaked with the carbon black of smoke and charred vegetation. A small and peculiarly shaped sidearm was clamped behind his right wrist, his smallest finger positioned on the long, curved trigger, which nestled in a complex trigger guard. The weapon's barrel was pointed at Joop's nose.

The saur rider's voice was low without being deep, fast and precise without sounding frantic.

"What is in your vehicle?"

"Weapons."

"Where are you from?"

"Offworld. I…"

"Why are you here?"

"To create an alliance with your…"

Another of the small missiles Joop had seen arced over their heads. Joop's captor spun around in the cockpit and grasped controls with both hands. The whine of the saur's turbine increased in pitch and the machine tipped up, leaping forward immediately into its brain-jarring gait. The man spoke to Joop without turning.

"Weapons are useful. We'll need to consolidate them. Fire be."

Joop was thrown down to the cockpit's floor. It was just a platform; on all sides were pipes and hoses and straight rods that might have been levers or pushrods. Joop squirmed around to face forward, his arms still tangled in the tight loop of the rope lasso. Each time the machine took a step, he was slammed bodily against the cockpit's metal deck.

The saur was leaning into a series of shallow turns. Joop guessed that the rider was doubling back toward his pod.

Between the spread legs of the rider Joop looked down into the heart of the machine, which was a mechanical nightmare. Dozens of hydraulic cylinders pushed and wheezed at linkages that drove the saur's legs. A spiderweb of thin, transparent tubes threaded all through the mechanism, singly and in woven bundles. Further forward Joop could make out by the machine's internal gas lamps (hissing like snakes and spilling more heat into the machine's sweltering interior) a system of two large spinning flywheels, each on an independent system of gimbals, constantly tugged and adjusted by a network of small hydraulic cylinders.

Gyroscopes! Each time the machine took a step, small gripping brake pads clamped down briefly on the sides of the flywheels. Joop shook his head in wonder. Put some drag on a flywheel and it kicked in the opposite direction. But how was it all controlled?

Just to one side of the rider's right foot was a large rectangular steel box into which hundreds of the transparent tubes vanished. Yellow fluid was coursing through them, making them twitch and pulse in response to the machine's gyrations.

Joop squinted to read the inscription on the box's side:

FLUIDIC NETWORK CONTROL COMPUTER
MODEL 4406-B
MANUFACTURED UNDER CONTRACT
TO GAMMA ALPHA SIGMA

The saur's rider turned and pointed the arm-clamped weapon at him. "Don't move!" he commanded. Joop gulped and nodded.

The saur danced through another dizzying turn. A burst of automatic rifle fire clanged raggedly against the machine's side. Joop made an uncomfortable decision: *Go with the primitives.* The IAR needed warriors, the dumber the better. People who used fluidic computers (Fluidic? What was that, anyway?) were smart. *Dangerously* smart. Hell was not what it appeared to be.

But then again, what ever was?

Joop inhaled and exhaled deeply, quietly, repeatedly, gradually loosening the loop of rope that hindered his arms. He waited, seeing yet another missile pass dangerously close, and hearing the mastodons trumpeting in pursuit.

Without warning, the saur heaved up and began another of its spinning one-legged turns. Joop pretended to flop over and in doing so pushed the rope far enough upward on his arms to move his right arm free. His hand darted out and grasped one of the several bundles of transparent tubes connected to the fluidic computer.

He pulled. *Hard.*

Half the tubes in the bundle came free, spraying hot fluid in every direction. The saur's flywheels screamed as their pads closed home, and the saur flipped violently into the air on the force of their stored momentum. The half-naked rider was thrown clear. Joop hung on as the machine fell heavily to the ground, then scrambled out of the cockpit and began to run. His pod, miraculously, was just ahead, lying on its side in the smoldering dirt. Its cloth covering, however, had been slit from top to bottom as though with a knife.

"Freeze, boy."

A man was lying on the ground, one leg bent grotesquely backward. He was leaning on one elbow, his hands holding the laser rifle Joop had handed him. Out of the gloom came other men, rough-looking men with long, sun-frizzled hair tied back in ponytails. Several were carrying the other fluorine chemical laser rifles Joop had brought in his pod.

Joop raised his hands.

"We ain't never seen anything like these," the wounded man said. If his leg was broken, he was exerting tremendous will against the pain. "We could use a few more. So what's the deal? You from Earth?"

"No. Not from Earth."

"The Numenor colony, then."

"No. Not Numenor. Another planet, an unknown planet…"

"Don't screw with us, son. Soon's the boys get a splint together for my leg, we're takin' you back to see the Boss in person. He don't like skinny little twerps messin' with his mind, an' bein' his oldest kid I don't much either. Truth be told, I'm not real comfortable right now, and I reckon you got three sentences to spill the deal, or I'm gonna judge you some kind of fluke and take your head off for my collection."

Someone brought up a gas lantern, which showed bloody scratches on the man's forehead, and eyes bottomless blue against a soot-streaked face.

Joop gulped. He smelled rain, and somewhere in the distance heard rolling thunder. "We'll get you as many of these weapons as you want…"

"Weapons ain't a deal, boy. Maybe a bribe. That's one sentence."

"We're fighting a war and we need help." The thunder was getting louder. Odd thunder. Odd—and familiar.

"Ain't a deal neither. More like a piss-ant whine. And that's two sentences."

Joop looked from one of the gathered men to another. He took a deep breath. If he could win them over, they would be ideal. The Missus would be pleased.

"Help us win our war, and we'll get you off of Hell."

The men looked from one to the other. There was a long moment of silence, punctuated by whispers in the gloom. Their leader, prone on the ground, nodded. "That'll interest the Boss, fersure. But if you're lyin', boy, we'll cook you for supper a piece at a time." The man lowered the laser rifle. "Now behave yourself while we get ready. There'll be a gun on your back every second, and you do anything funny you'll never know what hit you."

That wasn't thunder. But how…

The men looked up in the air. "Birk! Douse that lantern!"

One of the men pounced on the lamp and extinguished it. The thunder reached a crescendo and began to pass, its tone a falling Doppler roar.

Joop looked up with them. In the last faint light of the day he saw three delta-winged aircraft glinting in tight formation against the purple-blue sky. *Jet* aircraft. Joop's mouth fell open. "Those are impossible!"

The man on the ground chuckled. "No, boy. Those are the Ralpha Dogs. An' if you believe in God you better pray you never meet 'em in the flesh!"

Earth, August 27, 2374

"Kolitz holding on Line 1," the phone on the nightstand said. "Breathing suggests agitation."

A middle-aged man with disheveled blond hair sat up in bed and reached for the phone. The irritation in his voice was convincing but false. "*Now* what?"

The caller cleared his throat before replying. It was the key for the steganaural message that would follow. His audible speech seemed plodding and slow, but it carried a hidden burden. "Kolitz here. The Forfex Instruments shipment didn't get off on time. The port engine on CC-67 couldn't clear its Christmas tree, so we had to bring up CC-30 from dead cold and transfer cargo. Won't land in Rio until 0900 zulu. Forfex is pissed."

The leader of the Sangruse Society was only half-listening to his employee's clearsound report. Other words were streaming silently into his brain from his right ear, decoded by the distributed nanomachine in his bloodstream. The words had been hidden as calculated noise and irregularities in Kolitz's voice, and were now tapped out by the Sangruse Device as waveforms on the man's right stirrup bone:

|Nautonnier, the Governor General of America has confirmed that she is planning a "political action" against 1Earth. She's being close with details, but she wants to ensure that the Societies don't act against her. Her fear of nanotechnology indicates to me that whatever devices she may have under her control are old or weak. She won't explain her own interest in Hell, but she's willing to send our man and bring him back. She insists that he be sentenced for a real act. She can't—or won't—cook the books for us.|

The blond man was silent for a few seconds. The Sangruse Device watched his throat muscles as he rapidly subvocalized a reply, which would be hidden within the words he then spoke into the phone. "Forfex is always pissed. I'll deal with McConnell when he calls. We'll still get his crap down to Rio hours before anybody else could. I'm more interested in why you louts can't keep a practically new cargo jet alive for more than a week."

|Tell her she has a deal. We won't oppose her coup, and we'll provide a man to go down to Hell and scout it out for us—and try to determine what her interest in Hell is. 1Earth hasn't tried to pull anything off Hell's surface for over two hundred years. I would pay a lot to know how she intends to do it. Did she mention any of the other Societies by name? And her price?|

"Well, shit! You get what you pay for. Get me an engine mechanic who isn't some starving kid out of the slums and I'll keep your jets alive." Kolitz' angry response was pregnant with hidden meaning.

|She said we'll have to trust her on getting our man back. The price is what it's always been: She wants a free-range alternate of the Sangruse Device that will obey her alone. Won't trust it inside her body. She seems particularly afraid of Pequeño. She said she's cutting her own deals with Theometry and Pinhead. Didn't mention any other Societies. Who are we sending?|

"Crap. Let me quote you some numbers from your own record." The Nautonnier picked up a palmstone from the nightstand and tapped on its keyspots for a few breaths, while he framed his subvocal reply. "Your MTBF was eight months twelve days when you were younger and poorer than 'that kid,' and it was because I was managing you—if you get my drift."

|Tell her we'll keep Pequeño off her back—I like easy ones!—and suggest that the really nasty ones she hasn't heard of yet. Protea's the one that keeps me awake nights. Suggest that we'll do our best to deflect opposition from the Societies she isn't aware of. As for who we're sending, my choice is Peter Novilio. He's our junior initiate and doesn't know much, so he can't spill much. And every other week he makes me want to send him to Hell just to be rid of him. We can never trust him to act intelligently on Earth, but he'd be my choice to survive on Hell long enough to see what's there and whether we could found a chapter. The big puzzle is how to get him sentenced without risking a civilian or another operator.|

Kolitz said nothing aloud for several seconds. He let his breath go slowly as between lips pursed with withheld anger. "So you're saying it's my issue, not the kid's."

|The Governor General had a suggestion: She'll send an assassin to go up against our man. He'll attack Peter; if Peter kills him, he gets sentenced to Hell. If the assassin kills Peter, the assassin will sample the Device out of Peter's corpse, and she'll have it for free.|

"Bright boy! At this point I think the kid may be worth more to me than you. If you've got a plan to make sure we don't make a habit of this, I'll hear it." The blond man paused, waiting for an answer. The agent sputtered inarticulately for a moment, giving his leader the time to subvocalize a reply.

|She's dreaming. Emphasize that we pay on *delivery*. Our man must come back alive and uncompromised or she gets nothing—and tell her we're sending her a hired snoop who doesn't contain the Device or even know who we are. If she thinks Peter has the Device, she'll just send somebody with some SIS gimcrack that'll drop a man in his tracks from a hundred meters. I'll concoct a story for Peter. My intuition tells me something's going on down on Hell. If something is, we need to be there first. Just imagine what would happen if Protea beat us to it...|

"No plan. I'll…I'll do better from now on. Sorry to wake you up."

"*Tsk.* I'll just bet." This time there were no words within the words.

"Gone," said Kolitz. |It will be done, Nautonnier.|

The blond man put the phone back on the nightstand. The real challenge, of course, was one that had to remain unspoken: *How much do I tell Peter's copy of the Device?*

Fear was something he didn't admit to easily. Was he getting old? Losing his nerve? Or was there really something to be feared from the thing that lived in his veins?

He shook his head and reached for the lamp on the nightstand. He knew the Device affected the man it lived in. Supposedly the man had no effect on the Device—but years into the experiment that was Version 9, the leader of the Sangruse Society was beginning to have his doubts.

On the edge of sleep, the blond man realized his hesitation: *Peter is cocky, fearless in the pathological sense of aphobia, never one to duck an adrenaline rush. If the Sangruse Device grew too much like him—now, that would be something to fear!* ◼

ALSO BY JEFF DUNTEMANN

All of Jeff Duntemann's SF stories on artificial intelligence, gathered between two covers for the first time. The collection includes "Guardian" (nominated for the Hugo Award), "Borovsky's Hollow Woman," "The Steel Sonnets," "Silicon Psalm," "Marlowe," "Bathtub Mary," "STORMY vs. the Tornadoes,"and "Sympathy on the Loss of One of Your Legs," plus an excerpt from his nanotech AI novel, *The Cunning Blood*. $11.99.

Available from Lulu.com:
http://www.lulu.com/content/paperback-book/souls-in-silicon/3206657

www.ingramcontent.com/pod-product-compliance
Lightning Source LLC
Chambersburg PA
CBHW022014170626
46808CB00001B/398